too close for comfort

too close for comfort

A NOVEL

ellen feldman

Delacorte  Press

Published by
Delacorte Press
Bantam Doubleday Dell Publishing Group, Inc.
1540 Broadway
New York, New York 10036

Library of Congress Cataloging in Publication Data

Feldman, Ellen (Ellen Harriet)
Too close for comfort / Ellen Feldman.
p.   cm.
ISBN 0-385-30912-0
I. Title.
PS3556.F4584T66   1994
813'.54—dc20   93-48439
                                                       CIP

Manufactured in the United States of America
Published simultaneously in Canada

July 1994

10 9 8 7 6 5 4 3 2 1

BVG

In memory of
E. Russell Snyder,
who had
a talent to amuse,

and, of course, for
Stephen

Befriending a writer is a dicey business. The demands are great. The hours are long and irregular. The thanks are small but, in this case, heartfelt. I am deeply grateful to my sisters, my nieces, my stepson, and my daughter; the gang of five who sustain, and Liza, who listens and understands; and especially to my editor, Cynthia White, who has terrific sensibilities and an inspiring cat; and my agent, Binky Urban, who knows, among many other things, when to cut and run.

PROLOGUE

For as long as Isobel could remember, she'd wanted two things in life. She'd wanted to be loved and she'd wanted to be wild. Conventional wisdom said the two were mutually exclusive. Isobel figured out pretty quickly that conventional wisdom was wrong.

It was exactly that attitude, Pete said years later, that got her —correction, them—in trouble. None of it would have happened if for once in her life she'd followed the rules.

"Rules!" she repeated a couple of octaves higher. Though they were sure the episode was over, they were still pretty unhinged by it. "Fuck your goddamn rules!"

She regretted that as soon as it was out. She'd sworn to clean up her language, which Pete compared to a ghetto rapper's, but which she'd actually picked up in her youth at a variety of upscale political demonstrations, and for a while, before all this began, she thought she was changing. Before she'd started dreading the ring of the phone, and fearing the delivery of the mail, and getting a sick feeling in her stomach each night as she stepped off the elevator and crossed the hall to the apartment that was supposed to be her home; before he'd started blaming her, and suspecting everyone else, and, he told her once in a voice hushed with horror at the discovery of his own inhumanity, or maybe only humanity, figuring out how to do in the people he'd taken an oath to help; before they'd both started watching their own words and deciphering each other's looks, she really had been changing.

"Okay, requests." He corrected himself. "Requests that you adhere to the rules of my profession."

If he'd said that before the whole thing had started, she would have told him not to sound so damn pompous, but in the past months she'd seen him stripped of all the ordinary assumptions and innocent self-delusions that make life pleasant, or even bearable, so she let it go. He must have realized she had, because he went on in a milder voice to explain that all he was talking about was common sense. Common sense and reticence. Or at least discretion.

"So you're saying it was my fault."

"That's not what I meant," he insisted, but they both knew it was, and they stopped abruptly, because the last thing they wanted now was mutual recrimination. They'd had enough of that during the past months. What they wanted, they told each other with the stunned relief of earthquake victims who thought they'd finally felt the last aftershock, was to forget the whole thing. Besides, they both knew they couldn't blame it on him, or her, or the flouting of rules. All they could blame it on were the desperate dreams people hang on each other, like window dressers hanging clothes on mannequins, to give shape to their lives.

"It isn't anyone's fault," he said. "This kind of thing comes with the territory."

The territory he meant was psychiatry, but it was also the physical territory of his apartment. Five mornings a week, at seven twenty-five, Pete closed the door to the main part of the apartment, crossed the entrance hall that, by virtue of two Barcelona chairs, a steel-and-glass coffee table, and a stack of *Nation*s and *The New York Review of Books*, served as a waiting room, and went down another short hall past the closed kitchen door to the study that was kept perpetually dim, but was, at least, free of African masks and pre-Columbian figures to wait for his first patient, who was scheduled for seven-thirty. When Isobel had begun spending nights in the apartment, she'd found the proximity of those patients the next morning strange and faintly titillating. She used to lie in bed with the *Times* and the mug of coffee Pete brought her before he left and try to imagine what was going on in that small paneled room.

There was something else she used to wonder at on those mornings. How had she been lucky enough to get mixed up with a man who brought her the paper and a mug of coffee before he went to work? Then she realized the gesture was more preventive than tender. He didn't want her breaking one of his, or Freud's, ten commandments. Thou shalt not set foot in the professional part of the apartment during professional hours. Not, as Pete pointed out later, that she paid much attention to Freud's rules or Pete's requests. She was always sneaking through the waiting room to get more coffee, or look for a pair of gloves she was sure she'd left there the night before, or tempt fate. She was, Pete said when things began to get worse, like her cat. She couldn't resist leaving her scent around the place. What did he expect? she shouted back, because by that time she was doing a lot of shouting, given his goddamn uncle's will and the goddamn history of that goddamn apartment.

Half the New Yorkers Isobel knew would have killed for Pete's apartment. Pete hadn't had to kill for it. All he'd had to do was wait until his childless uncle, who'd made a fortune in bathroom fixtures and was, according to the family party line, determined to lose it backing Broadway shows, keeled over one afternoon in the paneled library where Pete now saw patients. The fact that the uncle was entertaining a twenty-three-year-old chorus boy when he keeled over hadn't endeared him to the family either. A few months later Pete, his former wife, and their two children had taken up residence in the seven rooms with their twelve-foot ceilings, and long privacy-giving halls, a view of Central Park, and two fireplaces that couldn't accommodate any blaze bigger than a matchbook but boasted beautifully carved marble mantels. That had been eleven years ago. The new apartment had sent a terminally ill marriage into remission. Later Pete had come to think of all the paraphernalia of renovation and redecoration as the equipment in an ICU. But the disease had exacerbated, and three years later the patient had died. Pete's wife, in keeping with a stipulation in the uncle's will, had moved out, leaving Pete with painstakingly restored moldings and mantels, a master bath full of state-of-the-art Italian fixtures—not off his late uncle's assembly lines— and a vast, newly renovated kitchen with four long tilt-and-turn windows opening into the morning sun. She'd also left enough guilt to keep him locked in that apartment, brooding and lacerating himself for some time. Or maybe, like the original moldings and carvings beneath the layers of paint, the guilt had been there all along. The divorce had merely stripped away the overlays to bring it out in all its striking detail.

At any rate, by the time Isobel came along, the guilt had begun to erode, though the apartment was still in pretty good shape. It was certainly in a lot better shape than her one-bedroom rabbit warren. So it was only logical that she began to spend more and more time at Pete's. And it was only sensible, once they decided to get married, that she move in.

Isobel wasn't naive. She'd known the dangers of taking up residence in that apartment. At least she'd thought she had. One of the first laws of second- or third- or fourth-times-around was that since you couldn't really start over, you'd better start neutral. She remembered the new husband of an old friend who'd gone berserk and threatened divorce when he'd come home one night and found she'd moved the furniture and taken down the curtains in his Mario Buatta–designed apartment. She thought of her poor uncle whose second wife still wouldn't let him sit in her late first husband's easy chair. And she'd seen more than one murderous glance fired across a dinner table at a spouse's casual reference to *my* place. But Pete's apartment had skewed her judgment—just as Pete had undermined her principles, or at least her convictions.

Isobel had never had much faith in marriage. Her feminist creed told her that it was unjust, her agnostic doubt that it was irrelevant, and her personal experience that it was impossible.

Pete hadn't argued with her reasoning. He'd merely pointed out that he was a conventional man. The statement had surprised her. All her life she'd had a weakness for people who'd rather die than be considered ordinary.

But Pete hadn't tried to convert her to his point of view. In his place she would have waged war, or at least pulled out some of the stops she'd learned fighting for peace, and consumers' interests, and the environment, and abortion rights, but he'd just stood his ground, certain that it was the logical high ground and she'd eventually move to it. His brand of perseverance, she realized now, was particularly masculine. It was encoded in the genes, or at least learned at fathers' knees. She wouldn't go so far as to say it was the old when-a-woman-says-no-she-doesn't-mean-no school of thought. But it came close.

Yet, knowing that, she'd still agreed—no, not agreed, because the whole point was that Pete had never pushed—decided that they might as well get married. Though she hadn't told Pete until mid-September, she'd made up her mind more than a month earlier. They'd been anchored off Fishers Island in a sloop they'd chartered for the weekend. It had been about seven-thirty or eight, whenever the sun set in that part of the world in mid-August, and she'd been sitting in the cockpit reading a volume of Edith Wharton's letters while Pete stood in the stern fishing. He'd looked nice that way with the mauve sky backlighting him as if he were a well-designed ad for one of those products, like support hose or beeswax night cream or personal banking services, that were guaranteed to change your life. And all of a sudden she knew she was ready to buy. It might have been the drink, because there was a half-finished vodka tonic next to her on the nonskid deck, or it might have been the feeling of clean clothes chafing against tender sun-burned skin, or, most likely of all, it was the afterhum of sex, which was even better than a shower of hot pressurized water and clean clothes after a day of sailing. It had probably been all of those things, but more, too. The afterhum had been stronger than any Isobel had ever felt, not a cat's purr but the faint vibration of a solid-state electronic device that was designed not to burn out. It was an unusual feeling, so unusual that it had taken her awhile to figure out what it was. She hadn't had a lot of experience with contentment.

The sensation had been so foreign to her that she hadn't trusted it. That was why she'd waited a few weeks to say anything to Pete. The funny thing was that when she finally did say something, he wasn't surprised. He simply placed a few calls to track down a judge who was a friend of a friend and made arrangements for them to go down to his chambers one afternoon. There was nothing for Isobel to do then except move the rest of her clothes, a couple of dozen cartons of books, and Joseph Welch, a dignified black cat with a creamy mark like a bow tie beneath his chin and a conviction of the justice of his own causes in his heart, into Pete's apartment.

ONE

It wasn't Isobel's fault that she had to break the rules again on the morning of the day she and Pete were scheduled to go down to the judge's chambers. It wasn't even the cat's. If they were going to blame anyone, it ought to be Pete, but you couldn't really blame him because he wasn't accustomed to living with a cat, though God knew he was trying. He was trying to learn not to leave food on the kitchen counter, and not to jump when he felt something walking up and down his legs in the middle of the night, and not to lose his temper when, one morning a week before they were to see the judge, Welch managed to find his way into Pete's office, giving his patient a perfect pretext to stop talking about what Pete had finally got her to start talking about and ask if he'd just got a cat.

"Did you tell her it was mine?" Isobel asked.

"She's not supposed to know anything about my personal life."

"Not even that the woman you're about to marry has a cat?"

"Not even that there's a woman I'm about to marry."

That gave Isobel pause. She'd known she'd have to be discreet in the apartment, but she hadn't thought she'd have to be invisible.

Still, Pete was trying so hard that when Welch followed him

1

into the kitchen that morning and began rubbing against his leg, he opened a can of Science Diet, dumped half of it into a bowl, and put the bowl on the floor in the corner. It was a sweet gesture, especially for a man who claimed not to like cats. Then he carried his mug of coffee and an English muffin to the long trestle table in the center of the kitchen, turned to the business section of the paper, and forgot about the cat. He didn't re-member him fifteen minutes later when he closed the kitchen door behind him and went into his office to wait for his first patient.

Isobel didn't blame Pete for forgetting, but then she didn't think he ought to blame her either. She was just trying to get Welch back to the part of the apartment where Pete said he belonged.

When she realized what had happened, she picked up the shirt Pete had tossed on a chair in a corner of the bedroom the night before and pulled it on. It was a striped shirt with a white tab collar, and it didn't really suit him. Dressed casually in rough tweeds and sweaters and khakis, as he usually was, he looked like a tortured Slav poet. There were a lot of angles in his face. But when he tried to spiff up, he came off looking like a Mafia button man. She pulled on the shirt because it was there on the chair, and besides, she liked the faint aroma of Pete that still clung to it. Anyway, it wasn't the shirt that Pete would object to. If fact, sometimes on weekend mornings, when she came back to bed from the kitchen or the hall where the paper was delivered wearing one of his shirts, he didn't even bother to take it off. She said if you thought about it clinically, there was something narcissistic about doing the things he did to his own shirt, but he pointed out he wasn't doing them to the shirt, he was doing them beneath the shirt. At any rate, it wasn't the shirt he objected to. It wasn't even the fact that the shirt was all she was wearing when she crossed the entrance hall to get to the kitchen. It was the fact that she crossed the entrance hall. She hated that part of it, no matter what Pete thought. She hated having to open the door a crack to make sure there was no one in the waiting room, and having to leap across it as if she were dodging traffic, but once she was past it and down the hall, she liked the way the big kitchen sat in the morning sun, warm and fragrant as baking bread. On that particular morning, the sun lay in yellow pools on the terra-cotta tiles, and her bare feet splashed through them silently as she crossed the big open space. Welch was asleep on one of the Shaker chairs, his fur gleaming like jet in the shaft of light, his sleek body rising and falling in unconscious bliss. Isobel had planned to sneak into the kitchen, grab him, and dash back to the living part of the apartment, but the sunshine hung like bunting, and the floor felt so warm beneath her feet, and Welch looked so peaceful that she figured as long as she was there, she might as well stay for a while. She returned to the door, glanced back to the waiting room to make sure there was no one there, though she'd come through only seconds ago—Pete really had made her paranoid—and closed the door. Then she poured a mug of coffee, carried it to the table, sat in one of the Shaker chairs, and propped her bare feet up on another. The air conditioners were on, so the double-paned windows were neither tilted nor turned, and she couldn't hear the shrieking whistles of doormen, or the screeching brakes of taxis, or the ominous wail of sirens, or any of the other nerve-stripping sounds of the city nineteen floors below.

She spent perhaps half an hour that way, paging through the paper, sipping coffee, and basking in the fragrant, silent safety of that room. The paper was black with bad news. On the front page people halfway around the world were looting and burning their neighbors' villages, and in the second section people thirty blocks north of her were raping and knifing and shooting each other, and in the financial section empires were collapsing. Isobel read all about it and tried to work up the sense of horror and grief and despair that the news demanded, but the tranquillity of that room kept the world at bay. The more she read, the more the silence of that soaring space and the buttery light spilling through the windows and the hum of all those gleaming appliances lulled her into a state of solitary well-being. Her soul purred along with Welch and the appliances.

At one point she was startled by the sound of footsteps on the handsome but creaky parquet of the hall on the other side of the closed door—at least she thought they were footsteps—and she put down the paper and sat listening, but then there was only silence, so she went back to reading. She knew what was waiting for her at her office, and she was still a little nervous about what she was going to do after she left her office, and no matter what Pete said later, she wasn't looking for trouble, merely for a moment of peace.

The longer she sat there, the longer she wanted to sit there, but gradually she began to sense the big round clock—of Italian origin, like the bathroom fixtures and the floor tiles—on the wall behind her. The clock didn't tick; it didn't even hum; it merely bored into her back like a reproachful eye. She twisted her head around to check the time, awarded herself two more minutes, and went back to reading. But she could still feel the clock watching her. She turned her head to look at it again. That was when she noticed that the door to the hall was open a crack. She was sure she'd closed it behind her. Absolutely certain. She wouldn't dare sit in the kitchen during office hours without making sure the door was shut. Pete had hammered that much into her.

She glanced at the chair next to her. Welch hadn't moved. She couldn't pin this on him.

She stood. Though her bare feet made no sound on the

terra-cotta tiles, she moved to the door with exaggerated stealth and angled herself so she could glance down the hall to the waiting room without being seen, or at least without having much of her visible. From that position she had a view of one Barcelona chair and half the other. Both were empty. The two stacks of magazines were still perfectly aligned, but Isobel noticed, though she hadn't when she'd raced through, that there was a copy of *New York* magazine on top of the pile of *Nation*s. Occasionally Pete picked up a copy of *New York* and put it out to inject a trendy note into the waiting room. She found his definition of *trendy* endearing.

She closed the door and went back to the table. The clock said eight forty-seven, which meant Pete was already into his second session. That was when she realized what had happened. The force of air from the first patient leaving the apartment or the second arriving had blown open the kitchen door.

She figured she'd better make her getaway while the second patient was still in Pete's office and before the third showed up. She finished her coffee, put the mug in the sink, and picked up Welch. He was limp as a piece of velvet. On her dash through the waiting room, she detoured past the blue and white porcelain stand to grab her umbrella. The sun was out, but the paper said there was a chance of thundershowers that evening.

The stand was empty. Though she was worried about being caught, she stopped and moved it to make sure her aim hadn't been off and the umbrella wasn't stuck behind it. There was nothing. Damn. That would teach her for leaving it there in the first place. Some kleptomaniacal patient had pinched it. She was glad it was just the old beat-up Knirps she kept in her office. If it had been her oversized hand-painted umbrella, she would have been really angry.

* * *

5

The phone was ringing as Isobel walked into her office. It wasn't an unusual occurrence. Neither was the fact that her secretary, Megan, was not at her own desk. Isobel picked up the phone.

"I've asked you!" Pete was as close to shouting as he ever got. "Christ, I've pleaded with you. There are six other rooms in the apartment. All I ask is that you stay out of my office during hours."

She unbuttoned the jacket of her linen suit, though when she'd walked into the building a few minutes earlier, her first thought as a creature of comfort as well as an environmentalist had been that the air-conditioning was turned too high again.

"I wasn't in your office."

"In the office part of the apartment."

"I was in the kitchen."

"How did you get to the kitchen, Isobel? You didn't go out in the hall and around to the service door in my shirt and nothing else, did you? I mean, even you wouldn't do that."

"How did you know I was wearing your shirt?" She slipped off her jacket and hung it on the back of her chair.

"The patient told me. She asked who that woman running around my waiting room in a man's shirt was."

She sat behind her desk. "That was your out. You should have told her I had nothing to do with your personal life. I was another patient. A cross-dresser."

"It's not funny. It took months for her to begin to talk. Now we're finally starting to do some good work, and you come larking across my waiting room half undressed and set her God knows how far back."

Isobel didn't ask why the sight of a strange woman in a man's shirt should drive the woman off the deep end. She knew all about transference and countertransference and the analytic relationship. Well, not all, but enough.

She swiveled her chair to face the window, the closest thing to getting a breath of fresh air in an hermetically sealed modern office building, and as she did, she noticed her old beat-up Knirps on the windowsill. So much for kleptomaniacal patients.

"I wasn't larking across the waiting room. I was sitting in the kitchen, drinking coffee, reading the paper, and minding my own business."

"You have to cross the waiting room to get to the kitchen."

"There was no one in the waiting room when I sneaked through."

"You didn't think there was anyone in the waiting room. She must have been in the closet hanging up her coat—"

"Her coat! It's ninety-five degrees out."

"—or something like that."

"Or maybe she was the one who was sneaking around. Maybe she pushed open the kitchen door because she wanted to find out what went on in the rest of the apartment. She wanted to penetrate the doctor's inner sanctum, enter the forbidden."

"She said there was a woman in the waiting room."

Isobel hesitated. There was something wrong with this conversation. It took her a couple of seconds to figure out what. This wasn't just a she said/she said scenario. This was a-patient-who-might-be-crazy-or-at-the-very-least-highly-neurotic said/the-woman-you're-about-to-marry said. But Isobel didn't protest, because that was the point. Patients did that kind of thing. That was why they were patients. Isobel held herself to a higher standard.

"I'm sorry."

He sighed. Some men couldn't handle tears. Others caved in at the sight of hysterics. But Pete, who saw so much of both, was a pushover for apologies. She felt the anger go out of him with that sigh.

7

"Still want to meet me downtown this afternoon?" she asked.

"I have to go to work."

"I'll understand if you've changed your mind."

"Cut it out."

"I mean, a shrink needs someone who plays by the rules. Caesar's wife and all that kind of thing."

"Just try not to be late," he said, and she knew how he looked as he spoke. The heavy brows that fanned out over his eyes like wings would be drawn together in a single line. The brows were still jet black, and the contrast with his graying hair gave him a Faustian air. Isobel sometimes wondered if it made his patients uneasy. Imagine going into treatment with a board-certified psychiatrist and looking up from the couch a few months later to find you're cutting a deal with the devil.

By three o'clock that afternoon Isobel had forgotten Pete's patient, though when the trouble started, she'd remember her again. She and Pete both would. But she didn't have much chance to think about her that day. She was too busy waging a war to save a row of town houses in the East Nineties from a developer whose proposed building would adhere to local height restrictions and still manage to plunge the entire block into darkness by midafternoon.

Isobel's first job out of school had been for the Women's International League for Peace and Freedom. A few years later she'd moved to a consumer advocacy agency, then on to an environmental organization, and after that to an abortion rights group. For the past year and a half she'd been the director of Urban Heritage, which was devoted to saving New York's architectural gems from the wrecking ball of condo-crazed developers. She'd taken the position around the same time she'd met Pete, though she didn't think the two occurrences were related, even if he did. Most of her friends had been surprised at the job. As surprised, she suspected, as they were going to be at what she was planning to do that afternoon. They'd thought she was selling out. It had been one thing to go clean for Gene when she was a kid, but the patron saints of her new cause, old friends had pointed out, were Philip Johnson and Jackie O and Prince Charles. Her grandmother had put it differently. Hannah's heart ached for man's injustice to man. Her blood boiled at man's injustice to woman. But buildings? How worked up could you get about a building? It was the first job her grandmother hadn't celebrated and her mother hadn't fretted over. Still, she'd felt she had to take it. It meant more money and more control—no one in her right mind would call it power, and Isobel wouldn't be caught dead using the word anyway—and she'd been ready for a change.

"You really think that's why you went to Urban Heritage?" Pete had asked once.

"Why else?" Isobel had answered, but he wouldn't say why else. Pete insisted he'd no more analyze her mind as a shrink than he'd operate on her body if he were a surgeon. What he really meant was he wouldn't tell her the analyses he made.

Megan called from the outer office—it was an informal as well as a nonprofit group—that Ed Becker was on the phone. Becker was the attorney for Leon Gorsky, the developer. He called himself Gorsky's mouthpiece. Becker was convinced he had a sense of humor. He also called Isobel "cookie." At first he'd almost seemed to mean it. "I know we're going to be able to work together, cookie," he'd told her at their initial meeting. But now Gorsky was getting angry, and Becker was running scared, and the way he pronounced "cookie" made her think of those candied apples booby-trapped with razors that her mother used to warn her against on the Halloweens of her childhood.

9

"Cookie, I'm gonna make you an offer you can't refuse," Becker began.

"What would your Harvard Law School classmates say, Ed, if they knew you worked for a slumlord and talked like a Mafia don?"

"Are you kidding? Half those guys are out of work, and the ones who've managed to hang on to their white-shoe jobs wish they were pulling down a small piece of what I am."

"Okay, lay offer number one hundred and twenty-seven on me."

"My client will drop the plans for that site in the Nineties if you'll call off your dogs on that landmarking we're going to get reversed in the Seventies."

"You're kidding me, right? This isn't a serious offer?"

"Come on, cookie. You know the court isn't going to uphold the landmark status of those buildings."

"If you believed that, you wouldn't be offering this trade."

There was a moment's silence, and when Becker spoke again, it was in the voice he thought was sincere. "Listen, cookie, maybe you're too busy saving old broken-down tenements to notice, but the real estate market in this town has gone down the toilet. Now I'm not saying my client is in trouble, but if he gets in trouble, you think it's going to be good for this city?"

"You mean, what's good for Leon Gorsky is good for New York?"

"You can joke, but how do you think it's going to look when the banks start foreclosing and the several thousand people my client employs are out on their asses? Are you ready to take responsibility for that? Because I plan to point the finger at you. I know you think you're saving the world—"

"Just a little architectural heritage."

"Boy, I can't wait to hear you say that on the six o'clock news to a bunch of guys who're picketing to save their jobs. You're going to knock *Wheel of Fortune* right out of the ratings."

"I won't have to say it. The people who live in those buildings can speak for themselves."

"That's where you're wrong, cookie. Let me explain something to you. Before you came along, you know what Urban Heritage was? A bunch of little old ladies and limp-wristed guys running around screaming wasn't this dump divine and wasn't that hellhole *ex*-quisite."

"I'm really glad you took that workshop in political correctness, Ed."

"Screw political correctness. I'm telling you the facts of life. Then all of a sudden, you turn up fresh from the bra-burning wars, or Ho Chi Minh's school of guerrilla tactics, or some seventies time warp and start making trouble. Every time I turn around you're staging some happening—I bet that's a word from your past—or enlisting some rich bitch to save some building nobody even noticed until then. So, the way I figure it, it's not Urban Heritage I have to worry about; it's you. And in case I haven't made myself perfectly clear, I'm no Boy Scout."

"Aw, shucks, and here I was hoping you'd help me across the street."

"You know something, cookie," he said, and his voice was honeyed again. "I like you. When you're looking for a job, give me a call. Maybe I'll be able to help."

Isobel thanked him for the offer and hung up.

"I think I've just been threatened by Gorsky's mouthpiece," she said as Zoe Haywood, the assistant director of Urban Heritage, came barreling into her office. Zoe always led with her upper body. The stance made most people think she was putting her shoulder to the wheel, but Isobel knew it was merely the result of a daily jog behind a three-wheeled baby buggy and a twenty-five-pound toddler. "Not cement shoes or anything

11

like that," she added because she didn't want to sound melo-dramatic. "Just a few allusions to my lack of job security."

"That's ridiculous," Zoe said, but she didn't meet Isobel's eyes, and Isobel knew why. It wasn't that Zoe wished her ill. It was merely that Isobel was the only thing that stood between Zoe and the directorship of Urban Heritage. Isobel didn't blame Zoe for her reaction. It would be like blaming the lioness for the law of the jungle or, in this case, of the wildlife preserve.

Zoe asked if Isobel had a minute to talk about the awards dinner, because the woman who'd signed on as honorary chairperson had just hit the top of the Whitney's waiting list, and let's face it, who would take the honorary chair of a minor-league group when you had a crack at the next best thing to the Modern?

Isobel told her it would have to wait until Monday. "I have an appointment way the hell downtown, and I'm already late."

"Corporate sponsor?" Zoe asked.

Isobel made a noncommittal sound, took her handbag from the bottom drawer of the desk and her jacket from the back of the door, and started out of the office. It wasn't that she was ashamed of what she was about to do, but if she told anyone, it would become a public occasion, and that was the last thing she wanted.

She slipped into her jacket on her way down the hall, then stood in front of her reflection in the bronzed elevator doors, tugging and smoothing it into place, but good tailoring was no match for genetic deficiency. Her shoulders formed two sharp wedges. She was the only woman she knew who had to cut shoulder pads out of her clothing. Her breasts were nonexistent. The only part of her that had any flesh on it was her behind, and as far as she was concerned, that had too much. It was, her mother assured her, an inescapable family trait. The

12

Baum bum. Her grandmother had been a Baum before she'd married.

Isobel stepped into the elevator and thought again of Zoe's question about where she was going. She'd told Pete, when they'd decided to do this, that she wanted something private and seemly. What she'd meant, though she hadn't known it at the time, was that she didn't want the two people who thought they had the most right to be there. She didn't want her mother and her grandmother.

Isobel had used the words *private* and *seemly*. What she ended up with was closer to *furtive* and *criminal*. The judge had the florid, tight-skinned face of an alcoholic and the hearty insincerity of an old Tammany Hall appointee. He got her name wrong twice. The way he rolled "by-the-authority-vested-in-me" around in his mouth made Isobel think of political skulduggery and under-the-table payoffs. Though the peck on the cheek he gave her afterward was physically chaste, it somehow smacked of salaciousness. The whole operation—Pete said you couldn't dignify it by calling it a ceremony—was over in fewer than ten minutes.

Afterward they stood in front of the Family Court building under an awning of gathering humidity that might or might not build to a thunderstorm, feeling dazed and vaguely violated.

"Like victims of a hit-and-run accident or a mugging," Isobel said.

"But a private accident or mugging," Pete pointed out. "What do you want to do now?"

"I thought I'd go back to the office."

"You're kidding."

"I'm kidding. Come on, I'll buy you a drink."

13

"Aren't you afraid it might seem too much like a celebration?"

"We'll find a bar with a shamrock on the window and a steam table inside."

They managed to do a little better than that, and when they came out of the restaurant an hour later, the threat of a storm had passed. Pete said they ought to go somewhere for the weekend.

"Don't panic, I'm not talking honeymoon. Just some seedy motel with mirrors on the ceiling and rates by the hour."

She said she'd settle for a country inn, but first they had to stop at Central Park West. "Millie will never forgive me for not telling her. Hannah will just never forgive me."

Pete stood staring down at her from under those heavy brows.

"You don't understand," she insisted, because the frayed elastic band of love and guilt and need didn't pull and push and stretch his life out of shape.

"One small minute for us," she pleaded, "one big moment for Hannah and Millie."

He shrugged and lifted a long arm to hail a cab. "Why don't we just invite them along for the weekend?"

"Don't even joke. Millie would say yes in a minute."

The cab pulled up, and Pete opened the door for Isobel and slid in after her. She gave the driver her old address and put her hand on Pete's fly. He put his hand over hers. She started to tug at the zipper. He pushed her hand away. She went for the zipper again. This time he grabbed her hand and held it.

"You weren't so hard to get in the cab that time we went to the ballet when I first knew you," she said.

"We weren't caught in rush-hour traffic in broad daylight then."

She wrenched her hand free from his and went for his zipper again.

"That's not the reason."

He caught her hand.

"For Christ sake, Isobel." Despite the bulletproof divider, he was whispering. The habit of confidentiality died hard.

She tried to pull her hand free, but he held on to it.

"The reason is that we're married now."

"We've been married for about an hour."

She gave up the struggle and let her hand rest in his.

"Exactly, and you're already taking me for granted."

They got out of the cab and went into the lobby she used to come home to from school and dates and college terms. Most of the doormen were new, but Louie, who remembered her from her childhood, was on tonight. "Hi, Isobel," he said. "Good evening, Doctor," he added.

In the elevator she started again. She was quicker this time and managed to get his fly unzipped while he was still pressing the button for the twelfth floor. He caught her wrist. She dove into his trousers with the other hand.

"Jesus! Do you want me to be able to walk in the door or not?"

She was inside his boxer shorts now. He held on to her wrist. She held on to him.

"I knew it was a mistake," she said.

"What was a mistake?" His teeth were clenched almost as tightly as his hand on her wrist.

"Marriage."

She tried to move her hand. He tried to stop her.

"Isobel!"

"It's making you stodgy."

The dial above the elevator door inched from six to seven.

"Okay," he said, and, with the quick, sure grace of a natural

15

athlete, slid one hand beneath her skirt and pushed the stop button with the other.

A bell loud enough to call an entire village to worship clanged.

Her hand froze.

"What are you doing?"

His hand slid up the inside of her thigh.

"Stopping the elevator."

The bell clanged again.

"Why?"

He began to unbutton her blouse.

"I don't like quickies."

She took her hand out of his trousers.

He reached inside her blouse.

The bell clanged a third time.

She put her hand over his to stop him.

"Every doorman and porter in the building is going to be up here in a minute."

She was trying to hold his hand, but he wriggled two fingers inside her bra.

"Yup," he said. "And the super."

The bell clanged again.

She managed to pull his hand out of her blouse. Of course, he wasn't really fighting her.

He took his other hand out from under her skirt, pushed the start button, and picked up the telephone intercom.

"Sorry, Louie. I pushed the wrong button by mistake." After he hung up the phone, he looked at her and grinned. It wasn't only the effect of the dark brows against the graying hair that made the smile diabolical.

"You're in the major leagues now, slugger," he said as he followed her off the elevator. "Don't start things you're not prepared to finish."

16

TWO

H ANNAH SAT IN THE STUDY OF the Central Park West duplex trying to hear the television and trying not to hear the noise in the maid's room on the other side of the wall behind her back. No, not hear it, feel it.

Knock. Knock. Knock.

She didn't want to say anything because she was afraid if she did, the girl would leave, and who knew what she'd get next. Homemakers, the agency called them. Some homemakers. Half of them couldn't even make a cup of tea, and Hannah didn't want to think about what she'd find on the counters and the floors, if she could still see crumbs and spills. Except the one before last. She was immaculate. Did everything by the book. A regular Nazi. Even her mustache reminded Hannah of Hitler. And the one after her was a thief. Hannah didn't care what Millie said or how much the woman denied it. Who else had been in the house to take the silver frame with that baby picture of Isobel? Hannah had said to her, "Look, I'll forget about the frame, just put the picture back because it's one of my favorites and the negative disappeared years ago," but the woman went on insisting she hadn't taken it. This letting strangers into the house was no good. You never knew what you were going to end up with. That was why Cruz was such a find. She made a nice piece of cinnamon toast, and you could tell by the way she

17

kept herself that she kept the kitchen neat, too. She had a sweet laugh in a register Hannah could hear. And she was so honest she even brought the small change back from her errands. So Hannah didn't complain when Cruz sneaked her boyfriend in through the service entrance. But that didn't mean she wanted to listen.

Knock. Knock. Knock. Knock.

The young believed they'd invented sex.

Hannah knew the thought wasn't original, but that didn't make it any less galling. The irritation was like the burning sensation she got in her chest when she ate tomatoes. She used to be able to handle those, too.

They thought it was something new, like computers and video games. Hannah's upper lip, which Cruz tweezed for her so she wouldn't look like the Nazi, curled at the thought. She could have told them. They used to do the same things way back when. Manually then. Without all the shouting and the carrying-on, without the songs and the paraphernalia and the movies. Hannah knew about the movies because once, when she'd asked Isobel what they were like, Isobel had shown her. She'd waited until Millie was going out to one of her dinners and rented a movie. She'd even brought popcorn with it. No butter or salt, she'd explained. "I'm wayward but not crazy." She'd made them drinks, too. Nobody ever made Hannah apricot sours anymore. The doctor said they were the last thing she needed, as if the doctor with all his shiny equipment that rolled here and swung there and hummed and beeped knew what an old woman needed. But Isobel had made her an apricot sour that night. Then they'd sat at opposite ends of the sofa right here in the study, with Hannah's sour on one end table and Isobel's scotch on the other and the bowl of unsalted, unbuttered popcorn between them, and watched the rented movie.

To tell the truth, she hadn't thought much of it. The camera

18

kept getting in so close you couldn't tell what you were looking at. It could just as well have been an elbow or a leg as the other thing. And there was nothing new about the story either. Her friend Zelda-the-Blacklisted-Actress used to tell the same stories—fantasies, they called them now—about what she wanted to do with her mailman. Pat Reilly, his name was. For all Hannah knew, Zelda had actually done them, but she wouldn't have talked about that. People didn't in those days. They might joke about what they wanted to do, but they didn't come right out and tell you what they were doing. If you asked her, it was better that way. A little mystery was nothing to sneeze at. Not that Reuben had been what you'd call a mystery man. Unless you thought keeping the lights out through the whole thing was mysterious. But she wasn't complaining. In that department, at least, Reuben had been all right.

Knock knock knock knock knock.

You'd think a smart girl like Cruz would figure out how to put a pillow between the headboard and the wall so they wouldn't make so much noise. That was what she and Reuben used to do when there was someone else in the house, and when Millie had married Harry—poor Millie—Hannah had taught her the trick.

Knockknockknockknockknockknock.

A pillow, Cruz. A towel, even, would keep anyone from hearing.

Hannah started to shake her head, then stopped suddenly. That was it. As far as they were concerned, there was no one in the house to hear. A ninety-four-year-old woman was no one. Hannah saw it when they looked at her. They looked, but they didn't see. She was invisible. And when they did remember she was there, all they saw was a bunch of brittle bones they had to worry about breaking, a sack of crepy skin they were reluctant to touch, a couple of wisps of white hair someone had to wash.

19

Just a worn-out object that took up a little space and too much of their time. She could do things herself, but no, they were in too much of a hurry. So they put her here, they put her there. They stuck her in front of the television and didn't even care what they turned on, as if she were a baby who needed noise and color and movement to keep from fretting. They sat her in front of the windows to get the sun, as if she were a plant. She'd said that to Millie this morning, and the look had come across Millie's face again. As if she were sorry, and embarrassed, but more than that. Scared. Because she was next. As she tucked in the red and white afghan, the one Hannah had crocheted after Isobel was born, though Millie had asked for pink, she wondered how long before Isobel would be doing the same thing for her. Hannah had said that once, too, and Millie had laughed and shaken her head. "Isobel will slap me into a nursing home so fast it'll make your head spin. It'll be an integrated, equal-opportunity nursing home, and she'll come visit me once a week, but it'll be a nursing home. Isobel can barely take care of herself." But the joke hadn't hidden the fear. As long as Hannah was around, Millie was still a daughter. As long as Hannah was around, Millie still had someone to take care of, no matter how much she thought she resented it.

Hannah saw Millie coming across the living room toward her now. She'd had her hair done this afternoon. That was because Isobel had called yesterday and said that when she came by tonight, she was going to bring that man, that shrink she was mixed up with. What was his name again? After all these years, she could still remember the name of Zelda-the-Blacklisted-Actress's mailman, but she couldn't think of the name of the man her granddaughter was practically living with. Nelson? No, Nelson was the one she'd married. What a mess that had been. Hannah had warned them. What's the big rush? People are going to figure it out anyway. But Millie wouldn't let them

20

wait. Millie had been the one in a rush. She'd been planning that wedding since the day Isobel was born. It had been crazy. Worse than crazy. Immoral. All that money on a party, and Millie smiling and crying and carrying on in that dress that was too bridelike for the mother of the bride, though Hannah hadn't had the heart to tell her that. And then Isobel had lost it anyway. But that was Millie for you. Millie and marriage. Millie and men. She was always saying that if Isobel had any sense, she'd marry this one, whatever his name was.

"What does she have to marry him for?" Hannah had said the other day. "For sex? She's getting that anyway."

"You think that's all marriage is?"

Hannah hadn't answered. The issue was dead. Just like poor Harry. Let it rest in peace. "For money?" she'd gone on instead. "She works. She earns a good living. She'll get what I have."

"For security," Millie had answered.

"Ha! 'When a girl marries—' "

"Spare me the old Polish folk wisdom you got from that neighbor back on Hester Street."

" 'When a girl marries—' " Hannah had started again.

"The worst anti-Semites in the world. Worse than the Germans."

"Maybe, but whichever Pole said this knew what she was talking about. 'When a girl marries' "—Hannah had started a third time and managed to keep going—" 'she is buried alive.' That's what you want for her?"

As Millie got closer now, her features began to blur, but Hannah could still make out the colors. She'd had her hair tinted as well as washed and set. Too much blue. Hannah had told her that before, but Millie wouldn't listen. Because it came from Hannah. If anyone else had said it, she'd rush to the mirror to see if it were true. Hannah didn't understand the aging pro-

21

cess. The body disintegrated, the mind frayed, but the resentments grew stronger and sharper. Maybe because the time for righting old wrongs was growing short.

Millie kept coming toward her, growing larger and more blurry with each step. Her shoes, good Italian pumps Hannah knew without seeing, clicked across the wood floor between the Chinese rug in the living room and the Indian one in the study. The sound reminded Hannah of the puppy she'd bought Isobel when she was small. Hannah had said every girl should have a dog. Millie had said the phrase was "every boy," and the dog was dirty. When it had eaten a pair of those good Italian pumps, then thrown them up on that same Chinese rug, Millie had taken it back to the pet shop. Isobel had been heartbroken. Hannah was sure of it, no matter what Millie said or how well Isobel hid it.

The wavy figure sank into the chair across the room, directly beneath the portrait of herself that Harry had commissioned right after Isobel was born. The shoulders and face of the young Millie bloomed like a pale camellia from the dark silk décolletage of the dress. Millie loved that portrait. It had been painted, she liked to say, in the days when women were ladies.

Hannah looked from the portrait back to her daughter. "You had your hair done."

"It needed it."

The short silence echoed back through the years.

"It looks nice," Hannah said. "Do you like it?" Millie asked at the same time.

"She's late," Millie said after a while.

"She's busy," Hannah corrected her.

"I called her apartment. In case she went home instead of coming straight from the office. But I got the machine. I hate that machine."

"What are you talking about? Telephone answering machines are the greatest invention since the wheel. I wish we had them in the old days. All those people I wouldn't have had to talk to."

"If I said I liked answering machines, you'd say they were awful. Last week I called, and for once I didn't hang up. I left a message, and she didn't call back anyway."

"She always calls back when I leave a message."

"She said she never got it. She said she's been getting a lot of crank calls, so sometimes she misses the real ones when she fast-forwards."

"What kind of crank calls?"

"What do you mean, what kind? With her jobs it's one thing or another. Like that maniac who threw a bottle of blood at her. I told her not to take that job."

"You told her not to take every job she's ever had. If everyone felt like you, women would still be going to back-alley doctors or using coat hangers. And if she listened to you, she'd still be living at home, doing nothing, scared of her own shadow."

"If she'd listened to me, she'd still be married to Nelson."

"That's what I mean. You ought to be proud of her."

"I am proud of her. But I worry about her, too."

Hannah's laugh was low and hoarse, as if she'd smoked all her life, rather than just the years after her husband had died and before the doctor and her daughter had made her give it up. "It gives you something to do."

Millie sighed, and when she spoke again, Hannah heard the conscious attempt at gentleness. Her daughter's voice reminded her of the lotion the night nurse had rubbed on her when she'd been in the hospital after her heart attack. The lotion had been soothing, but there'd been a chill to it.

"Did Cruz give you your digitalis?"

"She gave it to me. You don't have to ask every day."

"I just wanted to make sure."

23

"So now you're sure," Hannah said, and was immediately ashamed of herself. Millie was just trying to take care of her. It wasn't Millie's fault that she hated being taken care of.

"Remind me to give Isobel that letter," Millie said after a while.

"What letter?"

"I know it's silly, but it's up to her to decide what to do with it."

"What are you talking about?"

"Just some crazy letter that came here addressed to her."

"And you opened it?"

There was a moment's pause, as if Millie were a child caught in the act and trying to think of an excuse. "I had to find out if it was something urgent or if it could wait until I saw her," she said finally.

"And?"

"It's a chain letter."

"Then why didn't you throw it out?"

"I wouldn't throw out someone else's mail." Righteousness stiffened her words like a backbone. "It lists all these awful things that happened to people who broke the chain. One woman was murdered in her bed. I know none of it's true," she rushed on before Hannah could make fun of her, "but still. Besides, it came from one of her old college friends so I thought I ought to let her decide for herself."

"What you ought to do is let her open her own mail."

Millie said nothing to that, and they sat in silence again.

"She's bringing Pete," Millie said finally.

Pete. That was his name. "You told me."

"This one's been going on for a while."

Hannah didn't say anything.

Millie shook her head. "I don't understand why they never last. She's my daughter, and I love her, but I have to say I think it's her fault. She doesn't try hard enough. She's not—I don't know—loyal."

"You want loyalty? You go to Bide-A-Wee and bring home something in a cardboard carrier."

"Don't talk to me about cardboard carriers. Now she's moved that cat into his apartment. If she had any sense, she'd think more about him and less about that animal."

"That's what happens when you take a pet away from a child."

Hannah saw the amorphous form float higher in the room and felt a pinprick of shame, or maybe it was fear. She'd gone too far. "Where are you going?"

"To answer the door. Didn't you hear the bell?"

"Of course, I heard the bell."

From the chair Hannah watched Millie cross the living room to the front door and open it to Isobel and that man. Pete. At this distance the figures were sharper. Millie and Isobel leaned forward to kiss, then pulled back. The effect of those identical profiles—Millie's chin rounded and sagged with age, and Isobel's jawline was still clean, but the high foreheads and sharp noses and long, unbending necks were the same—was eerie, like the twin faces of a Janus head, but instead of facing out toward the world, they turned in on each other.

Then Isobel said something and laughed, and Hannah saw the difference. When her granddaughter laughed, Hannah always said, she looked as if she were taking a big bite of life. Millie had never exactly disagreed with her mother. She'd merely begun teaching Isobel at an early age how to apply makeup to make her mouth appear smaller. For a while Isobel had taken her mother's lessons to heart and fought her image with a paint box of brazen hues. Then she'd gone to the other extreme, renounced all makeup, and walked around with a colorless dare on her face. Now she'd settled somewhere be-

25

tween the two and even begun restoring the red highlights to her hair. That was okay with Hannah. She'd never been one of those women who confuse a drab appearance with a high moral purpose.

Millie went up on her toes, and the man, Pete, bent to kiss her cheek. Hannah didn't have anything against him. He was better than most of them Isobel had brought home. She just wished Millie wouldn't make such a fuss about him. Anyway, you'd think Millie would know by now. The more fuss she made, the sooner it would be over.

The faces grew soft and fuzzy as Millie and Isobel and Pete came into the study. Hannah felt Isobel's cheek against her own. It gave off a lot of heat.

"How are you, Nana?"

"Ask your mother. She'll tell you I'm crotchety."

"You said it. I didn't."

That man, Pete, told her she was looking well. He said it like a compliment, not a diagnosis. Hannah knew she shouldn't be annoyed. Hypocrisy was just another word for charm.

"I was beginning to worry," Millie said.

Isobel sat on the sofa across from her mother and grandmother. "We were way downtown, and the traffic was awful."

"Friday afternoon," Millie said. "You should have left earlier to give yourself time."

"What were you doing way downtown?" Hannah asked, and Isobel thought again that it was funny what her grandmother did and didn't hear.

Pete looked at Isobel. Isobel glanced from her mother to her grandmother and back again. She smiled and shrugged.

"Getting married."

Millie clapped her hands together and let out a sound so girlish it didn't seem to come from her, but no one else in the room was young enough for it either. "I don't believe it."

"It's true."

Millie turned to Pete. "She's not teasing me, is she?"

"Nope. She made an honest man out of me."

"What did you say?" Hannah asked.

All three of them answered at the same time. "They got married." "We got married." "I said she made an honest man out of me."

"You don't have to shout," Hannah said.

"Now you have to stay for dinner," Millie insisted. "Or better yet, we'll go out and have a real celebration."

Pete cleared his throat.

Isobel said they couldn't.

"What do you mean you can't? It isn't every day you get married. The bride's family is supposed to make a celebration, and we're the bride's family."

"We're going away for the weekend," Pete explained in the professional voice that always made Isobel uneasy. It wasn't exactly insincere, only so gentle and reassuring that it sounded as if he were talking someone in off a ledge.

"We're going to a motel with mirrors on the ceiling and rates by the hour." Isobel shot Hannah a conspiratorial grin.

Hannah didn't smile back. Millie pretended not to hear. Or maybe she really didn't hear, because she was talking about a pair of cuff links she'd found in her drawer the other day.

"They belonged to Isobel's father. Now there was a man. I wish I could have known him."

"What are you talking about?" Hannah asked.

"Harry," Millie shouted. "I said I wish Pete could have known him."

"You said you wish you could have known him," Hannah pointed out.

"No, I didn't. Anyway, it's the excitement." She turned to Pete. "I was going to have the cuff links made into earrings for

Isobel, but now I want you to have them. Now that you're in the family. I'll go get them."

"We don't have much time," Isobel said.

"It'll just take a minute." Millie touched Pete's arm as she started out of the study.

"Everybody says I'm crazy," she called back from the living room, "to keep this big place just for the two of us. With stairs no less. But I always wanted Isobel to have a home. . . ."

As the sound of Millie's voice grew fainter, Isobel moved to the side of Hannah's chair and reached an arm around her shoulders. Their fragility made her think of the times when she was small and used to help set the table with Millie's fine china and crystal. The possibility of disaster had always yawned so enormously.

"Are you disappointed in me, Nana?"

"Thanks a lot," Pete said.

"This has nothing to do with you. I'm talking about principles."

Isobel turned back to her grandmother. Hannah lifted her face to Isobel slowly. Her skin was translucent as parchment. Behind the thick lenses of her glasses, her eyes had an unfocused glaze, like hard little marbles.

"If you're happy," Hannah said flatly, "I'm happy." Then her fading lips turned up at both ends so her mouth looked like a slice of unripe cantaloupe. "At least he's monogamous."

Pete looked surprised, but before he could say anything, they heard Millie's voice growing louder again. She was saying now that Isobel was married, now that Isobel had a real home and not that closet she'd been camping out in, maybe she'd put this place on the market after all and—

There was a faint scream and a thud, or maybe the thud came first. Isobel and Pete were on their feet in an instant, but he beat her through the double doors into the living room. By the time they got to the foot of the stairs, Millie was trying to stand.

"I've been meaning to call the handyman to tack down the runner on that stair for weeks." A quiver of fear ran beneath the indignation in Millie's voice.

Pete and Isobel were reaching down to help her, as Hannah came up behind them. "What happened?"

"It's nothing. I caught my heel in the runner."

They'd managed to lift Millie up, and she was still hanging on to Pete's arm with one hand while she smoothed her skirt with the other.

"Most serious accidents occur in the home," Hannah said.

"This was not a serious accident!" Millie snapped.

"All the same, maybe you ought to get off your feet," Pete said, and slid his other hand under her elbow to help her to the couch in the living room. As she put weight on her left foot, her mouth pulled back in a grimace.

She half hopped to the sofa, and Pete lowered her onto it, and Isobel put a pillow behind her back, and Hannah said maybe they ought to call the doctor.

"What do you mean, call a doctor?" Millie said. "Pete is a doctor."

"How do you feel about the fall?" he joked, but he was touching her ankle as he said it. Then he slid off the good Italian pump, and examined her toes with their pedicured scarlet nails glowing through the silky stockings, and moved her foot around one way, then the other. "The foot's okay," he said finally, "and the leg's not bad either. Must run in the family."

Millie smiled—no, beamed—at Pete. Hannah cleared her throat with a sound like a door swinging on a rusty hinge. Isobel asked if she should tell Cruz to get a basin of water to soak it, but Pete said it would probably be okay if Millie just stayed off it for the rest of the night. That was when Millie noticed that it was close to eight, and said that by the time Isobel and Pete went home to get their things and picked up the car, it would be after nine, and they had to eat something, so they might as well stay for dinner after all. They could leave for the country in the morning. Isobel saw the way Millie touched her ankle as she said it, and knew they were trapped.

They were halfway across the park before Pete brought it up. Isobel was surprised he'd waited that long. In his place she would have cornered him going down in the elevator.

"What was that line about my being monogamous?"

She kept her head turned to the open window while she debated her answer. The hot wind assaulted her face. She could say, "I don't know, I guess Hannah just thinks you look reliable," or she could tell the truth.

"Remember that conversation we had about a ménage à trois?"

"What are you talking about?"

Isobel reminded him of an evening when they'd first known each other. They'd gone out to dinner and found themselves at a table next to an unsavory threesome. She couldn't remember the sexual breakdown of the trio, but she remembered the aura they'd given off. There'd been a lot of under-the-table groping and mutual finger sucking.

"Have you ever been to bed with more than one person at a time?" she'd asked. They were still at that stage when she thought they had to swap a lot of information about *before*.

"No." The word had come out as a growl. For a man who made his living listening to other people talk about their most intimate thoughts and acts, he could be strangely reticent about his own.

"Neither have I." She hadn't meant to sound wistful, because it wasn't something she wanted to do, but she couldn't get over the feeling that at some point in that brief window of time after the sexual revolution and before the arrival of AIDS, she should have.

"Then I guess that's one more thing we don't have to worry about," he'd announced, and changed the subject.

"You told Hannah about that conversation!" he said as he paid the driver and climbed out of the cab.

She waited until they were past the doorman and in the elevator to answer. "She wasn't shocked."

"I wasn't worried about her sensibilities. I was thinking of my privacy. Is there anything that goes on between us that you don't tell them?"

"I don't tell them anything that goes on between us," she said as she followed him off the elevator. "I just told Hannah one thing that didn't go on between us."

He took a key ring from his pocket and bent to the lock. "Hell!"

"You're making too much of it."

"I'm not talking about that. The damn key won't turn."

"Are you sure you have the right one?"

"Of course, I'm sure." He went on jiggling the key in the lock. "I could swear someone's been messing around with this."

"Of course, someone's been messing around with it. This is New York City. Seven million people, six hundred and fifty thousand of whom, maybe six hundred and seventy-five thousand of whom don't live as well as you do, and resent it. Why wouldn't they want to trash your apartment?"

He took the key out and looked at it. "It's not funny, Isobel. Someone's been at this."

She took the key and moved in front of him. "Come on, slugger." She slipped the key into the lock. "You have a doorman, a concierge, and a couple of dozen porters." She turned the key. "Everything short of barbed wire and bloodhounds."

31

She pushed open the door. "No one could even get upstairs to tamper with your lock in this fortress." She stepped into the entrance hall and flicked on the light. "You're just rattled at your newly married state."

He followed her into the apartment. "Didn't I ever tell you about my *Pentagon Papers* incident?"

She stopped and turned back to face him. "You were mixed up with the *Pentagon Papers!*"

"My God, I married a celebrity fucker. I meant my *Pentagon Papers*–like incident. One afternoon when I came back from the hospital, the door was unlocked. I figured I'd forgotten to lock it, except I'm usually pretty careful about that. Then a couple of days later I noticed a file was missing. The file belonged to a patient who was thinking of running for office."

"You're kidding! Did you report it?"

"To whom? This is a country that reveres Richard Nixon as an elder statesman and thinks Ollie North's a national hero."

"Still, there must be someone, some agency or something."

"You have too much faith in the system. I warned the patient and let it go. Do you want a drink?"

"If you do."

"After tonight I don't want one, I need one." He started down the hall to the kitchen.

She started toward the bedroom, then changed her mind and followed him to the kitchen. "I still want to know how they got up here, with all your doormen and concierges and security."

"Piece of cake. All they had to do was flash a fake badge and produce a ten-dollar bill. Five if Angel was on duty."

She stood in the door watching him move around the room. The grace of his gestures always surprised her. Sometimes it made her wish she'd known him when he was young and still carried himself with the faint swagger of athletic and sexual pride she'd seen in the old photographs, though she knew in those days she never would have spotted it beneath the conventional camouflage.

"What would have happened if you'd been here at the time?"

"They knew I wouldn't be. That's the point. It was my morning at the hospital."

"That's even worse."

"Why? I didn't want to meet them."

"But that means they watched you and tracked your movements and knew all about your life."

"Not all, I hope."

"I'm serious."

He looked up at the sound of her voice. "I'm sorry I ever mentioned it."

She didn't like the look on his face. It was the same one he'd worn when she'd said she couldn't believe he spent most of his time at the hospital in locked wards. The look was tender, but it packed a patronizing wallop. She pulled herself up and away from the doorjamb. "If I'd known your apartment wasn't any safer than mine, I'm not sure I'd have gone through with this afternoon."

He looked up at her again, and this time he grinned. "You'd have gone through with it."

She went back down the hall and through the waiting room. She was halfway to the bedroom when she stopped, retraced her steps, and crossed to the front door. She turned the knob back and forth to make sure it was locked, then checked the bolt. She knew it was a dumb thing to do, but she couldn't help herself. Just as she couldn't help feeling that there was something upside down about working in locked wards and living in unlocked apartments.

When Pete came into the bedroom a few minutes later, carrying two glasses, she was standing beside the bed, holding the

33

phone to her ear with one hand and wriggling out of her jacket with the other.

He put the glasses down on the night table and tugged the knot of his tie loose. "If you're talking to any member of your family, even a distant cousin, I want a divorce."

She dropped her jacket on the bed and began unbuttoning her blouse. "Why not go for an annulment? We haven't consummated this deal yet."

He began unbuttoning his shirt. When he was half dressed at the beach or naked walking around the bedroom, she barely noticed the patch of silky dark hair on his chest, but the first view of it through an open shirt always struck her as strangely promising.

"I'm not the one who stopped in the elevator, slugger. Who're you talking to, anyway?"

She unzipped her skirt and stepped out of it. "I'm not. I'm listening to my machine. My lesbian heavy breather's at it again."

He stopped with his suspenders half off and looked at her. "Your what?"

She began tugging at her panty hose. "Some woman who calls and asks for Linda or Fred or Frank. It's a different name every time. She tries to use a different voice, too. Sometimes she even goes in for accents. My favorite is a kind of husky Garbo. 'I vish to speak to . . .' She's a good mimic. Once she asked for Peter. No accent that time, but it threw me a little, so I said, 'Peter who?' and she hung up."

He sat in the chair beside the bed and began unlacing his shoes. "What makes you think she's a lesbian?"

She sat on the side of the bed to peel off her panty hose. "Because after I hang up, the phone always rings again, right away, and there's just the sound of someone breathing, heavy-duty breathing, on the other end of the phone."

He took off his trousers and draped them over the chair. Welch pawed at the suspenders. "Did you report her to the phone company?"

Isobel shrugged as she slipped out of her blouse. "It doesn't happen all that often. Anyway, it isn't as if it were a man."

He sat again, tugged off his socks, and dropped them on the floor. She was glad because there was something faintly absurd about a man in long over-the-calf socks and boxer shorts.

"What's that supposed to mean, that the only crazies in this city are men?"

She unhooked her bra. "Of course not, but she isn't chasing me around with a kitchen knife or anything like that. She doesn't even know who I am. And somehow, it just doesn't feel threatening the way it would if she were a man. Annoying, but not really frightening. Half the time I feel sorry for her. I mean, what kind of life can this woman have if she gets her kicks listening to some strange woman's voice on the phone?"

"She ought to see you now."

"Maybe next time she calls I'll give her the name of the Women's Counseling Service."

He took off his watch and put it on the night table. "I'd give her the name of the New York Telephone harassment prevention office."

She slipped out of her bikinis. "Ah, the infinite compassion of the helping professional."

He dropped his boxer shorts. "I gave at the office. All day long."

They stood on either side of the bed looking at each other.

"What now?" she asked.

"I could go out and ring for the elevator," he said, but he lifted one side of the comforter and got into bed. She started to lift the other side, then stopped.

"We have to change sides."

35

"What?"

"You're supposed to be on this side; I'm supposed to be on that one."

"We've been sleeping this way for a year and a half."

"The husband is supposed to sleep on the left, as you're facing the bed."

"Whose rule is that, your grandmother's or your mother's?"

"Both. But for once they're right. Move over."

He moved over, and she got into bed beside him. He'd left an indentation warm as a nest. She settled into it and molded herself against him. He put his right hand on her hip. She put her left on the patch of silky dark hair.

"Is there a reason for this?" he asked as he slid his hand up the curve of her midriff. "I mean, are we warding off the evil eye or propitiating the goddess of fertility or something?"

She let her hand trail down his stomach. "More practical than that. You're right-handed."

He put his left hand between her legs. "Obviously neither your grandmother nor your mother ever went to bed with an ambidextrous man."

"You have a point."

They stopped talking for a while, but they didn't stop what they were doing.

"They also must have had remarkably stationary sex lives," she said as she climbed on top of him.

He put his hands on her breasts. They disappeared like peas in a street hustler's shell game. After a while his hands moved to her hips and began inching her up his chest. "Not to mention," he murmured, "a lack of imagination about the uses of other body parts."

Then the words turned into other sounds, and the world lurched into gear, and she stopped thinking about her family or anonymous callers or tampered locks. She simply stopped thinking, and that, when you stopped to think about it, was quite an achievement.

As Millie came into the study, stepping gingerly because her foot was still sore from her fall the night before, she saw the letter lying on the end table. In all the excitement she'd forgotten to give it to Isobel. She picked up the envelope and looked at Isobel's name and the Central Park West address again. The combination seemed fitting, as if even after all these years this was still her home. Then she remembered what was in the letter. Hannah was right, for once. No reasonable woman would give a letter like that a second thought. Certainly, no mother in her right mind would pass it on to her daughter. She crossed the room, careful to keep her weight on her good foot, and dropped it in the wastebasket.

THREE

THE FUNNY THING ABOUT BEING married, Isobel discovered as the sky over the park, which she could see from the living room of Pete's apartment, grew dark a little earlier each evening, was that it altered her life in small ways rather than large. Now when she talked to the cleaning woman or the doormen, she didn't have to refer to Pete as "the doctor," which she found pretentious, or "him," which was merely awkward, but could say "my husband," which struck her as archaic but effective. And now when she saw something silly in the paper or stupid on the news, or when she needed something from the top of a closet, or when she woke in a panic at three in the morning, Pete was there, though she knew he couldn't do anything about the things that terrified her in the night. Still, she liked his presence in her life. It reminded her of one of the anchors on the sloop they'd chartered the previous summer, the one Pete had called the luncheon anchor. Though it wasn't heavy—she could handle it on her own without a winch—it did the job.

She moved the few pieces of furniture that were worth taking from her apartment to Pete's. The wooden chair from an old Cunard liner, the thirties tea trolley shaped like an O on wheels, and the art nouveau hall stand called attention to themselves in the painstakingly decorated spaces like raffish intruders at a polite party. Pete didn't mind. He said they gave the place a lived-in air. The cleaning woman didn't agree.

"Where do you want me to put that stuff?" Mrs. Zelinski asked Isobel a few days after she'd moved the pieces in.

"What stuff?"

"That old wooden beach chair in Emily's room and the thing on wheels in the dining room."

"I don't want you to put them anywhere. I mean, they are where they belong."

Mrs. Zelinski looked as if Isobel had just asked her to wash her personal laundry by hand.

"That beach chair in *my* study is from an old Cunard liner."

Mrs. Zelinski shrugged. "That don't make it an antique," she said in a voice that was supposed to be under her breath, but actually carried to Isobel, who was already halfway down the hall.

Isobel didn't go back to argue. She knew there was no winning against Mrs. Zelinski.

In the beginning Isobel had thought the woman's disapproval of her was moral. The first time they'd met, Isobel had been coming out of the shower in Pete's terry-cloth robe. At a subsequent encounter several months later Mrs. Zelinski had come into the bedroom as Isobel was packing up her briefcase to leave for the office, held out a handkerchief with lace edging, and announced that she was paid to take care of the doctor and wasn't about to have everybody and anybody who spent the night in the apartment leaving laundry for her to do. Isobel had apologized and explained that the handkerchief had found its way into the doctor's laundry by accident. Mrs. Zelinski's long, sharp features had composed themselves into a sneer that said she could imagine what unsavory acts had led to Isobel's handkerchief ending up in Pete's hamper.

Isobel had thought she understood Mrs. Zelinski's disapproval. She'd been wrong. Mrs. Zelinski didn't resent her because of her illicit connection with Pete. She resented her because of her connection with Pete.

One morning Mrs. Zelinski found some underwear that Isobel, in a rare marital or at least domestic gesture, had laundered and put away in Pete's drawer. Mrs. Zelinski stood staring at the open drawer for a long moment before she spoke, though the ominous silence was lost on Isobel. She had to go on after work to an opening of one of those shows where celebrity designers turn a succession of uninhabited spaces into a series of unlivable rooms to benefit delinquent boys or drug-addicted girls or minor diseases, and she couldn't decide what to wear. She'd frequently had that problem since she'd gone to work at Urban Heritage. It hadn't taken long for her to look around and figure out that you could cross the picket line of an abortion clinic or demonstrate against a company that dumped hazardous waste in jeans and an Eddie Bauer parka that protected against a little mild manhandling as well as the cold, but conning a socially ambitious woman out of her husband's ill-gotten gains at La Côte Basque or talking Urban Heritage's way into an article at the Century Club required a costume with more cachet. On the other hand, she didn't want to look as if she'd gone over to the establishment. So during the past year she'd worked out a simple rule of thumb. First she'd ask herself what Tipper Gore would wear, next she'd figure out what Madonna would turn up in, and then she'd put together an outfit that came in somewhere between.

Mrs. Zelinski cleared her throat. "The doctor doesn't like his shorts folded in half like this."

It took Isobel a moment to look up from her jewelry box. "What?"

"The doctor's shorts. He likes them folded one side, then the other, then in half." As she spoke, Mrs. Zelinski turned a pair of

Pete's boxer shorts into a cunning little packet that reminded Isobel of those thin sheets of airmail stationery that become their own envelopes.

Isobel took off a string of pearls, put on a 1940s retro silver necklace, and told Mrs. Zelinski she was pretty sure her husband didn't care how his undies were folded, or, for that matter, if they were folded.

Mrs. Zelinski took the pile of incorrectly folded shorts from the drawer and began refolding. "Mrs. Arlen used to say the same thing."

"Mrs. Arlen!" Isobel said to Pete when she got home that night. "Who the hell am I if your first wife is Mrs. Arlen?"

"Ms. Behringer. You insisted on it, remember?"

"Rebecca to you, slugger. I'm living in a goddamn Hitchcock movie."

Isobel could joke about Mrs. Zelinski. When she wasn't lurking around the apartment, looking dark and malevolent, Isobel could even feel sympathy for her, because Isobel knew about the empty, hungry lives of domestic help. Mary, the maid Millie had hired when Isobel was small, used to take Isobel along on her days off. She'd tell people Isobel was her daughter. "I gained all this weight when I was carrying her," she'd confided to the saleswomen in Lane Bryant. "She takes after my husband," she'd explained to the waitresses in Schrafft's as she'd pulled a snapshot of Isobel's father and herself taken at some family gathering from her wallet. There'd been another copy of that snapshot in an album at home, but Isobel's mother hadn't been cut off the end of that one. Millie had fired Mary when Isobel was five or six. Not because of the lies she'd told saleswomen and waitresses, but because of the rash. The doctor hadn't been able to figure out what was wrong with Millie. Then one day she'd walked into the bathroom and found Mary scrubbing the toilet with her back brush. Isobel still found it hard to believe that her father had aroused such passion, but she'd never doubted that poor obese Mary had harbored such dreams. That was one of the reasons she did her best to put up with Mrs. Zelinski. Sometimes it wasn't easy. It wasn't easy the morning of the missing shoes incident.

Isobel had a lunch date that day with Grace Feyer, a woman who'd made it clear she'd bring her checkbook to the table if Isobel could promise an article or at least several paragraphs describing Mrs. Harlan Feyer's work on behalf of preservation causes in a reputable magazine, and by *reputable*, she did not mean *Quest* or *Avenue* or one of those giveaway rags that pile up on the fake Louis Quinze/Chippendale/Biedermeier tables in Upper East Side lobbies. The lunch was at Le Cirque, and style as well as neatness counted, but Isobel couldn't find her good black Robert Clergerie pumps, which would be a mere step above Keds to Grace Feyer but were the best Isobel could do.

She went through her closet from bottom to top twice, through what felt like miles of shelves and racks and cubbies. The spirit of the first Mrs. Arlen still hung in that closet: the spirit of a woman of compulsive orderliness who, from all appearances, had owned as many sweaters as Jay Gatsby had shirts and could have given Imelda Marcos a run for her money in the shoe department. Swinging from the few padded satin hangers left, Isobel's wardrobe reminded her of a thin crowd of subway riders who planned to get off at the next stop.

Finally, after she'd gone through every cubbyhole and even climbed up the ladder that slid back and forth across the shelves to get to the top a third time, she swallowed her pride and went across the hall to her study, where Mrs. Zelinski was rearranging the few things Emily had left in the drawers of the built-in wall unit. "You haven't by any chance seen a pair of black shoes, have you?" Isobel asked in a voice so sweet it made her teeth ache. "Plain black pumps with a medium heel."

43

Mrs. Zelinski went on taking sweaters out of the drawer, refolding them, and putting them back.

"Black calf," Isobel pleaded, and hated herself for doing it. "They say 'Robert Clergerie' inside."

Mrs. Zelinski finally looked up. She shook her head no and went back to folding.

"They were in my closet."

"I go in the big closet to vacuum," Mrs. Zelinski said. "Not that it does any good. I vacuum, an hour later everything's covered with cat hair. I don't understand how the doctor puts up with it. With his allergy and all."

"What allergy?" Isobel asked, then cursed herself for taking the bait.

"His allergy to cats."

"He isn't allergic to cats."

Mrs. Zelinski unfolded and refolded another sweater. "You don't do the laundry. You don't see the handkerchiefs. There are twice as many since that animal came."

Isobel went back to the bedroom and checked her closet once more. Then she looked at her watch, put on another pair of shoes, and left the apartment by the door at the end of the bedroom hallway so she wouldn't have to go through the waiting room.

She forgot the incident as soon as she got to her office, but it came back to her that night in a cab on the way to the Metropolitan Museum when she looked down and noticed the spot on her black silk pumps. When she'd first told Pete about the opening, he hadn't been able to believe he had to put on a black tie to stand around and look at pictures.

"Why don't we wait one more night and go to a regular preview?" he'd asked.

She'd sighed. He still didn't get her job. "Slugger, why do

you think people give money to organizations like Urban Heritage?"

"Because they want to save buildings?"

"Because they want to put on their black ties and go places where other people in black ties will see them."

"You mean you're going to be hitting people up for money at this thing?"

She'd never thought of him as naive before. "I'm not going to be walking around with a tin cup, if that's what you mean. I'm just going to be visible. So are you." He'd looked stricken. "Don't worry. All you have to do is drop the occasional fatuous comment about the artist's palette or the horizontal plane, and smile."

"Are you saying Mrs. Zelinski stole your shoes?" he asked as the cab nosed its way into the line of limos pulling up in front of the museum.

She waited while Pete paid the driver. Behind them a woman emerged from a limo and stood for a moment with her nose lifted to the evening air and her eyes to the pollution-streaked darkening sky. Farther up the sidewalk, another woman stepped out of a limo and stood the same way. Inside they'd size each other up. Out here at street level they didn't dare look around. There was no telling what they might see.

"All I'm saying," Isobel went on as they started up the stairs to the museum, "is that I had them a few days ago, and I don't have them now, and she's the only one in the apartment besides you and me. Unless you count a few dozen patients, but they aren't mucking around in my closet. At least I hope they're not."

As they reached the top of the stairs and stepped into the pool of light flooding out of the museum, she saw the expression on his face. "What are you smiling at?"

"The idea of a patient taking your shoes." He handed the

45

invitation to the man at the door, and they passed into the main hall. "The image is perfect. She'd be standing in your shoes."

She took his arm. "Just where every patient wants to be," she said, then pasted a smile on her face and plunged into the crowd.

She mentioned the shoes again on the way home. She didn't want to make too much of them, but the problem kept tugging at her.

"You must have misplaced them," he said.

"I don't misplace things." She remembered the theater tickets that she'd insisted she'd given to him and that he'd found in her jewelry box ten minutes before curtain time. "At least not favorite pairs of shoes," she added.

"Even if Mrs. Zelinski hadn't worked for me forever, have you noticed her feet? Like Fats Waller said, they're too big."

"I wear an eight and a half quad. I wouldn't call that tiny."

"Your feet are aristocratic. Mrs. Zelinski's are gunboats."

That took the wind out of her argument. She thought of the line about a patient wanting to stand in her shoes. The simple thing to do, the logical thing to do would be to put a lock on the door to the living part of the apartment, but she felt silly making the suggestion. She was still sure a patient had spied on her in the kitchen, but she couldn't believe one would sneak into her bedroom and steal her shoes. Her husband, if the patient could, sure, but not her shoes. Unless the patient was really off the wall, and then Pete would have seen to it that she was behind the locked doors of the wards and not wandering the unlocked rooms of the apartment. Isobel decided not to mention getting a lock for the inside door. It would sound worse than silly. It would sound paranoid.

"You misplaced the shoes," Pete said in the same tone he probably used to tell patients the hour was over and he'd see them next time. "They'll turn up eventually."

* * *

Since Pete had relinquished the big closet he'd taken over after his wife—correction, his first wife—had left, and made sure that Isobel's name as well as his was on the tenants' list at the concierge's desk in the lobby, and never even mentioned the allergy he might or might not have to cats, Isobel made a real effort to play by the rules. When she got home before he was finished with his last patient, she went through the service entrance and stayed in the kitchen, or used the other door at the end of the bedroom hallway and stayed in that part of the apartment until she heard the front door close and Pete come out and lock it.

She was even scrupulous about running into patients in the lobby. Three times in a row now she'd come home on Wednesday nights and passed the suicidal architect getting off the elevator as she was getting on. She was pretty sure that was who he was, because the architect was Pete's last patient on Wednesdays, and she could tell from the panel above the elevator that it came straight from nineteen to the lobby, and there was only one other apartment on the nineteenth floor. Isobel tried not to look at him, but she couldn't help noticing that his eyes had a sore, red, puffy appearance, like abscesses that needed lancing, and that he was wearing a muffler exactly like one of Pete's, which struck Isobel as creepy or at least pathetic. When did imitation cross the line from flattery to cannibalism? But she was careful not to stare, or smile, or even look sorry for him.

It was more difficult to keep her cover the evening she came home from the office and ran into Isabelle Fowler getting off the elevator, which had descended straight from nineteen to the lobby. For a time Isobel and Isabelle, who'd lived on the same floor of Pembroke West for their last two years at Bryn Mawr, had been good friends. At least people had always assumed they were, and given the proximity of their rooms and

47

the coincidence of their names—though both of them were always eager to point out to anyone who was interested and some who weren't that they spelled it differently—and the fact that though they didn't look alike, the similarity of their physical types and coloring made people think they did, it had been easier to play the role than fight it. Besides, they must have had something in common because they'd even attracted and been attracted to the same men. A year after they'd graduated and shortly after Isobel and Nelson had agreed to their perfectly amicable separation, Isabelle and Nelson had taken up together. Isobel hadn't been jealous. If anything, she'd felt flattered that Isabelle was emulating her. Standing in her shoes, as Pete would say. At least she'd felt that way until Isabelle and Nelson had split up and Isabelle had started telling people that Nelson was so boring he was the Typhoid Mary of narcolepsy. After that the imposed friendship had dwindled and, when Isobel had moved to New York, finally died.

Isobel spotted Isabelle immediately, but it took a minute for Isabelle to recognize Isobel. Of course, that might have had something to do with the fact that when the elevator door opened, Isabelle was staring at the space where the door used to be with glazed eyes and an air of crystalline preoccupation. Isobel's first thought was that her husband must be one hell of a shrink.

After Isabelle recognized Isobel and they went through the usual long-lost-friend routine, Isabelle asked what Isobel was doing there. Isobel said she lived there, and Isabelle said that was a coincidence because her shrink lived in the building, too. Isobel didn't know what to say to that, but then Isabelle said she was late, told Isobel they really had to get together for lunch, and headed for the revolving wood-and-glass door, and Isobel didn't have to say anything at all.

She did, however, plan to say something to Pete. And she

would have if Pete hadn't been on the phone when she used her key to let herself into the apartment. The door to his office was open, but he held his finger to his lips in warning. He still hadn't forgiven her for that time before they were married when he was talking on the phone to a patient whose mother had just died, and she'd come bounding into the apartment shouting, "Hiya, sweetballs," at the top of her lungs.

Tonight Isobel was quiet. She put her briefcase down on the hall floor gently. She tiptoed into his office silently. She bent and gave him a kiss on the top of his head wordlessly. She went back to the waiting room and hung up her coat without rattling a single hanger. She didn't even turn on any music when she went into the kitchen, though she did do a double take. Someone had moved the Cuisinart and the KitchenAid and the coffee grinder. The fact that they'd been rearranged didn't surprise Isobel, but the way they'd been rearranged did. When she'd first moved into the apartment, she'd shifted some of the appliances from one counter to another in what she'd thought was a more efficient arrangement. Mrs. Zelinski had moved them back. The battle had gone on for a few weeks, but in the end Isobel had given up. She really didn't care where things stood in the kitchen, and Mrs. Zelinski seemed to. But the strange thing about the current rearrangement was that someone had put the appliances back where Isobel had placed them originally. She should have been glad, but instead she just felt uneasy. Mrs. Zelinski wasn't given to graceful surrenders. Besides, it was Monday, and Mrs. Zelinski came in on Tuesday and Friday. Of course, Pete could have moved things, only she knew the man she married wouldn't spend his ten-minute breaks dashing into the kitchen to rearrange appliances. As she took the bin of ice from the freezer, she remembered the black pumps and felt even more uneasy. Then she opened the refrigerator to take out the siphon of seltzer. She should have known.

The shelves overflowed with plastic containers and foil packages and handsomely wrapped delicacies.

It wasn't that Millie thought there were no stores on the East Side or that Isobel couldn't cook. Actually she had her doubts about the latter, but she never mentioned them. At least she tried not to. It was merely that she knew how busy Isobel was and just wanted to take a little of the burden off her daughter and onto herself.

Pete came striding into the kitchen and announced that there was a lot of pain and suffering in the world, in case she wasn't aware of the fact. She closed the refrigerator door. She wasn't trying to hide anything, but she knew how Pete would interpret Millie's care packages, and the world's anguish and longings sat heavy on his shoulders tonight. The remittance girl was refusing to take the medication that was finally stabilizing her, and the lawyer whose lover was leaving him for a younger man was so broken up he was having trouble functioning at work, and the architect had made another reference to suicide during his hour, he told her in a single breath.

Pete was funny about his patients. He didn't mind talking about them. In fact, sometimes during dinner he'd begin telling her about an insight or a breakthrough or a new patient and get so carried away that her plate would be empty while his was still full. But he wouldn't give her any information that might allow her to identify the individuals. One Sunday afternoon when he was sending out bills, she'd come up behind him and asked what he was doing. His hand had flown to cover the name on the envelope the way someone caught naked might rush to cover an erogenous zone. "Jesus," she'd said, "talk about overreaction," but she'd known from the way his shoulders had hunched forward to protect the patient—against what? against her, of course—that he hadn't thought it was funny. So she'd come to know the women and men who peopled his days not by names or places of employment or any other identifiable details, but by symptoms and causes and generic careers. There was the graduate student who'd been sexually abused by both her twin brothers, and the architect who'd found his mother lying in a tub of cooling water as the blood seeping from her wrists turned it crimson, and the magazine editor who still couldn't forgive her father for abandoning her —forget her mother—when she was on the verge of puberty.

He poured himself a drink, sat at the long trestle table, and began telling her about the magazine editor, who'd been his last patient of the day.

Isobel started to say something to stop him—she really did—but he went on before she could.

"Don't start that business about her being my favorite patient and countertransference and all that again. I'm serious. I thought we were making progress, but she walked in today and announced she was having an affair with the husband of one of her closest friends. A year ago she was in love with another friend's fiancé."

"Tell me about it," Isobel said as she took a container of brussels sprouts from the refrigerator. She was thinking of Nelson, and meant it as a slang expression. He took her literally. In three minutes Isobel learned more about Isabelle Fowler than she had living on the same floor of the same dorm for two years, and certainly more than she ought to know.

"About this last patient," Isobel said without looking up from the brussels sprouts she was trimming. "I think I know her." Then, with her eyes still on her work, she told him about their rooms on the same floor of Pembroke West, and Nelson, and their meeting in the lobby half an hour earlier.

He sat staring at her for a minute. She felt his gaze, stopped cutting, and finally looked up to meet his eyes.

"Freud was right," he said.

51

She knew what was coming, and she resisted the impulse to throw something at him. Not a knife, just something harmless, like a brussels sprout.

"Women have no sense of morality."

She should have ignored it because in his more rational moments Pete admitted that the Father of Psychoanalysis, the God of Insight, Our Hero was also an uptight, penis-obsessed Victorian misogynist. If anything, Pete went out of his way to compensate for the bias. But she couldn't ignore it because the slur struck a chord that resonated deep within her. Hannah had seen to that, Hannah and Millie both.

She couldn't remember when the argument had started, or when it had petered out, for that matter. If she'd been a boy, it would have begun with the rituals of her infancy, but she was a girl, and there were no rituals. That was Hannah's point. All she knew was that the noise of her mother's and grandmother's disagreement had been the long discordant riff that had run through her youth. Her earliest memory of it went back to the time Millie had enrolled her in religious school.

Hannah had been outraged. "Why not just send her back to the shtetl?"

"Temple Emanu-El is not exactly a shtetl." Millie's voice had been quiet, not only because she knew she was right but because she knew she was in control. The men, Isobel's father and grandfather, were on her side.

"Temple Emanu-El!" Hannah had spit out the words. "I didn't even know they had a school. What do they teach there? How to tell a Chanel from a Norell?"

The school would teach Isobel, Millie had said as the years had passed and they'd played their variations on a theme, spiritual values and moral lessons and a sense of belonging.

"Belonging!" Hannah had sneered. "To a religion that starts

every day, at least the men are supposed to start every day, with the prayer 'Thank you, God, for not making me a woman.' "

Isobel put the knife down and turned to face Pete. "Terrific. From Yahweh to Freud in four short millennia."

That stopped him for a moment.

"You still should have told me you knew who the patient was." There was conciliation in his voice, but it was grudging.

She thought about that for a minute. She could say she'd tried, but in fact, she hadn't tried hard. On the other hand, she didn't blame herself much, either. There wasn't a woman she knew who would have resisted the temptation to pick up a little information, and if a man had acted differently in the same situation, she was willing to bet it had more to do with an absence of interest in people than an excess of moral scruples. But she knew that wasn't the point. She might have been acting normally, but she wasn't playing by the rules. It was all right for patients to be curious about her, to scheme and snoop and search for clues, but she measured herself against a more exacting moral standard. "You're right," she said finally. "I'm sorry. I should have."

There wasn't much he could say to that, so he stood, carried his drink to the counter, and helped her finish trimming the sprouts.

They stayed away from his patients during dinner, and by the time they finished they'd just about forgiven each other their transgressions. Then, at a little after eleven, the phone rang.

"Who'd call at this hour?" Pete said.

Isobel didn't answer, because she had a good idea who'd call at this hour. Millie still hadn't been thanked for all that food.

He picked up the phone on the night table. "There's no Arthur here," he said after a moment. "You have the wrong number."

She sat watching him as he hung up the phone. His brows had come together the way they did when he was trying to figure something out. She had a feeling he was thinking the same thing she was, but before she could say anything, the phone rang again.

"Don't pick it up," she said. "Let her breath into the machine."

They sat on opposite sides of the bed, books open and ignored on their laps, listening to the sounds from the study across the hall. All they heard was the series of clicks on the machine that meant the caller had hung up.

"What happens when you call your old number?" he asked.

"What do you mean?" she said, though she already knew what he meant.

"Do they give you this number or do they just say the phone has been disconnected?"

"They say the phone has been disconnected."

"So she isn't a random caller after all," he said. "She's a woman who knows your name and was interested enough to call information to get your new number."

FOUR

PETE WANTED HER TO GET AN UN-
listed phone, but Isobel said she'd just changed her number a
few weeks ago, and only women who imagined pinches in elevators and a man under every bed changed their phone numbers each month. She was going to ignore the calls, she insisted,
just as she was ignoring the shoes that still hadn't turned up
and that incident the other morning when she'd come out of
the bedroom and found the door to the waiting room open.
She was especially going to ignore the open door, which might
have been the result of a patient's curiosity, but was probably
just the consequence of Welch's perseverance and an old latch
that didn't always catch. Though Isobel still didn't know
whether Pete was allergic to cats, she did know that this particular cat was here on sufferance, and she wasn't about to push
Welch's luck, or her own. Not now. Not when she was finally
happy. Before this she'd been triumphant when she'd helped
bring down a business scam or an environmental polluter and
proud when she'd contributed to saving a species or a spirit or
a freedom, she'd been euphoric at the beginning of affairs and
relieved at the end, but she'd never felt this slow, steady stream
of pleasure flowing from day to day.

The odd thing, though, was that she couldn't tell anyone.
Her single friends would think she was gloating. Several of her

married friends had asked how it was working out, but before she'd had a chance to answer, they'd gone on to say they knew how difficult it must be. "The adjustment." They'd shaken their heads. "After all these years." She hadn't had the heart to tell them it was just about the easiest thing she'd ever done.

She thought of telling Hannah, because ever since Isobel was small, her grandmother had insisted she could tell her anything, but somehow Isobel felt she couldn't tell her this.

The logical person to tell was Millie. Isobel knew exactly how Millie would smile and nod, not quite smug, just immeasurably pleased to be proven right. But when they spoke, Isobel never managed to find an opening between Millie's reports on white sales and furniture auctions and new outlets for kitchen equipment. It didn't matter how often Isobel explained that since she and Pete were combining two apartments, they had more than enough linens and furniture and kitchen gadgets, especially kitchen gadgets, as Millie must have noticed when she'd re-arranged all those appliances. They had two minichoppers, and two toaster-ovens, and two of everything, except knives. They had dozens of those. Butcher knives and carving knives, chopping knives and paring knives, bread knives and all-purpose knives. Pete's collection was the result of what Isobel thought of as a universal male kitchen obsession; her own, of a succession of too many males in her kitchen.

There was another reason Isobel didn't confide in Hannah and Millie. She told herself it had to do with privacy, but she knew it was more than that. She didn't confide in them because they were too hungry to know.

But as the days began to shrink, so that when Isobel got home in the evening, all she could see from the living room windows were the lights of the West Side glowing with secret security in the hazy autumn dusk, she found she was dying to tell someone. She ended up telling a young woman she barely knew. She ended up telling one of her Society Library pickups.

If the New York Society Library weren't already a city landmark, Isobel would have mobilized Urban Heritage to make it one. It wasn't just the Italianate facade, which was respectable, even pleasing, but nothing to write home about. It was the feel of the place. Like Pete's kitchen—our kitchen, Pete kept correcting her, but Isobel remembered the stipulations in the uncle's will—the library was a haven from the real world.

Isobel had started going there to do research when she'd worked for the consumer advocacy group and had been frequenting it ever since. During the week, when she had to write a speech or prepare a testimony, it offered asylum from the noisy circus that was her job. On Saturdays, when Pete was at the Harvard Club playing squash, it simply provided asylum. Isobel knew that most of her friends and her mother and maybe even Pete thought her attachment to the place was peculiar. Wouldn't she prefer, her mother and her friends insisted, to have lunch or shop or let the experts work over her nails or pores or cellulite? How could she stand, Pete asked, being cooped up like that? But she liked the ambiance of the old town house that made her feel as if Edith Wharton might turn up at any moment, and she enjoyed browsing through the slick magazines and self-important journals and dusty books, and she reveled in the escape. The only problem was that the library was such a haven, such a peaceful anachronism in the howling, menacing city lurking beyond those long French windows, that it attracted the disaffected the way sidewalk three-card monte games attracted tourists. Over the years Isobel had come to recognize some of the regulars. There was the nattily dressed man with pomaded hair and an Eastern European accent who read the library copy of the *Wall Street Journal* and preyed on the rich widows and trust fund tootsies who stopped in to keep abreast of *Town and Country* and *Architectural Digest*. There was the successful author of several sex manuals who claimed she came to the library to do research, which had confused Isobel until she'd stumbled on her in the stacks with a would-be writer who was young enough to be her son, or at least her protégé. There was the intense though unpublished novelist who always took the same seat in front of one of the French windows, spread thirty or forty pencils sharpened to lethal points out on the end table, and had a habit of muttering to herself while she worked. There was even, though she wasn't a regular, the current mother-in-law of Isobel's former husband, a hawk-eyed woman who had an unfathomable—in view of Nelson's enduring second marriage—habit of mailing Nelson newspaper clippings showing Isobel in a series of unflattering poses at a variety of unruly demonstrations. There were also a lot of lonely people at loose ends. Whenever Isobel came home with another story about one of the regulars, Pete said the Member's Room sounded more like a minimum-security ward than a library. Isobel said he was exaggerating. The people who hung out there were just average New Yorkers. Pete said that was what he meant.

He also said she was too trusting. She resolved to be more wary, but when a perfectly ordinary-seeming man asked to borrow a scrap of paper so he could make a note from a journal he was reading, or a young woman who was highlighting a copy of *When You and Your Mother Can't Be Friends* with a thick yellow marker asked the time, Isobel couldn't very well hide her pad or refuse to look at her watch.

"You couldn't refuse to look at your watch," Pete agreed, "but you didn't have to go for coffee and listen to her problems."

"I didn't go for coffee with her." Isobel's voice was indignant, because at that time she still hadn't. "We came out of the library at the same time and ended up walking up Madison Avenue together. We talked about graduate school. She's getting a Ph.D. in English lit."

"She's looking for a mother."

"I'm not that much older than she is," Isobel insisted, though she knew age wasn't the issue and feared Pete might be on to something. When Lucy Price had asked which way Isobel was heading and Isobel had said uptown, Lucy's face had creased with the kind of smile that had made Isobel think if Lucy had had a tail, it would have been thumping against the pavement. "I'm the same age as the photographer she lives with. The one she keeps breaking up with and going back to."

"You got that in your first conversation?"

"Second." She saw the way Pete was looking at her. "Women talk differently."

She supposed that was why she ended up telling Lucy Price how much she liked being married to Pete. Because women did talk differently. Still, Isobel wasn't the one who brought the subject up. Kay Glass did that.

Kay wasn't exactly another library pickup. She was a friend of Hannah's.

An extraordinary thing had happened to Hannah after her husband had died. As she'd grown older, she'd begun attracting younger women. Wherever she went, she made friends of women ten, fifteen, twenty years her junior. Friends, Hannah said, who still had futures.

But now that Hannah could no longer get around to museums and theaters and movies on her own, her circle had dwindled. They still adored Hannah; they still called her feisty, and fearless, and said they hoped they had as much spunk when they reached her age; but there were fewer of them. That was probably one of the reasons Hannah had taken such an interest in Kay Glass when she'd met her at one of the Friday afternoon concerts, that and the fact that Kay's mother had known Zelda-the-Blacklisted-Actress. Hannah had even asked Isobel to talk to Kay, who'd quit her job to have her first child fifteen years ago and was eager to get back into the work force now.

"It's the least I can do," Hannah had said, and Isobel had refrained from pointing out that she was the one who'd be doing it. "She's so helpful. Sometimes she picks up and drops off books for me at the Society Library. She said she thinks she's seen you there."

"How would she know me?" Isobel asked.

"She said you were wearing my face, only younger." Hannah hesitated for a moment, then laughed. "And I showed her a picture."

Still, Kay Glass wasn't a library crazy, though she was one of those thin, nervous women who give off a lot of brittle energy, most of which goes into dressing well. When she came up to Isobel's office to drop off her résumé, she was wearing an Armani jacket—at least, Isobel thought it was an Armani; Millie would have known for sure—and her hair had the expensive ash blond streaks favored by so many otherwise cautious middle-aged women. But beneath the slick packaging was a perfectly pleasant woman who'd spent the past fifteen years fashioning her life to her husband and children the way women of earlier generations used to fit the clothes they sewed at home to a dressmaker's dummy. It had taken Isobel about two minutes of conversation to figure out that the dummy had begun to fray and tear and spill its guts, or maybe Kay had merely grown or shrunk. Whatever the reason, Isobel knew a woman in the market for a new dummy when she saw one. So she wasn't surprised a week or so later when she came across Kay and Lucy together on the landing outside the Member's Room of the Society Library.

"A woman in search of a mother and a mother whose children are growing up," she told Pete that night. "If ever there was a match made in heaven."

"Stay away from them," he said, and she didn't blame him because he knew how needy people like that could be. It was his job to know. She assured him she was going to, and didn't mention the conversation they'd had that afternoon.

"Hannah told me you just got married," Kay burst out before Isobel had even said hello. There was an echo of relief in her voice that Isobel had heard in the congratulations of other married women. The happy ones were welcoming a renegade to the fold. The miserable ones were reassuring themselves that no matter how bad their marriages were, being single was worse.

Lucy's head swiveled to Isobel so abruptly her silky blond hair swung against her cheeks. "You didn't tell me!"

"We didn't want to make a fuss," Isobel said, though she knew a young woman she'd picked up in the library and barely knew was the last person she owed an explanation.

"You were smart to wait until you were a grown-up," Kay said.

The comment was such a naked admission that Kay might as well have come out and said she was one of the miserable ones. Isobel felt a twinge of guilt for her own comparative bliss and rushed to balance the scales. "Not so smart. I was married before. Right out of college."

"You were!" Lucy's words were another accusation of betrayal.

"Hannah never mentioned that," Kay said.

"She wouldn't. Anyway, it only lasted eleven months."

"That's not a marriage," Lucy snapped, quick as a shot. "That's a long date."

How could Isobel not take to Lucy after that? Still, she never intended to tell her how much she liked being married to Pete,

61

and she probably wouldn't have if Lucy hadn't brought the subject up again on the way home from the library that afternoon.

"I thought," she began as they were standing on the corner waiting for the light to change, "that you didn't believe in marriage. I mean, from the way you talked and all that." Lucy's tone was thoughtful and a little sullen, as if she were trying to figure out whether she'd been taken in, or Isobel had.

"I don't suppose I did."

Lucy looked over at her sharply. "What made you change your mind?"

Isobel thought about that evening anchored off Fishers Island, but it was too private to talk about, even to a stranger, so instead she told Lucy it had to do with Edith Wharton. After all, Lucy was a student of literature.

"But she had a terrible marriage," Lucy said.

"Exactly. And when she met Morton Fullerton, she was forty-five. She'd already made a name for herself and was hanging out with people like Henry James. What I'm trying to say is she wasn't exactly unworldly. Then along came this dyed-in-the-wool womanizer and knocked her for a loop."

"I don't understand. Are you saying your husband was a womanizer and you wanted to reform him?"

"God, no. Anyway, I don't believe women reform men. They just make themselves and everyone else miserable trying to. All I meant was that I'm not as old as Edith, but I was getting to a point in life when I was beginning to think the only surprises I had left were dire medical prognoses. Then I met Pete. I guess I just figured I ought to do something about it." She hesitated. This was her chance. "And I'm glad I did."

A sigh, round and rosy as the autumn sun sliding behind the buildings on the other side of the park, escaped from Lucy. "That's such a romantic story."

Isobel was so surprised she stopped walking. Over the years she'd received the requisite long-stemmed roses and slim volumes of Shakespeare's and Browning's love sonnets; a two-hundred-dollar black lace teddy—the kind you dress up with a whip or down with a chain—which she'd returned to the lawyer whose client had been running a mail-order scam; and protestations of undying love from an environmentalist who'd locked himself in a mountain cabin, which just happened to have a phone, with a half gallon of Clan MacGregor scotch and a confiscated hunting rifle after Isobel had told him things weren't working out between them. Though she'd found the ploys silly or tacky or scary, she knew they'd been intended as romantic. At least, that was the way friends had described them at the time. But no one had ever used the word about Pete before.

Maybe that was why Isobel turned to Lucy with the story in the first place. She knew the reflection she'd get back.

Isobel told one other person how much she liked being married to Pete. She told Pete.

At first she hadn't intended to say anything. Not only was Pete strangely silent about his own feelings, but he was, Isobel had learned early in their affair, a little squeamish about hers. She'd made the discovery one night after they'd known each other for two or three months. They were both covered with a film of sweat, and his voice, as he stopped her from what she was starting to say, sounded as breathless as it did when he'd just finished half an hour on the stationary bike that stood in a corner of the bedroom.

"Isobel," he'd said, and put a hand that, for the record, was still redolent of her, over her mouth. "Just because you feel it doesn't mean you have to describe it."

That was the night she'd put away her Anaïs Nin for good.

But she had to tell Pete, because she couldn't believe how happy she was, and how long it had taken her to get that way.

Sometimes the happiness didn't seem fair, especially when she thought of what was going on in that dimly lit library at the other end of the apartment. Whenever she went there after hours, she couldn't help noticing that the wastebasket had at least a few crumpled tissues in it. Sometimes it was half full. Once she'd seen it overflowing. She wasn't spying. She just couldn't help noticing. Occasionally, as she stood on the warm terra-cotta tiles of the big kitchen unpacking groceries or peeling vegetables, she heard stifled sobs or angry shrieks on the other side of the wall. Other times, when there was no sound at all, she imagined misery seeping under the door like noxious fumes.

But it wasn't just her imagination. It was the stories Pete told her. When she heard the tales of abuse and abandonment and heartbreak, she felt improbably fortunate, and faintly guilty, and more than a little uneasy. Sometimes a patient reinforced her feelings. One night the lawyer who was being left for a younger man saw Pete and Isobel in a restaurant. He, too, played by the rules. He didn't come to the table, or wave hello, or intrude in any way. In fact, they didn't even know he'd been there until his session two days later, when he turned on Pete. It wasn't fair, he protested. Everyone had someone. Everyone was happy. Everyone except him. It wasn't fucking fair, he shouted, and lurched forward in his chair as if he were about to spring at Pete.

"What did you do?" Isobel asked.

"Nothing. I knew he wasn't really going to come at me."

"I didn't mean that. I meant, what did you do about his misery?"

"We talked about why he was so angry."

Isobel didn't say anything to that. She respected Pete's profession, no matter what he thought. She never could have got mixed up with him in the first place if she hadn't. But she couldn't help thinking there wasn't a lot of mystery or even psychological subtlety behind a jilted man's anger at the sight of a happy couple.

She had a harder time fathoming some of the other patients. Like the one who went in for rough sex.

"She's started picking up guys again," Pete announced one night at dinner.

"Is that so terrible?"

He put down his knife and fork. "She took this one home and let him tie her up."

Isobel stopped eating, too. "You're kidding. Ropes and chains and stuff?" She'd been striving for a tone of clinical disinterest, but she'd hit prurience. Her voice reminded her of Millie's when her mother used to quiz her after dates. It wasn't fear of Millie's disapproval that had made Isobel clam up. It was dread of her hunger, so deep and intense that it verged on cannibalism.

"Belts and panty hose. And this time an Hermès tie."

"At least he was an upmarket pickup."

"That's what she said. She made a big point of the fact that he wasn't some bagman but an Hermès kind of guy. 'Our kind of people,' she said."

"Not mine. Does she do this sort of thing often?"

"She used to. Then we started making some progress, and she stopped. The last time she did it was that weekend last summer when we left on vacation."

"What made her do it again now?"

"I wish I knew."

Isobel began eating. "Maybe it's not so bad."

Pete picked up his knife and fork but didn't do anything with them. "What?"

"You know, two consenting adults and all that. I mean, don't get any ideas and start getting out your suspenders, but if that's what she likes, is it wrong? It may be kinky, but is it sick?"

"She goes into bars, slugger, picks up total strangers—I don't care how expensive their clothes are—takes them home, and lets them tie her up. Forget AIDS. We're talking more immediate death, not to mention dismemberment."

"I guess you have a point."

He started eating.

"There's one thing I don't get, though."

He stopped again and looked at her.

"How does she spot them? I mean, how can she tell the ones who'll tie her up from the ones who're just looking for your garden-variety blow job and fuck?"

"Boy, am I glad you decided to clean up your verbal act."

"Sorry, fellatio and fornication. How can she tell?"

Pete thought about that for a moment. "The infinite resourcefulness of the human mind." The phrase seemed to encourage him, and he tucked into his dinner.

Just as the physical presence of Pete's patients in the apartment shaped and shadowed Isobel's life, so his talk about them began to color her view. She didn't realize how differently she was seeing things until the afternoon she had coffee, as Pete had predicted, with Lucy and Kay.

She was in the Member's Room working on a speech she was supposed to give to a neighborhood preservation group. The speech was boring even to Isobel, maybe especially to Isobel, because she'd said the same things so many times before, and when Lucy came over and whispered that she and Kay were going for coffee, Isobel put away her yellow legal pad and pen and picked up her handbag and umbrella.

Outside the library, the sky, dark and damp as an old army blanket, sat low overhead, and coronas of mist hung around the streetlights that had gone on early to ward off the gathering dusk. As they started for the corner, Kay and Isobel opened their umbrellas and made room for Lucy between them, but she stepped back into the rain and stood with her hands hooked in the back pockets of her jeans, looking up at Isobel's umbrella.

"Cute."

It wasn't one of Isobel's favorite words, but she had to admit Lucy had a point. There was no other way to describe an umbrella decorated with a hand-painted portrait of the woman who was holding it. Isobel never would have bought it, despite the fact that it had been painted by Polly Markson, one of her oldest and dearest friends, if Polly's husband hadn't teased her that it would be cheaper for him in the long run if she gave up this new career and went back to tennis and shopping. After that Isobel not only ordered an umbrella but considered it a moral obligation to carry it.

They went to a Greek coffee shop half a block away.

The East European gigolo was sitting at the counter. He turned and gazed at them with espresso eyes. His mouth opened from one side to the other, as if he were unzipping it, and a knowing smiled darted out. It lingered briefly, maybe even longingly on Lucy, the youngest of them, skimmed over Isobel, and came to rest on Kay, the most expensively dressed of them. He pushed himself halfway up from the stool. His heels stopped just short of clicking together.

"He gives me the creeps," Lucy whispered as she slid across the plastic seat of the booth.

Isobel took the seat across from her. "You're safe unless he finds out you have a trust fund."

"He always makes me think of a snake," Kay said as she sat beside Lucy. Her eyes darted to Isobel. "Oops, I should know better than to say that in front of a shrink's wife."

"Not this shrink's wife. I'm terrified of snakes. Anyway, you know what Freud said. Sometimes a cigar is just a cigar."

"I didn't know you were married to a psychologist," Lucy said as soon as they'd ordered.

"Psychiatrist." Isobel wasn't a snob, but she didn't think it was fair that any college psych major could hang out a shingle and begin handing out pronouncements and interpretations at a hundred dollars a pop, more if the psych major really had hubris.

"That's even worse," Lucy said. "How do you stand it?"

"Stand what?" Isobel asked, though she knew. Pete's profession was like exotic food or experimental art. Some people admired it, others reviled it, but everyone was a little afraid of it.

"Living with someone who knows everything you think, and interprets everything you say, and understands what you're really doing when you think you're doing something else."

Isobel laughed. "What's weird is having him think he's doing all that."

"You mean he doesn't?" Lucy asked.

"I hope he does with his patients, but in private life shrinks are just as screwed up as everyone else. More so. That's why they go into it."

The restaurant was almost empty—even the gigolo had left— and a man two tables away glanced over and gave Isobel a filthy look. In this neighborhood, with her luck, he was bound to be a colleague of Pete's.

"I'm not giving anything away. Pete says the same thing," she

68

added more softly, and went on to tell them about his reaction to his daughter's first date, which was so classic she might have been reading from a textbook.

"Then how can they help other people?" Lucy asked.

"They say they can. I mean, they can. It has to do with proper training and professional distance."

Kay looked skeptical. "It's hard to believe there's no spill-over."

Isobel decided Pete was right. She ought to be more discreet. She ought to learn reticence. And she never should have told them about Pete and his daughter.

"Well, there isn't. Pete's a good therapist."

"I didn't mean that," Kay said. "I meant it seems hard to believe he wouldn't be easier, or at least more understanding, to live with."

That was when Isobel realized three things about Kay. There was trouble in her marriage, as Isobel had suspected. She was in treatment. And her transference was going like gangbusters.

A few days later the black Robert Clergerie pumps turned up. Isobel was rummaging around in the top of her closet looking for an evening bag, and there they were, sitting on the highest shelf of the shoe rack.

"I told you," Pete said.

"But who put them there?"

"They were there all along."

"They couldn't have been. I went through the closet three times. I wouldn't have missed them."

That was when he told her the story Freud had told on himself about walking past the sign for the train to Rotterdam, which was right in front of his eyes, too, thereby missing the connection that would have taken him to the brother he was

69

supposed to visit and enabling him to spend a day looking at the Rembrandts he'd wanted to see.

Isobel didn't mind the story. In fact, she found it fascinating. She just didn't like the smug look on Pete's face as he told it. She was glad she hadn't asked him to put a lock on the door to the living part of the apartment.

FIVE

I SOBEL HAD INSISTED SHE COULD live with the annoying calls, and maybe she could have if her picture hadn't run in the *Post*, and her name hadn't turned up in the *Times*, and she hadn't made an appearance on that talk show, though the show was aired at an hour when anyone with a life was sleeping or reading the Sunday paper or making love. But of course, that was the point. Whoever was making the calls didn't have a life.

The *Post* and the *Times* and the far-from-prime-time talk show were the result of Gorsky's sneak attack. In the dead of night, while all right-thinking citizens slept, he'd moved in bull-dozers and begun demolishing the two brownstones that were already vacant. By six o'clock the next morning Isobel had been on the phone to half the staff of Urban Heritage. By seven, when she arrived on the site, a human chain of neighbors and protesters was standing toe to tread with the bulldozers. Thanks to the calls she made as soon as she found out that the water and gas lines hadn't been disconnected, and therefore, she pointed out in case her media contacts didn't get it, the illegal demolition could have blown up the entire block, the incident made the seven-thirty news. By nine she and the Urban Heritage attorney were down at the city's Department of Investigation. By ten she was back on the site, and the sight was

71

familiar. It was more than familiar; it was bred in her bones. She'd been only two or three when Hannah and Zelda-the-Blacklisted-Actress had zippered and snapped her into her snowsuit, pinned a sign saying JOE MUST GO to her narrow chest, and wheeled her down to the demonstration.

Today was the kind of day organizers of protests dream about, sun-blinding and crisp as an apple. A line of twenty-five or thirty men and women, hands clasped, faces raised to the heavens as well as the drivers of the bulldozers, screamed and chanted, though they were hampered by the lack of a catchy jingle. Nobody had been able to come up with a rhyme for Gorsky. Other demonstrators held placards. One of the long-time residents carried a sign saying FIFTY-FIVE YEARS AT FIFTY-FIVE EAST, though, Zoe reported, she'd lived in her apartment for only fifty-three years and had insisted on running the placard by her priest to make sure she was using poetic license rather than telling a lie. Beside her a mother and small boy of about four in matching jackets complete with suede gun patches on the shoulders and polo players on the breast pockets waved posters demanding preservation of the boy's architectural heritage and protesting Gorskygate. Separated from them by a line of police, a covey of men wearing dark suits, Rolex watches, and furtive expressions on their faces—they looked a lot like Becker, though Becker wasn't among them—denied knowing anything about the demolition. A cop waved a limo through the police lines, and a famous architect and a famous actor and a famous socialite climbed out of it. A handful of men with cameras and women with microphones—fewer than Isobel would have liked, more than she'd expected—surged toward them.

Buoyed by their convictions, heartened by such celebrated leaders, encouraged by the press coverage, the protesters chanted and screamed louder, while the men with furtive faces stamped their feet and shook their heads like restive horses. Cameras snapped and whirred.

As the sun climbed higher over the endangered buildings, the morning air pulsed with fervor and violence and sex. A man and woman in the human chain rocked back and forth in ecstasy. The face of the mother in the hunting jacket contorted in orgasmic abandon. Even the longtime resident was caught up in the orgy. She clutched a gold crucifix to her long, flat breasts, while her breath came in jagged postcoital gasps. Isobel had seen it dozens of times before. The causes varied—faulty merchandise, small dumb animals threatened by large dumb humans, women's right to control their own bodies, world peace, destruction of the planet—but the passion remained unflagging and eternal. The passion was the magnet. Isobel was living proof of that. If LBJ hadn't announced he wouldn't run again, she never would have got so carried away on that sofa and lost her virginity. The funny thing was that she remembered less about the event than the aftermath. The next morning Hannah had been excited about the political news, and Millie had wanted to know all the details of Isobel's evening, and she'd just sat there, pale, exhausted, and stunned by her own recent history.

One of the men in the dark suits shot his cuff to get a better look at his Rolex, a protester shouted something at him, and a scuffle erupted. The contest was unmatched, Peter Pan had taken on the Mafia, and the photographers zeroed in, but the other suits were faster and pulled their colleague away.

People were passing coffee and doughnuts, and reporters were firing questions at the celebrated actor and the celebrated architect and the celebrated socialite, and the police kept telling people to stand in one place and not to stand in another. The crowd surged and swirled and shouted, and suddenly in the middle of all the chaos, two familiar faces swung into Isobel's line of vision. She didn't know why she was surprised. When Kay Glass had come to her office to drop off her résumé, she'd asked a lot of breathless questions about Urban Heritage and said, as she was leaving, that it must be wonderful to be doing something useful. She'd weighted the last word as if she were a hit man preparing to deep-six it. And just a few weeks ago Lucy Price had mentioned wistfully that she'd never demonstrated for or against anything. When they realized they had her attention, they both began waving wildly. As soon as Isobel waved back, Kay picked up a container of coffee and shouldered her way through the demonstrators.

"I had to come help," Kay said. "When I heard it on the news."

Warmed by the gesture and the cardboard container Kay had put in her hand, Isobel leaned across the small cloud of steam that rose from the cup and hugged Kay in thanks. And as she did, she saw, through the fine ash gold mist of Kay's hair, Lucy watching them.

"Thank Lucy, too," she said as she pulled away and turned back to the suits.

The whole scene, or at least thirty seconds of it, was played back on the local news that night. Though a group of Urban Heritage workers were watching it on the small television in the empty office they used as a conference room, Isobel missed the segment because she'd gone into her own office to answer her phone. She was just in time to hear the end of the report in stereo from the set in the next office and Millie's.

"Are you all right?" Millie asked.

"I'm fine."

"There was a fight."

"More like a scuffle, and I wasn't anywhere near it."

"I thought when you took this job, it would be an end to all the marching and picketing and protests. I didn't think people could get so worked up about something as unimportant as a couple of old buildings."

"What do you mean, unimportant?" Isobel heard Hannah shouting in the background. "That's our architectural heritage."

When Hannah decided to convert, she didn't fool around.

"The developer has a lot of money tied up in this," Isobel explained to her mother. "Feelings can run pretty high over ten or twenty million dollars."

"I saw. They look like gangsters to me. Machine guns and acid in the face."

"No one's going to throw acid at me. I'm not that important."

"What about those phone calls you keep getting?"

"They're from a woman."

"You think they don't have molls? I never thought I'd wish you were back with that abortion group."

"Stop trying to frighten her," Isobel heard her grandmother's voice from the background again, then some words she couldn't make out.

"Nana wants to talk to you," Millie said.

"It was a good demonstration." Wistfulness rose through Hannah's voice like smoke rings. "It reminded me of that antiwar sit-in. You remember. The one down at the university building on Forty-second Street."

Isobel remembered, all right. How could she forget sitting in the center of a couple of hundred chanting, screaming kids with a seventy-some-year-old woman who was shouting, "Make love, not war," louder than any of them. Everyone had said they envied Isobel, again, and she'd been proud of Hannah, really, and from this distance in time she couldn't be sure that

75

the memory of inching away from her in the crowd wasn't something she was imagining.

"We got some coverage," Isobel admitted.

"I saw you in the background. You had a look of righteous indignation. It was nice. I bet there'll be a picture in the *Post*."

As Isobel got off the phone, she wondered if there would be and if Nelson's mother-in-law would clip it and send it to him.

Isobel smelled the garlic as soon as she got off the elevator. She followed the aroma across the hall, into the apartment, and down the corridor to the kitchen. Welch was sitting in a corner, cleaning his whiskers with the languid satisfaction that followed a surfeit of people food. Pete was standing at the stove, shaking a skillet over the fire. He was wearing one of his button man shirts, and there was a tomato stain on the front.

She came up behind him and put her arms around him so one palm would have covered each breast, if he'd had breasts. "Thanks for feeding Welch, but didn't your father ever tell you you're supposed to comb your hair and put on fresh makeup before I get home?"

"Too busy making your dinner." He bent to put his cheek in line with her mouth. "I understand you were on the evening news."

She took a glass from one of the cabinets, ice from the freezer, and picked up the bottle of scotch he'd left on the counter. "That means Hannah and Millie called again."

"Hannah and Millie, everyone we've had dinner with for the past year, the entire hospital staff, half my colleagues, and my third-grade teacher."

"You're kidding."

"Only about the third-grade teacher. Your crank caller barely had a chance to get through. Only two measly calls on the tape and one since I've been in the kitchen." He turned and

76

leaned against the stove. "Still, it was pretty impressive. One of my patients even came in talking about it."

"Which one?"

"The Hermès tie. She said she went over to protest for a while."

"She must have been the one who chained herself to the building."

"I'm sorry I ever told you about that."

"Her story never leaves this apartment. Did you tell her your wife was the guiding force behind the demonstration?"

"Are you kidding?"

"As a matter of fact, yes. I know the rules, slugger. My bonds to you are even more top secret than that Hermès tie."

During the next week the brownstone war moved from the streets to a variety of offices and courts and the back pages of the papers. The real work—the work that Becker with his references to Isobel's Ho Chi Minh training and high-profile tactics implied she couldn't handle—began, and on Saturday, after setting up an elaborate schedule for Pete to call the answering machine when he finished his squash game or by four-twenty at the latest to tell her whether they were meeting the Tuckers, and if so, at which movie, at what time, and for her to call the machine between four-thirty and five to get the message, she took a briefcase full of files and set out for the Society Library.

She'd got as far as the lobby when she realized she'd forgotten her umbrella. She stood for a moment in front of the revolving door. The sidewalk outside the building was a dark-streaked khaki, and the air shimmered with mist, but she didn't see any open umbrellas. The concierge read her mind. "They say it's really gonna come down tonight, Mrs. Arlen." So much for Pete's making sure that her name as well as his was listed on the tenant roster.

She went back upstairs and let herself into the apartment. In the blue and white porcelain umbrella stand she found Pete's big black umbrella that always reminded her of an undertaker's, and the double umbrella Millie had bought them, and her beat-up Knirps, but the umbrella with her portrait, her moral-obligation umbrella, wasn't there.

She went down the hall to the kitchen, where Pete was still sitting with a cup of coffee, and asked him if he'd seen it.

"Maybe you left it in your office," he said without looking up from the paper.

"I remember bringing it home the other night when it was pouring. I remember putting it in the umbrella stand."

"It'll turn up."

"Sure. And now you're going to tell me Freud found his missing umbrella on the train to Rotterdam. Would you ask if one of your patients took it?"

He looked up from the paper. "What do you want me to do, slugger? Start every hour by asking if the patient has stolen an umbrella from the waiting room?"

"You don't have to say stolen. You can ask if someone took it by mistake."

"It's only an umbrella."

"How would you feel if some stranger, some crazy"—she saw the look he gave her—"okay, some emotionally impaired stranger were walking around town with a picture of you over his head?"

He went on looking at her for a moment. "All right," he said finally. "I'll put a sign on the umbrella stand. How's that?"

"Fine."

She went down the hall, took the beat-up Knirps from the stand, and put it in her briefcase.

* * *

The Member's Room was crowded with kids writing papers, and people reading magazines, and the elderly man who tended to fall asleep, and his wife, who had a habit of shouting across the room to him that he was snoring. In a chair in front of one of the French windows, the East European gigolo sat paging through the library copy of *Forbes*. Every few minutes he stopped to run a hand over his hair, and from across the room Isobel could see the way the thick stock of the magazine was beginning to wilt under his oily prints. By the time Lucy Price came in at around three-thirty, all the seats were taken except the middle place on the sofa beside Isobel. She picked up the pile of papers she'd spread out and moved them to the end table. Lucy thanked her and took the seat.

Isobel tried to go back to work, but she had trouble concentrating. Mutual awareness hummed between Lucy and her like an electrical current.

At four-thirty Isobel put her papers in her briefcase, stood, and picked up her handbag. Lucy looked up eagerly.

"I'm just going to make a phone call," Isobel said, and wondered again how she'd got in the position of having to explain her actions to an impressionable young woman she barely knew.

Isobel climbed the circular staircase to the telephone closet. The door was open, and the gigolo was telling someone in a voice as oil-slicked as his hair that he was counting the minutes until he saw her. She couldn't believe there were men in the world still selling lines like that, or women still buying them. He came out of the phone closet, executed a smart little dip of head, neck, and chest, and said he hoped he had not inconvenienced her. When she said he hadn't, he unzipped his mouth, one side to the other, and the smile oozed out.

Isobel moved around him into the phone closet. The cloying

stench made her queasy. When she picked up the receiver, it felt slippery in her hand. She took a tissue from her bag and wiped the phone off, then dialed her number. The busy signal surprised her. Then she realized someone must be leaving a message. She hung up, waited a moment, and dialed again. The same dull rhythmic sound buzzed in her ear.

The knock on the door startled her. She opened it to find Lucy standing with her hands hooked in the back pockets of her jeans and the tail-thumping smile on her face.

"I remembered, when you said you had to make a call, I promised Julian I'd call him." She pushed the fringe of blond bangs back from her forehead and ducked her head, like an embarrassed child. "I know. Everyone says he's possessive, but he says he just likes to know where I am."

"You don't have to apologize to me," Isobel said, though she knew the confidences she'd listened to, and the comments she'd made, and the interest she'd shown implied that Lucy did. She tried her own number once more, got a busy signal, and stepped outside the closet to let Lucy go in.

Lucy picked up the receiver, dropped a quarter in the box, and began to dial. Isobel closed the door and sat on the top step to wait.

A few minutes later Lucy came out smiling, and Isobel went back into the closet. She dialed her number, then stood with her hand poised to tap in the code that would play back her messages. The busy signal droned in her ear like an insistent insect.

"Fuck," she muttered, and dialed again. The busy signal sounded as if it had never been interrupted. She pressed down the lever, got the dial tone again, and dialed the operator. Isobel explained her problem. The operator asked if Isobel would like her to check the line. Isobel said she would. Isobel heard a series of clicks, then the busy signal again.

"The line is busy."

"I know it's busy," Isobel snapped, then caught herself. "But it can't be," she said more reasonably. "There's no one there. That's why I wanted you to check it."

"The line is engaged," the operator said.

"But even if someone were on the phone, we have call waiting. My call would click in. It must be out of order or off the hook or something."

"It's engaged," the operator repeated in a stern voice indigenous to public service employees and second-grade teachers.

"I keep telling you. How can it be engaged if there's no one there?"

Suddenly the severe voice turned confidential. "Do you have an answering machine on the line?"

"That's why I'm calling it."

"Someone must be talking to the answering machine."

"For half an hour?" Isobel knew she was exaggerating, but frustration bred hyperbole.

"The party calling you may have left their phone off the hook by mistake, which, depending on the kind of machine you have, could keep your machine and phone engaged. Have you considered New York Telephone's new voice message service? It allows you to unplug your answering machine for good. No more—"

"For Christ sake!"

"I beg your pardon." The second-grade teacher was back.

"I'm sorry. No, I don't want your new voice whatever service."

"It costs only pennies a month."

"I'm not interested." Isobel's voice bounced off the walls of the small room.

"Thank you for calling New York Telephone."

"Anytime," Isobel said, and hung up the phone. "Fuck," she muttered to the small closet.

She picked up the phone, dialed the Harvard Club, and asked the switchboard operator to page Dr. Arlen. Ten minutes and several dimes later, the operator told her Dr. Arlen wasn't answering his page. She hung up the phone and cursed again.

When she opened the door, she found Kay Glass standing on the other side of it.

"I didn't know it was you in there," Kay said. "Though I saw your briefcase in the Member's Room. Lucy was guarding it with her life."

"Please. I have enough problems without worrying about Lucy," Isobel said, and broke into a diatribe about her busy phone line that couldn't or at least shouldn't be engaged. "And all because of my anonymous caller."

"What do you mean?"

"Some crazy woman keeps calling and asking for strange names and then calling back and breathing into the phone. Only this time apparently she didn't bother to hang up. So now Pete's going to be standing in front of some movie with another couple, expecting me to turn up, and I don't even know which movie or what time, and it's all because of this goddamn crazy woman, only he won't see it that way because he wanted me to get an unlisted number or report her, and I didn't, so I'm the one responsible, and there goes the whole weekend shot to hell. Fuck!"

Isobel saw the way Kay flinched. "I'm sorry. Pete says I have a mouth like a ghetto rapper. But you have to admit whoever she is, she really has managed to screw things up."

"Hey!"

The cry rose from the floor below, and Isobel and Kay leaned over the staircase railing to see who it was. Lucy stood with her hands hooked in the back pockets of her jeans and her face lifted to them.

"Hey, you guys," she called again. "Have a nice weekend."

"Now will you report it?" Pete asked as he peeled off a wet tweed jacket to reveal the wet blue work shirt beneath that was stuck to his skin. At three o'clock he'd called and left a message on the machine. At five-thirty he'd met the Tuckers in front of the movie. At five fifty-five he'd sent them inside. At six-ten it had begun to rain. At six-fifteen it had begun to pour. At six-thirty he'd left.

"Why didn't you stand under the marquee?"

"Because it was a small marquee, and the usher or bouncer or whoever the hell he was said loitering was not permitted. If I wanted to wait for the next show, I had to get in the ticket holders' line." He handed Isobel two soaked movie tickets and headed for the shower.

"I'll report it," she said, but he'd already turned on the water, and if he heard her, he didn't acknowledge her.

She went into the kitchen, made him a drink, and took it back to the bathroom, where she left it on the sink. Then she went across the hall to the study, took out the phone book, and carried it back to the bedroom.

She sat cross-legged on the bed and opened the phone book. Welch came and sat on it. She pushed him off. He thought it was a game and went for her hand. She pushed him away again. He pounced again. This time she cuffed him harder. She disapproved of physical violence, but she didn't know how else to cope with Welch when he reverted to the wild.

A few minutes later Pete came out of the bathroom with a towel wrapped around his waist and the drink in his hand.

"The line's only open Monday to Friday," she said.

His answer was a monumental sneeze. It sent Welch running

for cover under the bed. It disconcerted Isobel, too. Pete couldn't fake a sneeze. He wasn't even a good liar.

He put the drink on the night table and stretched out on top of the quilt.

"I'm sorry. I really am."

He didn't say anything to that. Now she was really worried.

"We can still meet the Tuckers for dinner."

"Fuck the Tuckers." He put his hand over his eyes. "I'm beginning to sound like you."

"I'm not particularly interested in the Tuckers, but if you'd like to make that invitation more personal . . ."

"I've been standing out in the rain for half an hour. . . ."

She stood and unzipped her jeans. "Twenty minutes. You said it didn't begin to rain for a while."

"I'm wet, I'm cold, and I'm pissed."

She pulled off her jeans and bikinis in one move. "You had a hot shower, and I made you a drink. You're not wet and cold anymore."

"All right, I'm just pissed."

She climbed on top of him, but left his towel in place because she wasn't sure how angry he really was.

"So you're going to lie around all night wallowing in self-pity." She tightened her knees around his hips.

He picked up the glass off the night table and took a swallow. "Right."

She took the glass from him, sipped the drink, and put it back on the night table. "Bet I can make you change your mind."

He didn't say anything to that.

"Bet I can," she repeated.

It took awhile, but she did. And all the while she kept thinking that this was something else that was odd about marriage, or at least about ongoing sex. The moves tended to be the same, touch here, touch there, partly because it was so easy to fall into a routine, mostly because they knew each other's tastes, but the results could be so different. Like now, the familiar moves, do this, do that, that usually edged her body into another realm couldn't even stop her mind from racing. This, that was usually this, ahh, that, ahhh, sometimes lusty, and sometimes ardent, and occasionally transcendent, and once, though she wouldn't dare admit it to anyone, not even Pete, she could swear she'd lost consciousness for a moment. But sometimes the same moves, here, there, and nothing happened, which was what was or rather wasn't happening now, because of her damn mind, click, click, clicking away about Pete standing out in the rain, and the busy signal buzzing, and a strange woman spending half her life trying to ruin theirs, and come to think of it, damn it, stop thinking of it, succeeding because whoever she was, she was here with them now, standing in the shadows, sitting on the edge of the bed, insinuating herself between them.

Isobel began dialing the hot line for obscene, threatening, or harassing calls at nine-ten on Monday morning. At nine-twenty she finally made it through the busy signals and recorded announcements. She'd never dreamed there were so many people receiving anonymous calls.

A woman with a no-nonsense voice asked how she could help. Isobel had been expecting someone more maternal, or at least sympathetic. She told the woman about the phone calls.

"Don't say anything after the initial hello," the woman warned her. "And don't slam the receiver down. That's what the caller wants."

"I never slammed it down." Isobel was surprised at the defensiveness in her voice. Obviously the fact that she'd said more than hello had only encouraged the woman.

"Make sure that everyone in your home, especially young-sters, do the same."

"There are no youngsters in my home," Isobel said to the woman. "Youngsters?" she mumbled to herself in disbelief.

"Don't talk about the calls to anyone outside your immediate family. Not even close friends."

She was glad now she hadn't asked Megan to look up the number for her and had stopped dialing when Zoe had walked into her office a few minutes ago. She could kick herself for complaining to Kay Glass.

"In most cases, the caller knows either you or some member of the family. If he—"

"She."

"—if she hears about your anxiety either directly or indi-rectly, that's encouragement to continue."

"I understand."

"Thank you for calling New York Telephone."

"You mean, that's it?" Isobel looked down at the phone book on her desk. "You haven't told me anything that isn't written here. You even use the same words."

"We're trained counselors."

"Trained to read aloud from the phone book?"

"I made a record of your complaint."

"You didn't even ask me if I had any idea who the calls might be coming from."

"Do you?"

"I work for an organization called Urban Heritage. We're involved in a pretty ugly dispute at the moment. But I just don't think they'd do anything this childish."

"Harassing phone calls are not childish," the woman said, and again Isobel felt guilty. "Do you have any other suspi-cions?"

Isobel thought about that for a moment. She'd never considered herself a woman who made enemies. She couldn't even believe that Becker really disliked her. She knew he wanted her out of the way, but she didn't think he had anything against her personally. She thought of the other possibilities. Lucy Price was needy, but Isobel didn't believe she was vicious. Nelson's mother-in-law didn't even know her; she just didn't like the fact that Isobel had existed in Nelson's life before her daughter had. Isobel thought of past jobs and old battles. Part of her knew there were a lot of people out there who hated her guts, but another part of her couldn't believe that anyone really disliked her.

"Wouldn't it be easier if you just traced the calls?"

"We can't do that."

"What do you mean you can't do that? They do it all the time in the movies."

"We can't trace calls unless you file a police complaint."

"Then what's the point of this line?"

"To reassure our customers."

"You haven't reassured me."

"Keep a log of the calls. Then you can file a complaint with the police, and we can trace them for you."

"And that's your advice?"

"You might also try pushing the pound sign on your touch-tone phone. Do you have a touch-tone phone?"

"Yes."

"Next time you get a call, try pushing the pound button."

"What good will that do?"

"It simulates the sound of a call being traced. Sometimes it works."

"Thanks for your help," Isobel said.

But her trained counselor was impervious to irony. "We're always happy to be of service. Thank you for calling New York Telephone."

87

She waited till twenty minutes after the hour to call Pete's office.

"So much for New York Tel's harassment prevention line." There was vindication in her voice, but there was uneasiness as well. She hadn't wanted to report the calls because she hadn't wanted to make too much of them. It hadn't occurred to her that if she did report them, no one would give a damn. She felt betrayed. She felt worse than betrayed; she felt helpless. Maybe that was why it happened. Maybe that was why, later that night, she lost it.

They went to a screening after work. The invitation had come from one of Pete's patients. Isobel had been surprised when Pete said they could accept it. "I thought you weren't allowed to accept invitations from your patients."

"We're not going with her," he'd explained. "But she worked on the movie, and she wants me to see it."

"That sculptor wanted you to see his work, and you refused because you said you were treating him, not critiquing his talent."

"This is different," Pete said, though he wouldn't explain how, and Isobel didn't push it. Advance word on the movie was good, and who wouldn't rather walk into a screening than stand in line for half an hour, possibly in the rain, during the regular run?

The movie lived up to expectations, and by the time they got home that night Isobel hadn't exactly forgotten the woman on the hot line, but she was no longer angry at her. She went into her study to check the answering machine. The first call was from Millie. All the tests from her checkup had come back, and the doctor had given her a clean bill of health. Isobel had forgotten her mother's checkup. She stood in the small arc of illumination from a single lamp that felt like a spotlight on her flaws and listened to the five other calls on the machine. They flowed together into a single river of silence, but tonight Isobel detected a current she hadn't noticed before, a dark undertow of menace. She forced herself to listen to the entire length. Hate flooded the room.

"Five," she said when she went into the bedroom, where Pete was standing beside the bed unbuttoning his shirt.

"Did you make a note of them?"

Before she could answer, the phone rang again.

"I'll get it," he said.

"No."

She picked up the receiver and said hello into it.

Malice, thick as sludge, oozed into the room.

"Hello!" She shouted the word into the phone. It disappeared into the emptiness.

"Goddamn it," she screamed. The silence closed around her voice.

"Stop it! Whoever the fuck you are, stop—"

Pete took the phone from her hand and replaced it in the cradle.

"I think it's time to report the calls to the police," he said quietly.

Isobel made the call as soon as she got to the office the next morning. The woman on the other end of the line asked what sort of calls Isobel was complaining about. "Did he—"

"She."

"—threaten you with bodily harm?"

Isobel explained that the caller used to disguise her voice and ask for phony names. "Now she just calls and breathes into the phone."

There was a moment of silence on the other end of the line. Isobel interpreted the unspoken comment. You call that harassment? In this city? In this day and age? Give me a break.

"I know it doesn't sound like much," Isobel apologized, "but you have to live through it to understand. I mean, call after call of these weird voices and then this awful silence. After a while it gets to you. You begin to feel she's watching you or something. I mean, I know it doesn't make sense . . ." She let her voice trail off, then pulled herself together. "The phone company said they can't trace the calls unless I report them to you."

The woman told Isobel she'd have to come to precinct head-quarters to file a complaint. Her voice wasn't kind when she said it. Again Isobel heard the subtext. Lady, people are shooting children in the streets and raping old ladies in their beds and holding entire neighborhoods hostage to drugs, and you really expect the poor whipped NYPD to spend man-hours and tax dollars and the little energy it has left to track down some woman who calls you up and breathes in your ear. Get real.

When Isobel reported the conversation to Pete that night, there was no vindication in her voice.

"I think it's time for an unlisted number," he said.

This time she didn't argue with him. She wondered why she had in the first place. It was such a simple solution to the problem.

SIX

A<small>T FIRST ISOBEL HAD TROUBLE</small>
getting used to the fact that the calls had stopped. She still
circled the phone warily, as if it were Welch at those dispiriting
moments when he reverted to nature. Occasionally when it
rang, she felt her body tense. But after two weeks of picking up
the phone to Hannah's and Millie's voices, to Polly Markson
announcing she was taking a workshop in performance art, to
her uncles in Florida saying they were worried about Hannah
or Millie or both of them, she almost began to believe she was
free. She even got a call from her former husband, Nelson,
who'd heard about her marriage from a mutual friend, who'd
also passed on her new number. He said that if the picture in
the *Post* was any indication, this marriage agreed with her.
Isobel tried to keep the smirk out of her voice as she thanked
him. That ought to teach his mother-in-law. He also told her
he'd had lunch with Isabelle Fowler, who'd been in Philadel-
phia on business one day. He said she hadn't changed much.
Isobel asked in what way she hadn't changed much and wondered whether he was trying to tell her that Isabelle had made
a play for him. It would figure, since he was someone else's
husband again. Nelson said she still looked the same.

For a while Isobel waited for the calls to begin in her office,
but Megan didn't mention anything out of the ordinary, and
Isobel didn't ask. It would be like asking for trouble.

Life began to take on a veneer of normalcy. Mrs. Zelinski slipped once and called Emily's room the study. Hannah began remembering Pete's name. Millie went on dropping off precooked dinners and gourmet delicacies and household bargains.

Gorsky agreed to give the city two million for the restoration of landmarked public buildings and was permitted to plead guilty to the misdemeanor of reckless endangerment rather than the criminal charges Urban Heritage had called for. Isobel wrote a letter of protest to the op-ed page of the *Times* accusing Gorsky of buying public justice at a private sale, and Hannah had Cruz take the letter to a neighborhood shop to be matted and framed. "Your grandfather and your father should see that," she said as she put the letter on an end table in the study where the picture of Isobel with a JOE MUST GO sign pinned to her chest had stood before Cruz's predecessor had stolen it.

At first Isobel thought her grandmother meant her grandfather and father would have been proud, which was the kind of thing Millie occasionally said but Hannah never did, and Isobel was surprised. Then Hannah went on.

"They were always screaming at me, 'Whatever you do, don't sign anything. It's bad enough you march and carry on and all that, but don't sign anything.' " Behind the thick lenses of her glasses, Hannah's eyes slid to the past. "I used to feel sorry for Reuben when he said that, but he never seemed to get the irony."

"What do you mean?" Isobel asked.

"What?" Hannah's eyes came back to her granddaughter. "Oh. You know. McCarthyism. It made people afraid to put their names to anything."

The city lurched toward winter. One day Isobel turned the page on her calendar and found she'd been married for two months. She remembered the days when two months, almost the length of the summer vacation from school, had been a lifetime. Now it wasn't even long enough to have got around to organizing the books she'd shoved hastily into the bookcases when she'd first moved in. Still, she felt time moving. These days when she looked out the windows of the apartment, the trees around the reservoir shivered in their nakedness, but the buildings of Central Park West still strutted like an art deco chorus line beneath the platinum sky. The sight made Isobel realize that just as Pete had said, her job at Urban Heritage wasn't an accident. As she looked at the city through those double-paned windows designed to keep out dirt and noise and buffeting winds, she knew that what she felt for endangered rain forests and wetlands and savannas and rivers were convictions. What she felt for that skyline was passion of the worst kind, atavistic love. She'd looked up from her carriage to those gray stone slabs swaying gently against the city sky. She'd taken her first steps across those wide doorman-patrolled sidewalks. The primary colors for her were the red and yellow and green of traffic lights. The smell of the outdoors was the spicy tang of steam rising from a Sabrett's hot dog wagon. The constellations were the neat rows of lights glowing from other people's apartments and the garish blaze of theater marquees. The sight of a mounted policeman made her think not of the American cowboy and his lost frontier but of the cops who'd herded Hannah and Zelda-the-Blacklisted-Actress and a toddling or a childish or an adolescent Isobel at a series of demonstrations. The sound of wheels sizzling on a wet city street, like fat in a hot skillet, lulled her to sleep; the unnatural silence of a city morning told her before she opened her eyes that Central Park was dreaming under a comforter of snow.

She understood that the rudeness and frustration and violence of the city took a toll on her spirit. The previous summer when Pete had pulled into a country gas station to fill up the tank and the boy had started to wash the windshield, she'd reached over to flick on the wipers the way she did to shake off the addicts and muggers who slathered greasy rags across windshields on urban corners, then banged on the window demanding money. Pete had pushed her hand away, but not before the kid had jumped back, startled. "Sorry," Pete had told the boy. "She has a quick trigger finger." But the jangled nerves and the fear and the knowledge of her own hardening shell were no match for the old instinctive love. This was her natural habitat, as critical to her survival as the ozone layer. She knew it was flawed and filthy and inequitable, but she didn't want to tear it down, not even for Hannah's approval or Millie's attention.

"Now you get it," Pete said. "Or at least you get part of it."

Maybe that was why she broke the rules again. The feeling of having arrived where she wanted to be lulled her into carelessness.

When she got home that evening, Pete was still in his office with a patient, so she went around to the service entrance and let herself into the kitchen. She'd planned to stay there until the last patient left, but then she remembered she'd left the recipe she'd clipped from the Sunday magazine section on the desk in Emily's room. Mrs. Zelinski must be leaving subliminal messages around the apartment. The recipe she'd left on the desk in *her* study. She stood in the kitchen debating the problem for a moment. She knew the right thing to do was to go out the service entrance, around the outside area, come back in through the bedroom hallway entrance, and then retrace the entire route on the way back. It was the right thing to do, but it sure wasn't the logical or efficient thing to do. What was the point of being married if she had to sneak around like Susan

94

Hayward in *Back Street*, or like herself before the days of coed dorms?

She looked at the big Italian clock on the wall. The spidery black arms told her she had eight minutes before the end of Pete's hour. She could probably get the recipe and be back in fewer than sixty seconds.

The waiting room was empty. The magazines were still perfectly aligned, except for one issue, which lay open on the table. It wasn't a *Nation* or even an odd issue of *New York* magazine, but what used to be called, in simpler times, a woman's magazine, which meant a magazine designed to keep women abreast of what men thought, felt, wanted, and ate. She knew that instantly from the layout and the type and the title of the article. "How Well Do You and Your Mate Communicate?" Someone had highlighted paragraphs with a shocking pink marker. She kept going through the waiting room and into the study, picked up the recipe, and came back down the hall. On her way through the waiting room she glanced at the open magazine again. She didn't know why it bothered her. She wasn't an obsessively neat person. But she stopped and picked it up, and as she did, she couldn't help noticing a highlighted sentence. "The average two-career couple spend less than a hundred and forty minutes a week talking to each other." A note in ballpoint pen ran down the margin beside it. "I spend more time than that with Dr. Arlen." Three exclamation points followed the sentence.

Isobel put the magazine back on the table and went down the hall to the kitchen. Welch was sitting on the counter next to the bag from the fish market. She'd been so caught up in that stupid article she hadn't even seen him dart through the waiting room. She pushed him off the counter. He looked up at her with deep reproach.

Pete was unusually quiet at dinner that night. At least he

95

seemed that way to Isobel. She wondered if the newness was wearing off. She told herself she'd been reading too many women's magazines. Then she told him about Gorsky and Becker, and Grace Feyer's coming interview with the *New York Observer*, which was the best Isobel had been able to do, and Zoe's toddler, who refused to be toilet-trained so Zoe wanted Isobel to ask Pete's advice. She got a few un-hmms and an admonition not to worry in return.

"Either something's bothering you or this recipe is better than I think."

He looked up at her. There wasn't an ounce of guile in his face. He really didn't know what she was talking about.

"You haven't said a word since we sat down."

"Sure I have."

"What?"

"I said the scallops were good and kids generally know when they're ready."

She gave up. At least she tried to, but then she couldn't help herself. "Do you know the average two-career couple spend fewer than one hundred and forty minutes a week in conversation?"

"Where'd you get that?"

Isobel wished she'd stayed with the scallops. "I don't know. Some magazine. I think Kay Glass—you know, Hannah's Friday-afternoon-concert friend—pointed it out to me in the library the other day."

The lie spilled onto the table between them with appalling ease. Isobel knew where it had come from. A few days before, she'd gone to the library to return some books, and as she'd stood waiting her turn at the checkout desk, she'd spotted Kay sitting at the long table in the reference room. Kay's expensively streaked hair had hung lank and dull around her unmade-up face. Her rumpled raincoat had looked as if it had gone through a couple of wars. Her slumped figure had given off such an air of soiled dejection that at first Isobel had thought it was a bag woman who bore an uncanny resemblance to Kay. Then she'd noticed the title on the spine of the book Kay was holding: *The Intelligent Woman's Guide to Divorce*. Isobel hadn't gone over to talk to her. Remembering the incident now made her realize where she'd got the alibi, but the logic of the lie didn't make her feel any better about telling it.

"I'm not sure where I saw it, but I'm willing to bet it's true."

"It's funny."

"Some joke."

"No, I meant that you should mention it. My last patient said the same thing."

"The plaint of the married woman."

"She's not married."

"Then why—" Isobel began, then stopped suddenly. She was about to say, "Then why did she underline it and make that comment in the margin about spending more time than that with you?" "Then why did she bring it up?"

"I don't know. It just came up somehow during the hour." He shrugged, and Isobel let it go because she knew the answer to her real question. The patient wasn't complaining about her husband. She was exulting in Pete. She was saying she had more of Pete than most wives have of their husbands, more of Pete than Pete's wife had of him. But Isobel couldn't point that out to Pete because she wasn't supposed to be in Pete's waiting room, and she especially wasn't supposed to be spying on the private jottings of Pete's patients. Spying. In a Graham Greene novel or a book about Burgess and Maclean, the word resonated with glamour. In an apartment where patients came and went and Isobel and Pete were trying to live, it reeked of tawdry acts and petty paranoia. Hers as well as the patient's.

She didn't want to make too much of it. She hadn't had an

assignation with an old lover. She hadn't been holed up in a hotel room with a new man. She'd merely done something she was ashamed to admit to Pete.

The next morning she arrived in her office to a pile of opened letters on her desk and an unopened envelope lying beside it. The word *personal* was typed in capital letters on the left side of the envelope and again on the right. Isobel picked it up. The creamy stock felt thick between her fingers. Miss Waverly must be at it again.

Philomena Waverly was the eighty-four-year-old heir to an old Romanesque monstrosity of a town house on the West Side and twenty million dollars. The monstrosity had been designed and built by Miss Waverly's late father, and if Miss Waverly had her way and her millions their effect, it would be landmarked as a monument to him. During the past few months she'd taken to writing Isobel long letters describing the house's architectural fine points and her father's philanthropies. The last letter, which had also been marked "personal," had told the story of how the late Mr. Waverly, out of the goodness of his heart, had secretly supported a cook and her son long after she'd left his employ. The story smacked of backstairs sex and illicit issue, but Miss Waverly had insisted she wanted it kept quiet only because that was the way Daddy had always done his good deeds. Isobel didn't want to think about the unfulfilled needs and unrealized dreams that made an eighty-four-year-old woman refer to her late father as Daddy.

She turned the envelope over. There was no return address. She looked at her own name and the word *personal* again. The characters made no indentation in the thick stock. They looked as if they had come from a printer rather than a typewriter. The idea that Philomena Waverly was computer-literate sent a

98

chill through Isobel. She imagined reams of literature, a blitz-krieg, raining down on the offices of Urban Heritage.

She picked up the silver letter opener that Hannah had given her for her birthday years ago, slit the envelope, and removed the letter. Her first thought was that it couldn't be from Philomena Waverly. It was too short. The second thing she noticed was the salutation. The envelope was addressed to Ms. Isobel Behringer, but the letter said "Dear Mrs. Arlen." The third was the signature. Even before she read the letter, she knew it meant trouble. That was what "A well-intentioned friend" always had in mind.

> Dear Mrs. Arlen,
>   They say the wife is always the last to know. I guess you must be. And don't believe him if he says she's only a patient. My heart goes out to you.
>
>   A well-intentioned friend

Isobel sat behind her desk. She was still holding the letter in her hand. She read it again. It couldn't be Becker and Gorsky. Men who bulldoze buildings in the dead of night don't go in for psychological subtlety. But she didn't know who it could be.

She crumpled the paper into a ball, tossed it into the waste-basket, and turned to the stack of mail on her desk. A few minutes later she took the letter from the wastebasket, smoothed it out, and put it in her briefcase. Then she got down to work.

Not once during the day did it occur to her that there might be any truth to the letter. Not really.

That night Pete was still with a patient when she got home from the office, and again she went around to the service en-trance and let herself into the kitchen. She put her coat on a chair and her briefcase on the floor. Only after she'd made herself a drink and taken the salad greens from the refrigerator did she remember the letter. She took it from her briefcase and put it on the long trestle table. Then she got out the salad spinner and began washing the arugula. A moment later she put down the salad spinner, picked up her drink, and walked back to the table. She stood holding her drink in one hand and smoothing the wrinkles of the crumpled paper against the wooden table with the other while she read through it again. She knew she was being ridiculous—it was scattershot from a deranged mind, not a literary text to be deconstructed—but she couldn't help herself. She was still studying it when Pete, with Welch on his heels, came into the kitchen a few minutes later.

"Do you want me to go down and get whatever it is we're missing, or can we wing it?"

Isobel looked up from the letter. "What?"

"That recipe you're brooding over."

She handed him the letter. He read it once, pulled a chair out from the table, sat, and read it a second time. He was studying it as if it were the Rosetta stone to their lives.

"It doesn't take that long to read," she said, then remembered she'd done the same thing.

"You think it's related to the phone calls?" he asked.

"I don't know. I don't think it has anything to do with work. At least not with Gorsky and Becker."

Pete reached for her drink and took a swallow. Then he looked at the letter again.

"It could be a patient."

"If it's a patient, then it can't be Our Lady of the Phone Calls."

"Why not?"

"Because they started before we were married, before I was

really living here. In those days I was just one of a steady stream of women passing through. At least that's the way Mrs. Zelinski tells it."

"You were always the number one draft choice."

Isobel thought about that for a minute. "You don't think it's Mrs. Zelinski?"

"Not a chance."

He took the letter, crumpled it, and threw it in the trash bin. The one for nonrecyclables.

Isobel turned out the light, turned on her side, and molded herself against Pete's back. He lifted his right arm to let hers circle around to his chest. Her fingers settled in the light dusting of silky hair. Her nose rested against his scapula, which Millie had called Isobel's angel's wing when she was small.

"Are you asleep?"

"I was."

"That letter . . . about your affair with your patient."

"I know which letter you mean."

"You never denied it."

She felt his shoulders stiffen.

He peeled her arm off his chest and rolled over on his back. His eyes were open wide. She could tell even in the darkness because the whites caught the light from the full moon that hung just outside the bedroom window. He reached up and turned on the wall sconce over his side of the bed. Now she could see the pupils, too. They looked big and inky, absurdly like the comic book eyes of Little Orphan Annie.

"You've got to be kidding."

She put her hand back on his chest. "What I was trying to say was if your first response had been 'It's a lie' or 'I never looked at another woman' or something like that, I might have worried."

101

He looked at her for a long time. Then he turned the light off, turned on his side, took her arm, and wound it around himself again.

She freed her fingers from his and walked them down his stomach. He took her hand and put it back on his chest. She tugged her hand free again and went for his fledgling erection.

"It's after midnight, and I have to get up at six forty-five, and I'm not as young as I used to be. Hell, I'm not nearly as young as I was before I married you."

"Pretend I'm a patient," she said, and moved her hand up and down. "The one you're supposed to be having an affair with."

"Talk about a turnoff," he answered, but he reached a foot back and hooked it around her leg in one of those seemingly innocent gestures that over time become an erotic semaphore.

"Did you?" she asked later, when he was almost asleep again.

"Did I what?" he breathed.

"Pretend I was a patient?"

"You're certifiable."

"There's nothing wrong with a little healthy fantasy."

"Isobel"—he yawned—"did it ever occur to you that the fact that there's nothing wrong with something is not a compelling reason to do it?"

SEVEN

I SOBEL SAT STARING AT THE PILE OF pink phone messages in her hand. This was one thing Pete couldn't blame on her. She wasn't the one who'd suggested lunch. She hadn't even given Isabelle Fowler her number. But on the top slip the name Isabelle Fowler and a phone number were written in Megan's beautiful parochial school hand.

Isobel tucked the slip into the side of her blotter. She wasn't going to make a move on this without asking Pete.

She went through the rest of the messages, dividing them into the calls she had to return and the ones she could ignore, at least for the moment. Millie fell into the second category. "She was calling from a phone booth," Megan wrote. Isobel knew her mother well enough to know that didn't mean it was an emergency.

The doorman recognized Millie. The first time she'd come to the apartment with one of her surprise deliveries she'd worried that he might be difficult. She'd asked if the cleaning woman was still there. He'd said she'd just left. "And I forgot my key." Millie didn't have a key because Isobel kept forgetting to get to the locksmith to have one made, which was just like Isobel, but Millie did have experience dealing with doormen.

"No problem, ma'am," he'd said. "The doctor always leaves

the door to his waiting room open during office hours. That's why we're so careful down here. If I didn't know you, I'd have to call up, but being you're Mrs. Arlen's mother, I don't think we have to worry."

He'd smiled at his joke. She'd smiled at being Mrs. Arlen's mother. They'd bonded. Now he carried her packages to the elevator with a comment about the weather. Millie returned the pleasantry, the elevator door closed, and she looked down at the shopping bags at her feet with satisfaction.

It wasn't every day you found a sale like this. You could always get the patterned quilts with those designer names, as if a person slept better under Laura This or Christian That, but how often did you find an old-fashioned embroidered European duvet cover at half price? The sheets were on sale, too. Isobel said they had two of everything, but Millie knew better. She'd seen that bedroom. Pete's former wife might have lost the apartment, but she'd walked off with the linens. So now there were brown herringbone sheets, the kind a single man, awash in a flower-print-and-pastel linen department, would reach for like a lifeline. And the quilt, a different brown but just as ugly, was thin as a pancake. As long as Millie was getting the duvet cover, she figured she might as well get a new comforter, too. Then it had taken awhile to find a dust ruffle, because most of them were gathered, and Millie wanted the box-pleated kind. The saleslady, a woman Millie's age, whom Millie felt sorry for because she had to spend her days on her feet in Bloomingdale's linen department, had agreed.

"Tailored. It's the secret of a successful bedroom."

"Exactly," Millie said, though she didn't think it was that simple.

"I have women coming in here, putting flowers and lace and ribbons like you wouldn't believe all over the bedroom. Then they wonder why their husbands work late or fall asleep watching TV in the den."

Millie's head bobbed in agreement as she opened her handbag to find her charge card.

"I always tell my customers, you want to make a decorating statement, that's okay, but you gotta remember, your husband's gotta live there, too. If he's not comfortable in the bedroom, you may as well forget the whole thing."

Millie thought about it as the elevator rose to the nineteenth floor. Harry had been comfortable in their bedroom. That was one thing she was sure of. So what had gone wrong? Nothing had gone wrong. Their marriage had been a success. She only hoped Isobel's lasted half as long. And if Millie had to help by buying sheets and stocking the refrigerator and doing the things men expected in a marriage, because Isobel wouldn't or couldn't, she didn't mind. That was what mothers were for, though God knows her own mother hadn't been.

The elevator door opened, and Millie used her foot to keep it from closing while she slid her packages off. The comforter was bulky, and the linens were heavier than she'd expected, and she was glad she had to carry them only a few more steps.

She turned the knob and opened the door to the waiting room. The young woman sitting in one of the two Barcelona chairs looked from the wall where she'd been staring to Millie. Millie nodded and smiled. The young woman hesitated a moment, then nodded and smiled back. Millie bent to slide the packages from the hall into the apartment. The cord around the box with the comforter caught on the saddle, and she had to put down the bag with the linens to free it.

"Let me help you." The young woman stood.

"I can manage," Millie insisted, but the woman had already taken the box with the comforter from her.

"Thank you," Millie said as the young woman lifted the pack-

105

ages and carried them into the waiting room. "I didn't mean to bother you."

"It's no bother. I was just sitting here."

The woman was still holding the packages. Millie stood staring at her. She didn't mean to introduce herself because she knew she wasn't supposed to socialize with Pete's patients, but the woman was so helpful, and Millie couldn't help thinking that what Isobel called unethical or unprofessional or unhealthy was just plain uncouth.

"I'm Mrs. Arlen's mother," Millie said.

"I'm a patient," the young woman answered. "Where do you want these?"

Millie insisted she could manage, but the young woman said it was no trouble at all. "Hey, I'm from the Midwest. I even give up my seat on the subway when someone's older or pregnant or something."

Millie led the way down the hall to the bedroom.

"I thought I could manage them myself, but it was more than I expected. You know what linens are like. You think they're going to weigh nothing, but then you get a whole bunch of them wrapped up together. And then that comforter . . ." Millie turned into the bedroom.

The patient began to follow her, then stopped just inside the door and looked around. Millie recognized her expression. She saw it all the time on house tours. It was the look of someone who was trying to memorize everything.

The patient pushed her blond hair back from her eyes and went on staring. "I'll leave the stuff here," she said, and swept the room with one last furtive glance.

"Thank you." Millie took off her coat, shooed the cat off the bed, and began stripping the ugly brown sheets. "I'll tell my son-in-law how helpful you've been."

The patient was barely out the door when it occurred to

Millie that she'd never be able to get the dust ruffle on by herself. She'd just have to leave it for Isobel and Pete to put on later. She knew that was what she should do. But the image of the bed, as perfect and untouched as a bride, haunted her. She wanted Isobel and Pete to see it that way when they walked into the room. If you're going to do something, Harry used to say, do it right.

"I wonder," she called after the patient, "if I could bother you for one more thing."

Pete glanced at the old Tiffany desk clock, one of the few things of his uncle's left in the study, finished the note he was making, and put the closed file beside the blotter on top of his desk. Then he stood, crossed the office to the door, and opened it. That was the sign. The next patient always saw or heard or simply felt the door open and came down the hall to the office. But no patient appeared now.

He took a few steps down the hall toward the waiting room. It was empty. He turned and went back to his desk.

When she'd first started treatment, she'd been late for most of her appointments. The closer they'd got to confronting her resistance, the more elaborate her excuses had grown. She'd come racing into his office, collapse into the big wing chair, and launch breathlessly into tales of rush-hour traffic ground to a halt because of presidential cavalcades, and whole chunks of the city closed off by political demonstrations, and flooded subways, and burning buildings, and dire academic crises in the department where she was a teaching assistant. When he'd remarked one day that Job had had it easy by comparison, her small face had grown red and crinkled, like a baby about to bawl. That had surprised him because she prided herself on not showing any emotion, or weakness, as she called it. She'd opened her mouth. He'd waited. A laugh had spilled out. After

107

that they'd begun to talk about it, and little by little she'd stopped being late. But then, two days ago, she'd walked into the office and told him a joke about the woman scientist and the microscope, and instead of laughing, he'd asked her why she thought a joke that demeaned women's intelligence as well as their body parts was such a riot. She'd said he didn't understand, and it was just one of those jokes that went around the department, and she was damned if she'd turn into one of those women who were always screaming discrimination and harassment because they couldn't make it on their own abilities, and for Christ sake, Dr. Arlen, lighten up.

He looked at his watch. Seven minutes now.

He sat behind his desk thinking of Freud's question about what women wanted. Sometimes it seemed to him the only thing they could want in a society that kept working them over one way or another was to be men one way or another. Like his former wife. He could still remember the chill he'd felt the afternoon they were unpacking cartons of books when they'd first moved in here, and he'd opened her high school yearbook to the page with her name. Beneath the adolescent picture with the precociously sultry smile, beneath the list of clubs and honors and awards, was her ambition. She wanted to marry a great man and make a beautiful home for him. He'd told himself it was only her high school yearbook, people change, but when he'd come across her college yearbook, there had been no ambition listed.

He knew it wasn't her fault. All her life she'd been given everything and warned not to attempt too much. But it wasn't his fault either.

He looked at his watch again. Nine minutes. The patient had come of age in a different generation from his former wife and gone to the other extreme. Not only wasn't she going to be a dependent woman, but she wasn't going to be a woman at all,

108

because in her mind with her upbringing she couldn't separate the two words. That was the terrible rancid fact she'd got a whiff of in her last session, and he was willing to bet that was why she was late for this one.

He was about to check his watch again when he felt a presence and looked up. The first thing he saw was the patient coming down the hall toward him. The second was that damn cat, who was supposed to be locked in the other part of the apartment, close on her heels.

She reached the door, smiled at him, then ducked her head as she moved into the office. She settled into the big wing chair and went on smiling at him.

"This time I have an excuse," she said. "Ironclad."

Isobel got home a little before eight. The front door of the apartment was locked. She put down her briefcase and opened her handbag to get out the key.

The lights were on in the waiting room and the halls and the living room, but there was no sign of Pete. She went down the short hall to the kitchen. The parquet squeaked under her shoes. The sound struck her as unnaturally loud in the silent apartment. The light was on in the kitchen, too. He'd left the bottle of scotch on the counter, as he usually did, and a tray of melting ice beside it, as he never did. It was as if he'd been stopped in mid-action. She remembered the *Pentagon Papers* incident and told herself she was being melodramatic.

She called his name, but there was no answer. Not even Welch showed up at the sound. Now she was really getting worried.

She walked back down the hall, through the waiting room, and down the longer hall leading to the bedroom. The overhead light was on there, too, as well as the lamp beside the club chair where Pete was sitting with a drink in his hand and a mean look on his face. Welch was nowhere in sight, but then Welch was smart enough to stay away from men wearing expressions like that.

"Why didn't you answer me?" she asked.

He turned his face to the bed. She followed his gaze. The comforter was a fat cumulous cloud floating inside the starched duvet cover. The sheets made a neat embroidered border across the top. The pillows were plumped and perfectly aligned. The bed was clean and crisp and chaste. It had Millie's immaculate fingerprints all over it.

Isobel looked from the bed back to Pete. He was still wearing that mean look. It brought out the angles in his face. The floor lamp beside the chair turned them into harsh lines. Though Isobel understood his annoyance—he wasn't accustomed to having strange women tiptoing in and out of his apartment, at least not the private part of it—she was secretly glad. All that brown had been getting her down, but she hadn't had time to do anything about it.

She moved to the bed and sat on the end. The comforter even felt like a cloud.

"She means well. And you have to admit she has good taste."

"Fuck taste!" He rubbed his thick eyebrows with his thumb and forefinger. "This family really is getting to me."

"Come on, slugger, it's only some linens."

He took his hand away from his eyes. "No, Isobel, it is not only some linens. It's your mother coming into our apartment, unasked, unannounced, and un-fucking-believable."

Like your patients coming into the kitchen, she thought. "She brought the stuff herself?" she asked.

"Not entirely herself. How do you think she managed to lift a king-size mattress to get that thing—" He waved his hand in the direction of the dust ruffle.

"The dust ruffle?"

"—to get whatever you call it under the mattress?"

"Mrs. Zelinski?" Isobel prayed.

"Mrs. Zelinski was gone by the time Millie got here."

"Don't tell me she dragged you out of a session."

"Close, but no cigar. She dragged a patient out of the waiting room."

"Oh, my God."

"Millie was having trouble lugging all the stuff around, so the patient helped her carry it into the bedroom. Then Millie asked her if she'd mind, that was, if she had a minute before her appointment just to hold the mattress up so Millie could slide the thing under it."

"And she did?"

"Actually she was late for her appointment. Which happens to be a problem with this particular patient. But Millie told her she'd be sure to tell her son-in-law how helpful she'd been. It's the one thing my practice has been missing, a woman handing out MVP awards."

"Which patient?"

"The grad student."

"Was she upset?"

"That's not the point."

"I know. I was just asking what her reaction was."

"She found it fascinating that you'd taken the new Updike out of the Society Library."

"How'd she know it was from the Society Library?"

"How the hell do I know? Maybe Millie mentioned it when she read her a bedtime story after they got the goddamn ruffle on."

Isobel glanced over at the night table. A library postcard she was using to mark her place stuck halfway out of the book. "Either she's something out of a Le Carré novel or she has an unnatural interest in me."

111

"No, Isobel, she has a natural interest in me. That's the point." He covered his eyes with his hand again and slumped further down in the chair. "I used to run a responsible practice. Patients came and went, we did our work, I didn't have half-naked women running through my waiting room, or doormen interrupting hours to return delinquent cats on the loose in the lobby, or patients making my bed."

She still thought part of that sentence was a lie—the patient hadn't seen her in the waiting room; the patient had spied on her in the kitchen—but there was enough truth to keep her from arguing with it.

"She means well," she said.

"No, Isobel, she does not mean well. She means to hang on to you. She means to go on pretending that you're a fucking incompetent—that you can't buy your own sheets or make your own dinner or blow your own nose—so she has something to do."

"I can't just cut her off."

"You can stop playing the role. You can start realizing where you end and she begins. Hannah, too."

That's not fair, she wanted to shout back. I have stopped playing the role. If I hadn't, I wouldn't be here. And suddenly it occurred to her that liking marriage to Pete, and taking the job that was too tame for Hannah and still too rough for Millie, and being happy were all part of finally doing what she wanted rather than what Hannah and Millie expected. But she didn't argue with him, because the more she changed, the more Hannah and Millie dug in, and she didn't know what to do about that.

"And you can start taking what goes on here seriously," he went on in a calmer voice. "Because it might not be surgery, but there are other ways of cutting people open. And if this kind of thing keeps happening, we're going to wind up with patients bleeding all the fuck over us."

"So you're saying you don't want me in the apartment anymore."

Isobel tried to concentrate on the order slip she was filling out. She'd suggested the Harvard Club for a reason. Millie loved lunching among a certain caliber of men. The sea of somber pinstripe, polished cordovan, and neatly barbered hair whetted her appetite. The murmur of deep well-modulated voices, gently rising and falling like blue-chip stocks on the market, made her digestive juices flow. Hannah hated the Harvard Club, and not merely because Pete was their entrée to it. The one time Isobel had taken her there, she'd glanced around the baronial dining room and said all those men in their blue and gray uniforms made her feel as if she'd stumbled into a reunion of Civil War soldiers. But Millie couldn't get enough of it, so when Isobel had called to ask her mother to lunch, she'd suggested they lunch there. She'd thought, naively, she realized now, that the setting would soften the message.

She handed the waiter the slip, then turned back to Millie. "That's not what I said."

"Then explain it to me, because that's what I heard."

Isobel tried to explain. She talked about the psychiatrist-patient relationship. She talked about transference. She talked about plain old-fashioned privacy. She didn't talk about Millie's casting her in a role in order to hang on to her, but she still managed to make the point. At least she thought she did.

And Millie listened. She sat with her eyes downcast under lids drooping with age, and her lips pressed together so they didn't quiver, and her hands folded childishly in her lap, and listened.

"It has nothing to do with you," Isobel pleaded.

113

Her mother's painstakingly plucked eyebrows shot toward her hairline. "Do you see anyone else at this table?"

"Please try to understand."

"I understand. From now on I won't come unless I'm asked."

Isobel waited for the internal sigh of relief. Her mother was agreeing to her terms. And the terms weren't unreasonable. So why did she feel nauseated? She decided it was the lack of food and was relieved when the waiter arrived with their lunch.

They came out of the building onto Forty-fourth Street and began walking east. Isobel was eager to get back to her office, but she didn't dare hurry her mother, not after their conversation at lunch. Millie strolled with her back straight and her eyes alert to the passing crowds. She strolled like a woman who had all the time in the world.

When they reached Fifth Avenue, they stopped and turned to each other to say good-bye.

"Don't worry," Millie said, and her chin lifted imperceptibly. "I won't set foot in your apartment without a formal invitation."

"It doesn't have to be engraved." Isobel tried to joke, but Millie didn't even smile. "It isn't exactly a decree of banishment," Isobel pleaded, and her eyes scanned the crowd streaming around them, as if help might be on the way. That was when she noticed Kay Glass. She was standing on the opposite corner, talking to a man while she waited for the light to change. No, not talking. If their facial expressions were any indication, she was quarreling with a man.

"What are you staring at?" Millie asked.

"That friend of Hannah's who's looking for a job. The one I keep running into at the library."

Isobel saw the way her mother's eyes narrowed as she turned

to take in Kay and knew she was off the hook, at least for the moment.

"She looks better than when she came to drop off those books for Hannah," Millie said. "But she'd better start watching her skin. If she keeps that up, she's going to look like a prune by the time she's fifty."

"She must have gone south. I think her husband's a big tennis player or golfer or something."

"She went as far as the local tanning salon."

"How do you know?"

"The color. She looks like Hannah's old dining room table. Still, I like her jacket."

"Armani?" Isobel asked.

"That jacket hung on a rack next to an Armani. But it's still nice. And I'll make you a bet her husband's tie is from Sulka." The light changed, and she turned back to Isobel. "What are you smiling at?"

"Nothing. Just your expertise, and one of Pete's patients who has a thing about expensive name brand ties."

Millie's lips pursed as if she were drawing them together with a string. "If it's all the same to you, I've heard enough about Pete's patients for one day."

Considering the incident of the linens, as Isobel came to call it, it wasn't surprising that she forgot to tell Pete about Isabelle Fowler's call. But it was surprising that less than a week later Isabelle called again. Isobel figured maybe Isabelle didn't have lunch in mind after all. Maybe she was raising money for the alumnae fund or planning a reunion or something like that. As Megan sat at her desk, waiting for Isobel to decide whether she was going to take the call, she thought it was possible but unlikely. Isobel had never even seen Isabelle's name in the class notes of the alumnae bulletin.

115

Isobel motioned to Megan that she wasn't there, though she hated to because Megan had already said she'd see if Isobel was there, a dead giveaway that she was but didn't want to take the call, and swore that she'd remember to talk to Pete about it that night.

"It's not my fault," she insisted after she told him about the call.

"I didn't say it was. I just don't know what to do about it. Could you have lunch and be so dull she'd never suggest it again?"

"Me? Not a chance."

"I'm serious."

"Thanks a lot. So am I. I may be dull, but I couldn't set out to pull it off. What if I tell her I'm really busy with that brownstone fight and the holidays coming up and all, and promise to give her a call in January? By then she'll have forgotten she ever ran into me. Unless—" She stopped because she knew that what she was going to say would sound paranoid, but Pete had admitted Isabelle had a weakness for other women's men, even the ones who weren't her shrink.

"Unless what?"

"Unless she was cultivating me to get to you."

"You said she didn't know about us."

"She pretended she didn't. I mean, she acted as if she didn't."

"I think you're getting a little paranoid."

She wanted to tell him that disappearing possessions and anonymous letters and strange characters stalking the apartment had a tendency to make people that way, but she knew how paranoid the response would sound.

"You're right. I'll try putting her off."

As it turned out, Isobel didn't have to put Isabelle off until after the holidays. Isabelle did it for her. She'd only called, she

116

explained when Isobel finally called her back, because she'd had two tickets for an alumnae theater party that she couldn't use and thought Isobel might have liked them. "But when you didn't call, I gave them to someone else," Isabelle said.

"We really ought to get together," she added as they were getting off the phone. "Give me a call sometime after the holidays."

"I think I'm getting paranoid," Isobel told Pete that night.

"More like delusions of grandeur," he said.

Pete was right. The moral-obligation umbrella, like the shoes, turned up. One rainy night when Isobel came home from the office and put the dripping Knirps in the stand, she noticed the familiar white bone handle of the hand-painted umbrella. She picked it up and looked at it. Whoever had filched it had even returned the slipcase. She'd been sure she'd never see that again.

She bent to take the sign off the side of the stand, but it was already gone. Pete or Mrs. Zelinski must have taken it off, and she'd never noticed.

When she left for the office the next morning, it was still raining, so she took the umbrella from the stand and felt a surge of pity for Polly Markson, and a flash of anger at Polly's husband, and a little smug about how her own life had turned out. She didn't have to open the umbrella when she got to the street, because the doorman used his to shelter her from the awning to the cab he'd hailed for her. The driver managed to pull up right in front of her office building, so she tipped him generously, tucked her umbrella under her arm, and made a dash for the door.

It was still raining when she left the building for lunch. As she crossed the lobby, she held the umbrella in her left hand and had her right ready to slide it open. Polly's husband had kept

117

an eye on the costs, and when Polly had bought the umbrellas to paint, she hadn't dared spring for the more expensive kind that opened automatically with a button.

In one smooth move, Isobel pushed the door open with her shoulder, came out of the building onto the street, and slid open the umbrella. She felt the rain on the top of her head. She looked up. Through a large hole in the fabric she saw the angry battleship gray sky.

She stood staring up at it for a moment, though the rain sluiced into her eyes and down her face and over her chin and inside her collar. It was hard to tell because the wire spines were bent and the fabric was pulled all out of shape and shredding, and there was water in her eyes, but she could have sworn the hole was in the shape of her head.

As soon as she got home that night, she opened the umbrella and stood it on the kitchen floor. Millie would have gone crazy. She didn't like hats on the bed either. As Isobel moved about the room, taking off her coat, getting things out for dinner, opening a bottle of wine, she kept glancing at the umbrella. The hole was an empty Rorschach test. It changed shape every time she looked at it.

"What's that?" Pete asked when he came into the kitchen a few minutes later.

"My umbrella. The one a patient took and returned."

"You can write that off," he said on his way to the freezer. "Whoever took it must have got caught in some storm. The thing's in shreds."

"Those aren't shreds. That's a cut. Whoever took it cut my picture out of it."

He stood with the ice bin in his hands, staring across the room at her. "What are you talking about?"

"My picture is missing. Whoever took the umbrella cut it out and then returned the umbrella. It's creepy."

118

He put the ice bin on the counter, crossed the room, and picked up the umbrella. "Take a look at this, Isobel. The wires are bent and the material is coming off and hanging in strings. I don't call that a cut."

"But the hole is where my picture was."

"Probably because the chemicals in the paint did something to the fabric to make it shred more easily," the voice of scientific reason explained.

She crossed the room and stood beside him looking at the open umbrella in his hand. "Those strings could be from shredding after the cut."

He closed the umbrella and put his arm around her. "You're right, slugger. You are getting paranoid. It must be contagious. Another reason to keep you away from the patients."

EIGHT

Years of demonstrations and counterdemonstrations had taught Isobel a few useful, if not widely applicable, lessons. She knew when marching five or ten abreast never to take the outside position because that was where the hecklers could get you with food and spit and fists. She knew how to go limp in the arms of a cop. And she knew how to estimate a crowd. She figured there were between thirty and forty people milling around the long living room that had been carved from the front and back parlors of a nineteenth-century gray stone. She also figured that at least half of them were shrinks, more if you remembered that some of the couples were two-shrink families. The liaison struck her as incestuous, a sure invitation to thinning blood and burgeoning madness.

She left Pete talking to another shrink and made her way back to the dining room, where the bar had been set up. She had to wind her way around and through several groups to do it. Though most of the guests were strangers, she could place them as easily as she could tell a Central Park West apartment building from its Park Avenue cousin. The male guests from the West Side wore tieless flannel shirts, and shapeless sweaters and, in one case, a beret, which, whether for aesthetic, religious, or cosmetic reasons, had remained in place throughout

121

the party. Their female counterparts sported a lot of flowing fabric per square inch. When they gestured, as they tended to a great deal, the fringes of their shawls trailed through the dip for the crudités and the tartar sauce for the miniature crab cakes and each other's drinks. The East Side men, on the other hand, were trying to look like bankers. So were half the women. The other half showed either a lot of lingerie at the top or a lot of leg at the bottom, or both.

Isobel moved to a corner with her drink and watched the groups shift and re-form with amoebic sluggishness. She was probably the only person in the room who hadn't known everyone else for the past ten years, maybe twenty. A few of the women had been dismissive until they'd discovered she wasn't someone Pete had dragged along for the evening but someone he had married. A few had been simply dismissive, but in all fairness to the latter group, two of them were close friends of Pete's former wife and one had had an affair with Pete before she'd married her current husband. Isobel had spotted her even before Pete had let on. It was something about the tilt of her face as she'd lifted it to Pete and the timbre of her voice, which, like most artificial sweeteners, packed an acrid afterbite.

Isobel was still standing alone when the best dressed of the better-dressed shrinks sidled up to her. His double-breasted suit was cut for cruising the Via Veneto. His shoes looked as if they'd been made from the hides of milk-fed children. He said his name was Gabe Zeller. There was a moment's pause, as if he were waiting for her to say "oh" with a gasp of excitement, or at least "oh, yes" with a sigh of recognition. She tried for a smile of familiarity, because she figured he must refer a lot of patients to Pete, and if she wasn't shooting for helpmeet of the year, she didn't want to be an albatross around Pete's neck. Then Gabe Zeller went on to tell her he'd been quoted on the criminal mind in general and several mass murderers in particular in *Time*, *Vanity Fair*, and *McCall's*, not to mention on ABC News, and she realized Pete wasn't the one he was interested in. He asked about her talk show contacts. His PR firm, he confessed, had him within an inch of *Oprah*.

She spotted Pete across the room and thought again that she'd married an extraordinary man, at least for this day and age. Several months ago, when a CBS newswoman had called to interview him for one of those in-depth three-minute reports on a neurosis of the month, he'd actually passed up the chance to make a thirty-second appearance, or even be quoted.

Isobel wished Gabe Zeller good luck with *Oprah* and cut across the room to where Pete was standing in front of the French doors to the garden, talking to one of the imitation bankers. Pete introduced her to Martin Sasoon. Sasoon looked her up and down, paused for a moment as if he were thinking something over, then put his arm around her shoulders and squeezed them.

"Terrific," he said. "I was expecting a Jezebel. A real home wrecker. But you're okay."

She leaned back a little, a very little since Sasoon was still holding her shoulders. "A home wrecker? Pete was divorced for six years when I met him."

Sasoon squeezed her shoulders again. "You know what I mean. A trophy wife. A bimbo." He had trouble with the last word because he was salivating so heavily. "But I can see you're all right. You got him back on the straight and narrow." He let go of Isobel's shoulders and punched Pete's arm the way grown men do when they're trying to show they're kidding.

Pete looked as if he'd like to punch back, and no kidding.

"That's the first time I've ever been accused of getting any-one back on the straight and narrow," Isobel said. Though she wasn't keen on playing the Home Wrecker or Bimbo, she'd be damned if she'd let him cast her as the colorless Good Woman.

But Sasoon just patted her shoulder, told her to keep Pete up to the mark, and moved off.

When she turned back to Pete, there were two vertical lines, dark as crayon marks, between his eyebrows, and he wasn't smiling.

"He's your friend, not mine," she whispered.

"Come on," he answered, and started across the room toward the hosts. He told them he'd had a good time in a growl that sounded like a dog whose bone had just been taken away.

Out on the street she asked if he wanted to take a cab or walk. He started west toward Fifth Avenue without answering.

She fell in step beside him. "What are you so angry about? You're not the one he called a bimbo."

Pete turned north on Fifth. He still hadn't said a word.

"But I guess it makes sense when you think about it. Half the women there, three-quarters probably, were psychologists or counselors or psychiatric social workers, if they weren't full-fledged shrinks. They were all do-gooders. Except for me. I was the only professional troublemaker."

"You don't have to sound so damn proud of it."

His voice surprised her. It was sharp as the broken beer bottle lying in the gutter where they'd stopped to wait for the light to change. Pete nudged it with the toe of his shoe, then kicked it across the street. She might lack his formal training, but she wasn't stupid enough to think it was the bottle he was kicking.

"Anyway, it's sweet that he thinks you're back on the straight and narrow—no more incidents like that night in Vénasque— and all because of me. Naive but sweet."

Pete stopped walking and turned to her. "You want to know why he's so damn happy we got married?"

124

"Because now he can stop lying awake nights thinking of everything you're getting that he's not."

"It's a little more specific than that." He started walking again. "He referred a patient to me a year or so ago. She lives with a guy he's treating. Last week his patient came in with some cockamamy story about my making sexual advances to his girlfriend."

Now she stopped walking. "What?"

"It was a perfectly logical assumption when you think about it. How else did she know what my bedroom looked like?"

As she hurried to catch up with him, she noticed that *our* apartment had suddenly given way to *my* bedroom, but decided this wasn't the time to mention it.

"She even knew what kind of sheets were on the bed. She insisted it was all perfectly innocent, but her boyfriend was still suspicious, and, from the sound of things tonight, Marty was, too."

"Of you!"

There was no missing the indignation in her voice, but somehow he managed to.

"He said he wasn't suggesting anything had happened, but he just wanted to alert me. Sometimes patients misconstrue harmless words or gestures, he said. As if I weren't aware of the fact."

"That prick!"

Pete didn't say anything to that.

"So the implication is if you're married, you won't be doing and saying things to female patients that might get you in trouble. Or to put it in laywoman's terms, you'll be getting yours at home."

"Something like that."

They walked for a moment in silence. "If that's his view of marriage, or sex, or lust, I'm glad he's not my shrink."

125

"He's not the shrink under suspicion."

"Did you tell him what really happened?"

They went through the revolving door to the lobby of their or his—it depended on how you looked at it—building.

"That I'm a tower of professional virtue, but my mother-in-law recruits patients to help her make the bed? To tell you the truth, Isobel, I don't think it would have reassured him all that much."

"I'm sorry," she said as she followed him into the elevator.

Pete didn't say anything to that, but she thought she heard him mutter something under his breath. It sounded like "fuck."

The Well-Intentioned Friend wrote three more letters. Then the Other Woman took over. At least, that was what Isobel called her. The woman didn't bother to sign the letter. She simply warned Isobel that she couldn't stand in the way of destiny. She might as well give Pete up.

"It has to be a patient," he said.

"Then what does that say about the Heavy Breather? I still think the timing is off."

"The Heavy Breather started before you moved in, but not before you were larking through the waiting room in a variety of dressed and half-dressed states."

She put the letter she'd been holding down on the hall table —she'd shown it to him before she'd even taken off her coat— and walked away from him to the closet.

"I love it. Someone accuses you of screwing around, and it's my fault."

"That's not what I meant." His eyebrows gathered into a dark canopy over his eyes. "I was just trying to figure out who it might be. It doesn't fit anyone I'm seeing."

She hung up her coat and came back from the closet. "What

do you mean, it doesn't fit anyone? You don't expect whoever it is to come in and free-associate about the harassing phone calls she's making to the apartment or the anonymous letters she's sending to my office. Not to mention the shoes she swiped and the umbrella she destroyed."

"Nobody swiped your shoes."

"What about the umbrella?"

"A patient took it by mistake or borrowed it when it was raining."

"And cut my picture out?"

He sat in one of the Barcelona chairs. "Look, someone, probably a patient, is sending you these letters. It may be the same person who was making those phone calls. But that umbrella was falling apart. Let's not get paranoid."

"I never hated that word until I met you. Hell, I never used it until I met you."

Isobel put the four letters in a file, labeled it "Pete's Popsie," and stashed it in her bottom desk drawer next to another file labeled "Isobel's Heavy Breather." The drawer was narrow but deep, and the files didn't take up much room. It occurred to her that she had plenty of space for more evidence. She slammed the drawer closed.

As the city froze into a cold snap and the ancient radiators in the apartment clanged and groaned in protest, Pete warned her that things were likely to get worse. Psychiatry was a little like retailing. As the holidays grew closer, people who'd managed to stay out of Bloomingdale's, F. A. O. Schwarz, and his office for eleven months of the year suddenly began lining up outside the door. But the patient was craftier than that. Nothing disappeared or reappeared, and the letters stopped.

"Not even a Christmas card," Isobel said. "Maybe she went home for the holidays."

Isobel was joking, but later that evening she walked into Pete's office and found him studying his appointment book.

"What are you doing?"

"Trying to figure out who's canceled appointments because she's going away for the holidays."

"Has anyone?"

He shook his head as he went on studying the book. "The lawyer is planning to go to Barbados, but that's not till January. And the Hermès tie went to the Bahamas for a sailing course, but she managed to sandwich it in over a long weekend so she didn't miss any appointments."

Then about a week before Christmas Isobel came home to find a hat on the bed. It was a peaked baseball cap with "Brooklyn Dodgers" printed across the crown. She picked it up, not because she was superstitious but because she couldn't imagine what it was or how it had got there. As she stood studying it, she noticed something else, something she couldn't decipher, scrawled in ink on the peak. She was still trying to make out the letters when she heard Pete close the front door behind the last patient.

"Isn't that something!" he said as he came into the bedroom and saw what she was holding.

"The question is what."

"Are you kidding? It's a Dodgers hat. The real Dodgers. Did you see the autograph?"

"So that's what it is."

"Jeez," he said, and put his hand on the hat so they were holding it together. "It's Sandy Koufax's autograph."

"Wow!"

He took the hat from her, crossed the room, and put it on top of his dresser. "Nobody likes a cynic."

"Where'd it come from?"

"A patient."

"Which one?"

"The one who used to go in for rough sex."

She noticed his use of the past tense, but at the moment she wasn't interested in the patient's progress. "How'd she get it?"

"I don't know. Maybe she found it in some secondhand store."

"What do you mean, you don't know? You discuss her most intimate sexual secrets, but you won't ask her how she came up with an antique Dodgers' cap autographed by Sandy Koufax?"

"If you're going to look at it that way, how isn't important; why is."

"Okay, why?"

"Because she wants me to love her."

"What else is new?" Isobel stood staring at the hat for a moment. "Okay, that explains her, but what about you? I thought you weren't allowed to accept gifts from patients." She was still smarting from the tin of beluga that Pete had told the jilted lawyer he appreciated in theory but couldn't possibly accept in fact.

"I'm not, but something like this, with old Sandy's autograph and all the trouble she went to. How could I not take it?"

The next night Pete was still with a patient when Isobel got home, so she used the back entrance again and went straight to the bedroom. There was another gift for Pete at the foot of the bed. She knew it wasn't for her because the envelope attached to the gold paper that said "Peace on Earth" read "Dr. Peter Arlen." She wondered how this one got to the bed. If Pete had tossed it there on his way through the room during a break, as he'd tossed the hat, wouldn't he have opened it first?

While she got out of the suit she'd worn to the office and began putting together clothes that were festive enough for a holiday dinner party without making her look as if she'd been turned out by a department store wrap desk, she kept glancing at the package. It was flat and about six inches square, but it wasn't the gift that intrigued her; it was the giver. She bent over and picked it up. The handwriting was vaguely familiar, not Millie's—Isobel was both relieved and disappointed about that —but one she'd seen before.

She put down the package and looked at the clock on the night table. It said six twenty-four. Pete's sessions usually ended at twenty minutes after the hour. She wondered why this one was running over.

She didn't even wait till he came out to lock the front door. As soon as she heard it close behind the patient, she picked up the box, carried it down the hall and into Pete's office, and put it on his desk.

"Merry Christmas."

"What's that?"

"Beats me. Someone left it on the bed, and I don't think you can blame this on Millie."

He picked up the package and looked at the envelope attached to it. She sat in the chair across from his desk. It was still warm. She stared at the wastebasket. There were discarded papers, and a few Kleenex, and, on top, one of those small squares of tissue paper that's used to blot makeup. She noticed it had a perfect red kiss on it. If she were going to put on makeup after an hour of lip gnashing or crying, she'd do it in the waiting room or the hall.

"Mrs. Zelinski."

She looked from the wastebasket to him. "What?"

"It's from Mrs. Zelinski." He handed her the card. On the outside there was a reproduction of a baroque Madonna and Child. Inside, beneath the wishes for Peace on Earth and Good Will Toward Men, there was a note.

DEAR DR. ARLEN,

I told her you needed these, but she must have forgot. Merry Christmas and Happy New Year.

SOPHIA ZELINSKI

"I take it 'her' means me."

He tore off the paper and dropped it on the floor. Welch pounced on it. "Handkerchiefs." He handed the box to her.

A cardboard strip across the cellophane-covered cotton said "Baker's Dozen." The two top handkerchiefs were folded to show off large machine-embroidered *P*'s.

"Mrs. Zelinski insists you're allergic to Welch."

Pete nudged the wrapping paper with the toe of his shoe. Welch pounced again. "Not him in particular."

"You're kidding. I thought she was making it up."

He shrugged and stood.

"Because she's so crazy about you, I mean. She and about a dozen patients."

He started out of the room. "The patients have no choice. It's a psychiatric reflex. Mrs. Zelinski just has good taste."

She followed him down the hall. "Come to think of it, how did those handkerchiefs even get here today? It's Wednesday. Mrs. Zelinski doesn't come in on Wednesday."

He kept going through the waiting room and into the other hall. "She must have dropped them off. She works for other people in the building. And she knows the front door is open during office hours."

"But why didn't she bring them on one of her regular days?"

Now he stopped and turned back to her.

"You're kidding, right?"

"What about that patient who found her husband with the au pair?"

131

"Mrs. Zelinski isn't a nineteen-year-old French girl. More's the pity."

She shrugged. "I don't know. Those Slavic cheekbones are very Garboesque—in the right light."

"Like pitch-darkness." He started moving again. "You have a rich fantasy life."

At least he hadn't said she was paranoid. She followed him into the bedroom. One thing was still bothering her. "How come it's okay for Mrs. Zelinski to breeze in and out at will, but when Millie does the same thing, it's a criminal offense?"

He stopped and thought about that for a minute. "It's not all right. I'll say something to her about it." Then he put the box of handkerchiefs in his top drawer and closed it.

Of course, Isobel wasn't really worried about Mrs. Zelinski. She just liked to tease Pete about her, the same way she sometimes teased him about his patients. She knew what Freud had said about laughter as a discharge of hostility, but living in that madhouse with patients coming and going, how could she help making jokes?

"Haven't you ever been attracted to a patient?" she asked one evening a few days later after Pete had locked the door behind his last hour, come down the hall, stripped down to his boxer shorts, and climbed onto the stationary bike.

"What do you mean, attracted?" he said as he set the timer at thirty minutes.

Isobel was sitting cross-legged on the bed. "Now you sound like the East European gigolo. How you say in English? Lusted after? Was drawn to for sexual purposes? Wanted to fu—know carnally?"

"Your mouth's improving, but your mind is still prurient."

"My mind is inquiring. If you don't believe me, ask Hannah.

132

Come on, slugger, tell the truth. When the bondage queen lies there—"

"She sits."

"—sits there telling you about the chafe of Hermès silk against her milky white skin and the agony of soft purple bruises on her quivering pink thighs—"

"Forget prurient," Pete said through shortening breaths. "Pornographic. You have a pornographic mind. Hard-core."

"Don't you get even the tiniest little hard-on?"

His breath was coming faster now, and his words were coming slower. "She's . . . too . . . cra . . . zy."

"Okay, forget the bondage queen. What about the less weird ones? Haven't you ever had a patient who was a knockout, or even relatively attractive, and only mildly neurotic? From the sound of some of the women you were mixed up with before me, most of your patients would have been a step up in the world."

"Who's . . . talk . . . ing?" He was trying to cut down on the words. "Ne . . . ver . . . got . . . un . . . der . . . wear . . . from . . . fel . . . ons."

"That's not the way the doorman tells it. All I'm asking is, Aren't you ever attracted to any of your patients? What about Isabelle Fowler?"

"Not . . . her."

"What's wrong with Isabelle?"

This time he didn't bother to waste breath.

"Okay, but there must have been someone, once, a long time ago, when you were young and randy and didn't know I existed."

He was pedaling furiously now. If the bike hadn't been stationary, he would have escaped her long ago. He went on pedaling for a while before he answered.

"Oc . . . cas . . . ion . . . al . . . ly."

"Aha!" She leaned forward with her hands on her knees. "Who?"

The timer went off, and he stopped pedaling and sat staring at her. "I . . . should . . . have . . . known."

"Come on, you can tell me. Not names, just identifications."

He got off the bike and started for the bathroom. "You're a . . . sick . . . woman."

"Is that an opinion or a diagnosis?"

Through the open door to the bathroom, she saw a pair of boxer shorts sail past the hamper and hit the floor.

"Diagnosis."

She sat on the bed watching the pale Golden Delicious curve of his ass as he bent to put down the bathmat. The conversation didn't bother her. If anything, she found Pete's admission human and vulnerable and eerily sexy. But mostly she liked the fact that he'd made it at all.

Later that night, after they'd got home from a noisy Village party given by a friend from her environmental days—the wine had been raw; the food organic; and the napkins, paper, cloth, or otherwise, nonexistent—she lay in bed listening to Pete's breathing, which was even and peaceful now, and thinking about the sweet openness of his confession, even if she'd had to pry it out of him.

She turned on her side and molded herself against him. In the blue-white moonlight spilling through the windows, she noticed the shadow of the baseball cap on his dresser. She was still surprised he'd accepted it. Then suddenly it occurred to her. She wondered why she hadn't thought of it before. When she'd accused him of betraying his professional principles, she'd been talking about the fact that he'd taken a gift, but now a more serious transgression occurred to her. How had the patient known an old Brooklyn Dodgers' cap autographed by Sandy Koufax was the one Christmas gift he'd been pining for all his life? There were no Dodgers' artifacts in his office. There wasn't even a baseball book among the collected works of Freud, and the studies of his disciples and detractors, and the investigations of women's pathology and men's sexual dysfunction and the psychodynamics of loss. Pete's personal books were in her study, formerly the study, and still Emily's room to Mrs. Zelinski. That was how fastidious Pete was. He didn't leave telltale signs lying around his office. So how had the patient known?

She almost waked him to ask, but she knew he'd call her more than paranoid if she did. She decided to bring it up first thing in the morning.

Isobel opened her eyes to a dark gray city streaked and glistening with wet sleet and an unforgiving wind that howled off the park to rattle the windows and seep in through the cracks. It was Saturday morning. The paper was outside the door. The phone machine was on. She moved closer to Pete beneath the down comforter. Without opening his eyes, he hooked his leg around hers.

Later that morning, when she noticed the hat again, she realized that Pete frequently used sports analogies and baseball images and jock expressions, and there were a dozen ways anyone with the least little bit of intelligence would know he'd love a hat like that. Put that under "Paranoid" in your *Diagnostic and Statistical Manual*, American Psychiatric Association!

It was almost noon by the time Isobel went to the front door to get the *Times*. She wasn't wearing anything except the shirt Pete had worn the night before, so she opened the door a crack and snaked her hand around to pull in the paper. Only there was no paper there. The porter must have flung it from the elevator again. You'd think he'd be more careful this close to Christmas. She opened the door a little wider and stuck her head out. There was no paper anywhere in the hall. She closed the door, went into the kitchen, and picked up the house phone to call the lobby. The concierge answered immediately. He, at least, knew Christmas was just around the corner.

She asked what had happened to the papers that morning. He said, nothing, they were all delivered as usual. She asked if he was sure. He said he was positive.

"Do you think the Davisons took it?" she asked Pete when she went back to the bedroom.

"You lived in that disreputable brownstone for too long. People don't steal each other's newspapers here. Especially when there're only two apartments on the floor."

"Then who took it?"

"The same person who took your shoes and carved up your umbrella," he said, and grinned and scratched himself the way men do and grinned some more. And she had to smile, too, because disappearing papers were a staple of urban life, and only a paranoid—there was that word again—woman would make an issue of one, especially on a Saturday, when there was little news and not even a book review.

NINE

SOMEHOW THEY MADE IT
through the holidays not only unharassed by phone calls and
letters but generally unscathed. Isobel had worried about the
return of Pete's son from college and daughter from boarding
school, but they adjusted to Isobel's presence more easily than
Mrs. Zelinski had. In fact, on the nights they stayed over, they
slept so late the next morning, awakened so groggy, and spent
so much time on the phone arranging massive movements of
adolescents from movies to restaurants to other people's apartments that Isobel suspected they didn't even know she was
there.

On the afternoon of New Year's Eve she and Pete paid a brief
but *gemütlig* visit to Central Park West. The coffee and tea
flowed like champagne, the cakes and pastries and dried fruits
circulated, and the wishes for a happy and healthy New Year
reverberated through the apartment.

On New Year's Eve they took a rented movie and each other
to bed. As the fireworks sizzled in the sky over the park and
horns and whistles blared at their windows, they congratulated
themselves on their foresight and good taste. From the foot of
the bed Welch purred assent.

The next morning, on his way back from getting the paper at
the front door, Pete made a detour through the kitchen,

137

opened a can of cat food, and dumped half of it into Welch's bowl. Once again, it was such a sweet gesture that Isobel couldn't even blame him for what happened later in the day. She knew that if Welch didn't dog her heels into the kitchen and stay underfoot until food appeared, something was wrong, but Pete hadn't had her experience.

It wasn't until the middle of the afternoon that they noticed he was missing. Actually it was Pete who noticed. He'd grown accustomed to having a foot warmer when he stretched out on the bed to watch a football game.

Isobel went through the apartment calling Welch's name. She even went into the kitchen and rattled the box of cat treats as if it were a primitive musical instrument. There was no response. She looked under the beds and in the closets and even, though she knew she was overreacting, in the dishwasher and the washing machine and the oven. Then she went back to the bedroom.

"Did you see him when you put his food out this morning?" she asked.

Pete thought about it for a moment, then said he didn't think he had.

Now she was really beginning to worry. Welch might be impervious to human blandishments, but at the first whiff of Elegant Entree or Shrimp Surprise he developed round paws.

Pete got off the bed and made his own tour of the apartment. Isobel followed him in and out of the rooms. This time they both got down on their hands and knees and looked under the beds.

"The little bugger probably got out again," Pete said as he stood. He went down the hall to the kitchen and picked up the house phone to call the lobby. The concierge said he hadn't seen the cat.

"He must be in the halls," Isobel said.

They checked the front hall and the back service area. Both were empty.

"If he's been out since I opened the door this morning, he could be on any floor," Pete said.

"Or out of the building."

"Someone would have seen him go through the lobby."

"You didn't see him go past you into the hall."

Pete said he had to be in the building somewhere.

Isobel said she hoped so because he wouldn't last a minute on the streets. "Unless he manages to get a cab."

They went back into the apartment to put on shoes. Pete said he'd work his way up from the lobby while she made her way down from the top floor.

She took the elevator to twenty-one and began going through the halls and down the service stairs from one floor to the next. Under other circumstances she would have lingered to compare the decor. One floor had an original Julian Schnabel. She knew it was original because the crockery was falling off. But she didn't stop to look at it or the other paintings and prints and flower arrangements. When she'd said Welch wouldn't last a minute on the street, she'd been thinking of other cats that still had their claws, and speeding cars, and small boys given to random cruelty. She was trying not to think of a woman intent on more deliberate destruction.

As she worked her way from the sixteenth floor to the fifteenth to the fourteenth, the images kept pace with her. She remembered the dead dog left on the doorstep in *Cabaret*, and a cat carcass pinned to a wall in a book she'd read years ago, and horror movies awash in the blood of animals whose only crime had been taking up with the wrong humans. She muttered and cursed her way down another flight of stairs. It was one thing to harass her. It was something else to go after a helpless animal.

139

On the eleventh-floor landing she came face-to-face with Pete. They didn't have to ask each other if they'd found him.

"You don't think this could have anything to do with . . ." she started.

He shook his head, but she couldn't help noticing that he hadn't even let her finish.

They went back to the apartment. They called and whistled and pleaded. They opened drawers and moved furniture and peered behind the books in the bookcases. Finally, when they'd covered every inch of the apartment, Isobel sat at the kitchen table and rested her forehead on her hand. "He's not here."

Pete closed the door to the empty microwave. "He's never got out of the building before."

She lifted her head from her hand and looked at him. "Maybe he didn't get out. Maybe he was taken out. Like my shoes and the umbrella."

She waited for him to call her paranoid. When he didn't, she knew they were really in trouble.

He said he'd take a look around the block and went down the hall to the front closet. He was putting on his jacket when the bell rang. That was why he beat her to the door.

A girl of about nine or ten whom Isobel occasionally saw on the elevator was standing in the hallway. She had Welch, who was fussy about being held, slung over her shoulder like the strap of a handbag.

"He came in when my mom opened the door this morning," she explained. "I hope it's okay that we kept him for the day."

This time there was no question about it. It never would have happened if Isobel hadn't broken the rules. Again.

She was standing in the hall, waiting for the elevator and thinking about Philomena Waverly and her twenty million dollars, when it occurred to her that she didn't have any change to

140

call her office if the Landmarks Preservation hearing dragged on, as it was likely to. She could go around to the back door again and take change from the silver box on Pete's dresser, but she was already so late she'd have to take a subway because a cab would take forever to get that far downtown. Besides, she'd heard a patient go into the office only a few minutes ago, and no one had arrived since, so she knew the waiting room was empty. That was why she broke the rules, and for a long time after she couldn't decide whether she was glad or sorry she had. She'd never believed ignorance was bliss.

She opened the front door quietly and crossed the waiting room to the closet. Some kind of fur she couldn't identify but still didn't approve of hung beside Pete's trench coat. It was the trench coat she was after.

Like most men, Pete didn't think small change was money. When he took off his trousers at night, coins bounced to the floor. Half the time he didn't even notice them. Mrs. Zelinski was always finding nickels, dimes, and pennies when she went through his clothes to send them to the cleaner or put them in the washing machine. Even his bathrobes harbored change from late-night food deliveries. But his overcoats were treasure troves.

Isobel reached into the left pocket. It was empty. She slipped her hand into the right. Pay dirt. She should have known. Pete was right-handed. The metal felt cold and hard against her fingertips. Something else felt soft. That was another thing she could always count on finding in Pete's pockets. Crumpled handkerchiefs. Okay, so it wasn't the most savory surprise in the world, but no one was asking her to go through his pockets.

She didn't want the handkerchief, but as she pulled out her fingers clamped around the coins, the handkerchief came with them and fell to the floor. It lay there like a mangled pigeon, a gray-white clump soaked in blood. At first she thought it really

141

was blood and wondered if Pete had got a nosebleed or hurt himself and hadn't bothered to tell her. Then she picked it up and shook it out. The red stain opened like an explosion. A solid piece of it clung to the curl in the top of the *P*. Isobel ran her finger over it. It wasn't blood, and it sure wasn't Crayola, though it was greasy enough to be. It was lipstick. It was such an absurd cliché she almost laughed.

She started to stuff it back in Pete's pocket, because she was sure whatever it meant, it didn't mean what it looked as if it meant. Then she changed her mind, stuffed it in her own pocket, and left the waiting room so quietly neither Pete nor his patient would ever know she'd been there.

It wasn't that she wanted to keep touching it, just that the moist deep cold of midwinter had permeated the subway station. As she stood on the platform waiting for the train, she jammed her hands into her pockets. Even through the glove, she could feel the handkerchief.

Hannah and Millie came to stand on either side of her on the drafty platform. She heard the sound of their voices above the roar of the train thundering into the station.

"Harry never looked at another woman in his life," Hannah, twenty-five years younger, said.

From the next room, where they thought she was doing her Latin homework, where she had been doing her Latin homework until she'd heard her grandmother's words, Isobel listened.

"Not Harry," Hannah repeated. "Never Harry."

Isobel had gone on staring at the Latin text while she'd tried to decipher Hannah's words. She'd never heard her grandmother defend her father before, but then she'd never heard her mother criticize him. She couldn't hear her now, not the actual words, but she recognized the tone. It dripped out slowly, painfully, like the fluid in the bottle that had hung from Isobel's grandfather's bed before he'd died.

Hannah's voice snapped off the sound, the way Isobel had once seen the nurse unhook the tube and change the bottle. "The trouble with you is you have too much time on your hands. You sit around and imagine things."

Millie's next words carried to the living room. "I'm not imagining this."

Isobel never had found out for sure what her mother was or wasn't imagining. These days her powers of reason told her what it must have been, but her imagination still couldn't make the leap. It wasn't that she thought her father had been a saint, only that she had trouble fleshing him out as a man. He'd been like one of those expensive hand-dipped chocolates he used to bring her mother, dark and silky and inviting on the outside, but without a hint of what lay within.

The train lurched and clanked and squeaked to a stop. Hannah and Millie disappeared in the crush of exiting passengers. The clump of humanity pushing on carried Isobel through the doors.

It was a little after the rush hour, and she managed to get a seat. She didn't even realize she was toying with the handkerchief until the train had passed Fifty-ninth Street. When she did become aware of it, she took it out of her pocket and looked at it again. There could be a dozen explanations. Name one. Someone had kissed him on the cheek. Millie, for Christ sake. She wouldn't be giving it a second thought if it weren't for those stupid letters. He told her to ignore the letters. Well, what else would he say?

"I'm not imagining this," her mother had insisted.

She went on staring at the handkerchief. The color was such a dark red it really could have been blood, except it wasn't dry or brittle. The stain rubbed off on her fingers. Without realizing what she was doing, she opened her handbag and wiped her hand. Now her handkerchief was soiled, too.

She shoved Pete's handkerchief and her own back in her bag and snapped it shut. When she looked up, she saw a man watching her. He was wearing a torn storm coat covered with greasy black stains. Beneath it his chest was bare except for a long red plastic bicycle lock that dangled from his throat like a necklace. He took an imaginary handkerchief from the pocket of his filthy coat, shook it out, raised it to his white-crusted lips, then flipped his wrist and the imaginary handkerchief toward Isobel. Leave it to her to attract the Marcel Marceau of subway madmen. She was still debating whether it was more dangerous to stay where she was or to show her fear by moving when the train stopped and the man got off.

The hearing dragged on well into the afternoon. During a break Isobel opened her bag to get change to call her office and saw the handkerchief lying there with her keys and wallet and hairbrush. She was afraid the lipstick would rub off on everything in her handbag, but she didn't know where else to put it.

When she went into the women's room, she noticed a smudge of red lipstick on her nose. It wasn't the shade that had almost worn off her lips because she'd been biting them all morning, and she realized it must have come from her own handkerchief. She took a paper towel, the thick rough brown kind, from the dispenser on the wall and wrapped Pete's handkerchief in it.

"We can kiss good-bye to twenty mil." Zoe's voice had the sweet lilt that always lingered for a moment after she got off the phone with her Irish nanny.

"What do you mean?" Isobel asked as she took off her coat and hung it on the back of her office door.

144

"I was assuming from the way you looked that the commission refused to vote landmark status."

Isobel told her the commission hadn't decided yet, and fought the urge to tell her about the handkerchief. It was so outrageous, so impossible, so dumb that she had to tell someone, and then someone would tell her, "Don't be ridiculous." But not Zoe.

Pete was still with his last patient when she got home, but she went through the front door anyway. She dropped her handbag on the table and her briefcase on the floor with resounding thuds. She hoped they carried down the hall, through the door, and into his office. She still couldn't believe it was what it appeared to be, not Pete, never Pete, but suddenly she was furious at the patients who came and went, peering into her life and swiping her possessions and pilfering her peace of mind. And she was furious at Pete for letting them.

She crossed the waiting room and opened the door to the rest of the apartment. Welch streaked into the room and began wrapping himself around her legs. She reached down and rubbed his head. "No more low profile for us, Mr. Welch."

She took off her coat and hung it in the front closet next to Pete's trench coat and a red duffel jacket. The hangers rattled like a brass band. She started to close the closet door, then stopped and reached into the other pocket of the trench coat, though she'd checked it that morning. In ten hours she'd gone from blind trust to mean suspicion.

She picked up her handbag and went down the hall into the kitchen. Welch followed her. She left the door open in case he changed his mind, crossed the room to the radio, and switched it on. Innocuous Chopin filled the room. She fiddled with the dial until she found rock, then turned up the volume. She stood there listening to it for a moment. She hated rock. She

145

switched off the radio, went to the kitchen door, and closed it. Then she gave Welch his dinner. Pete came into the kitchen a few minutes later.

"Don't tell me. I can see from looking at you. You gave them hell at the hearing." He made a pass at her behind on his way to the refrigerator. She sidestepped it.

"Don't be so damn patronizing."

He took out the bin of ice, closed the freezer, and turned to look at her. "I take it your brand of hell wasn't enough. I'm sorry."

"They haven't voted yet."

"Then what's wrong?" He started to say something, then caught himself.

"If you just remembered that you're supposed to be a feminist and stopped yourself from asking if I was premenstrual, you made a smart move."

"You mean, this is just your natural charm oozing through?"

She crossed the kitchen to the table, opened her handbag, and pulled out the brown paper ball. She unwrapped the handkerchief and waved it in front of him as if she were the matador and he the bull.

"Do you want to tell me what the fuck this is?" It wasn't the way she'd planned to do it.

He looked at it. "I don't know." He put the ice bin down on the counter and wiped his wet hands on his shirt. "It looks like a handkerchief with lipstick on it."

"It's your handkerchief. But it isn't my lipstick." Her voice was measured. That was better.

"You're kidding, right? This is some kind of joke."

"It was in your trench coat pocket."

"I haven't worn my trench coat in weeks."

"You wore it to that party to raise money for your goddamn alma mater last week."

He thought about that for a minute. "Did I?" He spoke with the perfect calm of scientific inquiry.

She tried to match it. "You did."

"Then I guess you borrowed my handkerchief and I stuck it back in my pocket."

"Have you ever seen me in goddamn purple lipstick?"

He pulled a chair out from the table, sat, and looked up at her. "This really is a joke, right?"

"All right, forget disappearing possessions. I get weird phone calls. I get letters telling me you're screwing around. I find this" —she picked up the stained, crumpled handkerchief and waved it in front of his face again—"in your coat pocket, and all you keep saying is 'You're joking, right?' "

He took the handkerchief from her and looked at it. "This isn't even my handkerchief."

"Lenny Bruce."

"What?"

"It's an old Lenny Bruce joke. Deny, deny, deny. Your wife walks in and finds you in bed with another woman, and you say you were just giving mouth-to-mouth resuscitation."

He handed her the handkerchief. "All right. You ask if I've ever seen you in purple lipstick. Have you ever seen me carry a monogrammed handkerchief?"

"How the hell do I know? I don't pay that much attention to your handkerchiefs. That's Mrs. Zelinski's passion. As for 'ever,' I haven't even known you for most of your adult life."

"Thanks a lot."

They went on staring at each other across the table.

"Anyway, come to think of it, I have seen you carry a hand-kerchief with a monogram. Mrs. Zelinski gave you a goddamn baker's dozen handkerchiefs for Christmas, and there was a great big *P* on each and every goddamn one of them."

"I haven't used any of those yet."

147

"Like I said, Lenny Bruce."

He went on staring at her, then got up and walked out of the room.

She heard his steps receding down the hall and across the waiting room until they disappeared. He couldn't be walking out. It wasn't his style. And it was his apartment.

A moment later she heard the steps coming back down the hall toward her. He shouldered his way through the kitchen door as if there were a crowd in his way. His eyebrows made a single black line over his eyes. His mouth was thin as a thread.

He dropped a box on the table in front of her. The card-board strip that said baker's dozen was still in place.

"Count them."

She looked up at him.

"Count the fucking handkerchiefs. There are thirteen."

She looked at the handkerchiefs, then back at him. "I believe you."

He stood looking down at her for a moment longer. "Sure." Then he went to the counter, made himself a drink, and carried it into his office. And Welch, the little Quisling, followed him.

"It has to be a patient."

He spoke as if the conversation had been going on for the last half hour, though for the last half hour she'd been sitting in the kitchen trying to read the paper and trying not to think about the lipstick-stained handkerchief that she'd put in the trash and then, with some vague thought about evidence, immediately taken out, and he'd been doing God knows what on the other side of the closed door to his office. She wasn't sure what brought him out now—the empty glass in his hand, hunger, contrition—but she was glad he was here.

"It couldn't be anyone but a patient," he insisted. "It would

148

be the easiest thing in the world to stick something like that"—
his eyes darted to the handkerchief she'd put back on the table
because she didn't know where else to put it—"in my pocket
when no one was in the waiting room."

"Fine. Now all we have to do is figure out who's gone beyond
transference to obsession."

He pulled a chair out from the table and sat across from her.
"I'm not sure it's obsessive love. The letters sound more like
erotomania. They have that delusionary quality. In erotomania
the individual believes the love is reciprocated. In cases of obsessive love—"

"If I want definitions, I'll go to the fucking *DSM*."

The force of her words made him rear back in his chair like a
horse shying.

"I'm sorry," she said more gently. "I just want to know who's
doing this."

"Don't you think I do?"

"Of course, but you're not the one who's being hounded."

He went on staring at her without a word. He didn't have to
explain. She knew what he was thinking. She was the victim,
but he was the failure. He was the one who'd dedicated his life
to understanding the human mind, to going behind the ruses
and the subterfuges, the masks and the roles, to unlocking the
truth, or at least getting at the secrets. But not this time. This
time the role was so convincing it was as real as the real thing.

The letters started again. They arrived, two or three a week,
at Isobel's office, as if the sender didn't want Pete to know about
them but didn't care about the rest of the world. The envelopes
were no longer marked "personal," and the first one Megan
opened rattled her almost as much as the earlier ones had
Isobel.

"There's this letter," Megan began as she followed Isobel into her office. "I put it on top there." Her arm jerked toward Isobel's desk. "The envelope wasn't marked 'personal' or anything. You can see. I put it on your desk with the letter so you could see. That's why I opened it. I mean, I thought it was an ordinary—"

"That's okay," Isobel said before she even got to her desk. "It's just a crank letter."

"Oh, sure. I knew that."

"I've been getting them for a while."

Megan stood staring at her with curious, unintelligent eyes.

"Don't worry about them. I don't."

She was, in fact, beginning to get used to them. The sameness of the wording, the repetition of the passions, the reiteration of the pity for Isobel had begun to take on the insistent triteness of a popular song heard too often on the radio. Isobel knew it all by heart—sometimes she couldn't get the strains out of her head—but she no longer really heard it.

Then the letters began to change. At first the difference was so subtle Isobel almost missed it. The woman expressed her usual pity for poor blind Isobel and told her again that she might as well give Pete up, but this time she tacked a new phrase onto the end of the sentence. ". . . give him up and go home to mommy."

It was an innocuous phrase, a childish taunt that echoed from the playgrounds of youth. At least that was the way Isobel read it. The writer, whoever she was, hadn't meant that Isobel should go home to Millie. The idea that she had came to Isobel at four-nineteen the next morning. One of the great achievements of modern technology was that now insomniacs could mark the exact moment at which fear, despair, or panic struck.

She turned on her back and lay staring at the ceiling, though she knew she never fell asleep on her back. Welch waited to

150

make sure she wasn't going to move again, then draped himself over her ankles. If the writer was one of Pete's patients, how did she know about Hannah and Millie? The answer was so obvious Isobel was amazed it hadn't hit her before.

Hannah had loved to stay over in the dorm. Late at night she used to sit around with the girls, playing one of the girls in Isobel's navy blue flannel robe, cradling her mug of tea, passing the cookies and brownies she'd brought from a bakery on Broadway, talking, joking, and arguing. At some point in the discussions one of the girls would always ask what class Hannah had been. Then Hannah would admit she hadn't graduated from Bryn Mawr, but the fact that they'd thought she had always made her flush with pride.

Isobel's throat felt dry, and her mouth stale as a used ashtray. She smacked her lips sourly and turned toward the window. Welch tumbled off the bed. A figure stared down at her. Her heart stopped. The figure became the stationary bike.

Millie used to come to visit, too, though she hadn't stayed over in the dorm, even when she wasn't with Harry. She'd turn up at Pembroke West with shiny shopping bags, because Saks was having a sale or Bergdorf's had the exact shade of cashmere sweater to go with Isobel's blue skirt, and an ice chest full of food, and an invitation to as many girls as wanted to go out to dinner. Isabelle Fowler, whose father had never visited and whose mother's child support payments hadn't stretched to taking half the dorm out to dinner, always accepted the invitation.

She turned on her other side with her back to the window. Pete's profile took shape in the ghostly light. He was sleeping on his back with his hands crossed over his chest, peaceful as a sarcophagus. Welch had come around the other side of the bed and lay curled against him.

She pulled the comforter up over her shoulders. She wasn't

going to jump to conclusions. Other patients knew. The young woman Millie had enlisted to make the bed, for one. You didn't have to be in treatment to realize that a grown woman whose mother was still tiptoing around her bedroom was more tied up than she ought to be.

It was after five by the time she fell asleep again. The alarm on Pete's side of the bed went off at six forty-five.

"Which of your patients know about me?"

Pete's hand reached for the clock radio. His eyes opened. He made a noise, or maybe only cleared his throat. Isobel took it as a question.

"Which of your patients know about my life? About Millie and Hannah and the whole setup?"

He pushed away Welch, who'd gone from cleaning his own fur to Pete's eyebrows. "What are you talking about?"

She explained how both of them had missed the real significance of that phrase in the letter.

He lay there staring at her as if he were trying to put her in focus. Later he'd blame what he said next on the fact that he was still half asleep.

"Which of my patients know about you? Only the ones you and Millie keep accosting in the waiting room."

She fought free of the tangled sweaty covers and got out of bed. "Do me a favor. Next time I get a call or a letter or find some goddamn disgusting handkerchief that's been planted for my benefit, don't tell me we're in this together."

She went into the bathroom and slammed the door behind her. Usually, when she showered, she left it open a crack to let the steam out. The fixtures might be Italian state-of-the-art, but the ventilation was prewar inadequate.

A few minutes later she heard the squeak of the door over the sound of running water. On the other side of the frosted glass doors she could make out Pete's shadow.

"I'm sorry."

"I should have let you wake up first." She turned off the shower, opened the door, and took a towel from the heated rack. "Anyway, you have a point. The way I figure it, it's either Isabelle Fowler or the patient Millie conscripted into service."

"Not a chance."

"Why not?"

"The one Millie conscripted isn't sick enough. Besides, she'd never come up with all that stuff in the letters about star-crossed love and destiny and sacrifice. This is a woman who prides herself on being one of the guys."

"Then Isabelle."

He shook his head. "A few months ago I might have agreed with you, but not now."

"Why not now?"

"Because she's finally beginning to understand what she's been doing with all those men who belonged to other women."

"You mean you've raised her consciousness. You've shown her sisterhood."

He reached past her, opened the shower door, and turned on the water. "Like the morning light," he said in an exaggerated southern drawl, "bitchiness does not become you."

The next letter made no reference to Isobel's personal life, if you could call telling a woman that her husband was in love with another woman and urging her to give him up impersonal. Isobel decided Pete was right. The connection between the line telling her to go home to mommy and the fact of Millie's apartment on Central Park West was a middle-of-the-night hallucination, like the hovering figure who'd turned into a stationary bike.

Then, on a rainy February morning, when two Japanese men beat Isobel out of a cab at the corner of Fifth and Ninetieth—

the corner where empty cabs emerged from the park, which used to be a well-kept secret among native Upper East Siders— and the Fifth Avenue bus reeked of damp wool and steamed with the heat of too many hostile wet bodies, she arrived in her office to find another letter. Megan had put it on top of the pile of mail on her desk.

Isobel skimmed through the familiar first paragraph about Pete's and the writer's passion for each other. It had a tired, steamy feeling, like the air on the bus that morning. Then the second paragraph jumped out at her.

> *Don't blame yourself. No woman could have come between us, but especially not someone like you who knows so little about men, who was raised by women who never got along with men themselves. Your mother filled your mind with romantic garbage. Your grandmother fed you apocryphal crap about the love of books and the burning of books and the redeeming quality of books. Whichever way you look at it, neither of them understood the male psyche. Are you surprised I know so much? Are you surprised he tells me the things you told him? Are you surprised that we pity you and laugh at you and just wish you'd disappear from the face of the earth? I'd feel sorry for you if I didn't hate you so much.*

Isobel had come into the office still overheated from the bus. Now she felt the sweat running down her sides, like roaches scuttling beneath her clothing. The sensation reminded her of the days when she'd canvassed ghetto households for the consumer group. All the women who'd worked on the study had confessed that as they'd sat in those vermin-infested tenements asking questions and tallying answers, they'd squirmed at the hallucinated sensation of insects crawling up their thighs and in their pubic areas. When she'd told Pete about the feeling, he'd said it was a common delusion. She opened her suit jacket and slipped out of it, but the itching sensation continued. She sat behind her desk and read the letter through again. This was no childish taunt that had hit the mark by accident. This venom was coded to her genes.

She leaned her elbow on her desk and her head on her hand and closed her eyes for a moment. She had to keep her perspective. How many women of her generation hadn't been raised by romantics?

She opened her eyes, leaned back in her chair, and read the letter through a third time. Perspective, hell! This was no stab in the dark. It was her family history. It was one of the stories Isobel had grown up on. Millie had spun fairy tales. Hannah had talked about book burnings. Not the ones by the Nazis, but the one by Hannah's own mother.

It had happened on a winter night. That was why there'd been fires in the street. Hannah was a good storyteller. She'd made Isobel feel the wind howling down Hester Street, and see the flames in the big metal drums, and taste the grit and ashes in the frozen air.

"I used to wonder," Hannah had said once, "if it had happened during the summer, if I'd come home some night in July or August, when the air was steaming and the fire hydrants made rainbows of the garbage in the streets, and told her what the woman in the settlement house had said, I used to wonder what my mother would have done with the books then."

But it was winter the night Hannah came home and told Leah that the woman in the settlement house said, if you were smart, like Hannah, and a hard worker, like Hannah, you could go to college, even if you didn't have any money. Even if you were a girl.

First Leah had laughed. "Sure, and I'm Mrs. Astor's pet horse."

But it was true, Hannah had insisted. The woman from the

settlement house had even said she'd help Hannah with the applications.

"You know what my mother said then?" Hannah used to ask Isobel when the story had become a catechism.

" 'Sure, she's an old maid, so she wants you should be, too.' " Isobel mimicked her grandmother mimicking her great-grand-mother.

What the woman from the settlement house wanted her to be, Hannah had explained as she'd stood beside the chipped sink and watched her mother's hands fly back and forth pluck-ing the feathers from a chicken, was a teacher or a social worker or even a doctor. Hannah was counting on the last word to convince her mother. It was a golden word, more American than rabbi, more respectable than businessman, and more se-cure than money in the bank.

Leah didn't answer for a moment. Her hands picked up speed. Feathers flew. When she finally opened her mouth to speak, one of them caught on her breath and danced in front of her face. What did that troublemaker in the settlement house take her for, a greenhorn fresh off the boat, ready to believe stories about streets paved with gold and girls becoming doc-tors? But it was true, Hannah insisted.

Leah put down the chicken, turned off the water, and dried her hands on her apron. Then she went down the corridor, past the room where Hannah's brothers slept and the alcove where the two youngest girls slept and the room where Leah and Hannah's father slept, and turned into the room Hannah shared with two of her sisters. When Leah came out of the room and back down the hall, she was carrying Hannah's three books, not the ones she borrowed from the library or brought home from school or was lent by the troublemaker, but the ones Hannah had asked for as presents and saved her money to buy. One was called *A Tale of Two Cities*, another was called *Jane*

156

Eyre, and the third was called *Webster's Dictionary*. Leah carried them past Hannah, through the door of the apartment, down five flights of stairs, and out onto the street. At that time of year there wasn't a block on the Lower East Side that didn't have at least one metal drum with a fire going in it to roast chestnuts or sweet potatoes or warm hands. Up and down Hester Street, flames licked at the thin night air. Leah didn't have to walk far.

As Hannah knew, as all Leah's children knew, Leah had a primitive and pathological fear of waste. A morsel of uneaten food left on a plate begged for financial reverses. A coat or pair of shoes thrown out rather than passed on invited accidents. A light bulb burning in an empty room tempted illness or even death. Long after Leah had learned English and abandoned certain religious practices, she still went through the rituals to propitiate the god of profligacy. But that winter night when Hannah came home from the settlement house talking about college, Leah took three books that had cost good money and been made from fine materials and hurled them into the first flaming drum she found. She could have sold them. She could have given them away. She could have let the younger girls cut them up into paper dolls. But she burned them. While Hannah stood on the stoop of the tenement crying and begging and promising, she tossed them into the stinking smoking drum, not one by one, as if she were trying to make a point, but quickly and unceremoniously, the way she'd burned rags and contaminated clothing after the baby had died.

A week later Hannah's father brought home a young man. His name was Reuben. Hannah called him the stranger. Her mother told her not to talk crazy. He was Leah's cousin's husband's nephew, and he had a good little business with his brothers that had something to do with boxes or paper or cord or something like that. What else did you have to know about him? Leah asked.

157

Six weeks later Hannah married the stranger. Leah was right. There wasn't a lot more to learn about Reuben. Something, but not a lot.

That was the story Hannah had raised Isobel on, the story that later, after she was grown, Isobel continued to dine out on. It was such a perfect feminist parable. In dormitory smokers, in fresh-out-of-school studio apartments, over lunch and dinner tables, Isobel must have told the story to friends almost as many times as Hannah had told it to her. She especially liked to tell it to younger women who didn't understand what the anger was all about. Even now she could have gone through her roster of acquaintances and found several dozen people who knew about Hannah and the book burning.

She sat staring at the letter. But only one of them was a patient of Pete's.

She looked at her watch. It was eighteen after eleven. The second hand swept through one minute, then another. She forced herself to wait through two more, then dialed Pete's number.

"It's Isabelle Fowler," she said as soon as he picked up the phone. "I'm sure of it."

"How do you know?"

She read him the letter. She explained her reasoning. He admitted the circumstantial evidence pointed to Isabelle.

"Circumstantial evidence! Who am I talking to, the attorney for the defense?"

"What about the other hundred people who know the story?"

"You said you were sure it was one of your patients."

"It just doesn't feel right."

"Feel right! You sound like some New Age quack. The next thing I know you'll be casting chicken bones on your office floor to find who it is by goddamn divination."

158

"Would you please calm down."

"I'm calm." She rubbed the back of her neck. It was still damp beneath her hair. "I'm perfectly calm."

"You're perfectly off the wall. Look, that's my next patient. Can we talk about it when you get home?"

"Do you see Isabelle Fowler today?"

"No."

"Then we can talk about it when I get home."

They did, for most of the night. They went over the phone calls and the letters and the umbrella and the handkerchief. They discussed the patient who'd helped Millie make the bed and the patient who'd given him the Dodgers' cap and his need, because of his mother and his sister and his former wife and God knew who else, to give women, especially women who'd had a hard time, the benefit of a doubt.

"I thought you thought that was one of my virtues," he said.

"I used to," she snapped.

But mostly they talked about Isabelle Fowler. And finally Pete agreed to talk to Isabelle Fowler.

Isabelle Fowler had an appointment for six-thirty the following evening. Isobel decided to stay at her office until at least seven-thirty. She didn't want to take the chance of running into Isabelle in the lobby again.

The silence in the empty office wasn't peaceful like the quiet of the Society Library—this was an absence of something rather than the presence of serenity—but she managed to concentrate. By the time the cleaning woman came in to empty the wastebasket, she'd cleared most of the papers off her desk. When the cleaning woman left, she glanced at her watch. It was ten after seven. She could leave in twenty minutes, ten really. By the time she found a cab and got uptown, Isabelle Fowler would be gone.

The phone rang. Her hand reached for it automatically. She said hello into the receiver. A rush of garbled sounds greeted her. She could barely make out the words, but she thought one of them sounded like *letters*.

"What did you say?"

The unintelligible sounds came again.

"I can't understand you," Isobel said, then realized with a flash of heat and sweat that she was listening to one of those machines that altered voices. Her grip tightened around the receiver. "Who are you?" she screamed, though she knew she wasn't supposed to.

The electronic device was less successful at altering the sound of laughter. It screeched over the line. It was still building as Isobel put the receiver back in the cradle. Gently, the way the woman on the hot line had told her to.

The first thing she did was begin to cry, though when she thought about it later, she realized that was peculiar, since this had been going on for months and she'd never cried before. The second was look at her watch. It was twelve after seven. Isabelle Fowler was still with Pete, if she'd kept her appointment.

Isobel picked up the phone and dialed Pete's office. Pete's talking-someone-in-off-a-ledge voice came on and told her if she'd leave her name and number, Dr. Arlen would make everything all right, or at least return her call. She didn't even wait for the recording to end. She put down the phone, put on her coat, and left her office.

She noticed the envelope as she was waiting for the elevator. It was regulation eight-and-a-half-by-eleven manila with a neatly typed address sticker in the center. She picked it up. The sticker had her name on it. Damn the receptionist and Megan and everyone else who couldn't be bothered walking an envelope across an office before they went home for the evening. The anger made her feel better. At least it had an object.

She turned the envelope over and tore open the flap with her finger. She felt the sting of paper slicing flesh. Damn paper cuts, too.

She looked inside the envelope. At first she thought it was full of carbon paper. That struck her as odd because she hadn't seen carbon paper in years. Who had since Xerox machines had come on the scene? Then she realized it was fabric. Black, silky, starting to go a little rusty. She pulled the material out of the envelope. It unfurled. Her own face stared back at her. This time there was no mistaking the damage. Someone had taken a knife and slashed the painted face. Two neat holes penetrated Isobel's eyes. A dozen smaller wounds lacerated her cheeks. Her lips had been cut away. When she stuffed the material back in the envelope, she noticed that her hands were shaking.

In the lobby the security guard sat behind the desk, reading *Penthouse*. At the sound of Isobel's footsteps, he looked up from the magazine and leaned back in his chair so that his belly strained at the buttons of his thin white shirt. He beamed at her with a wet smile and the small shifty eyes of a confirmed felon. It was the same look that made her dash past him with a curt good night every evening, but now she stopped in front of the desk.

"Did you let anyone up to sixteen tonight?"

"Lemme see." He ran a fat tongue over his lips. Spittle glistened in the harsh overhead light. "Yeah, I think I did. A gal. Not bad-looking."

"Did you make her sign in?"

He smirked at her. No tight-ass executive bitch was going to catch him out. "Sure did."

"Could I see the book?"

161

His tongue slithered over his lips again; then he shrugged and turned the book toward her.

There were ten or twelve entries. She ran her finger down the numbers that corresponded to the floor the visitor was going to and stopped at 16. Her finger traced the line back from the number to the name. "Isobel Behringer" was written in a large, confident hand.

Isobel let herself into the waiting room. As she closed the door behind her, she glanced down the hall to Pete's office. He was sitting in the big black leather chair staring into the middle distance. He looked far away and diminished, as if she were staring at him the wrong way down the lens of a telescope.

She went down the hall to his office. He took a moment to look up at her, though he was facing the door and had to have seen her approach and heard her footsteps.

"It isn't Isabelle," he said.

"I know."

He looked surprised. That was when she realized he was expecting an argument. She realized one other thing as well. He was usually expecting an argument these days. They both were.

She sat in the chair across from him, the one for patients.

"How did you know?" he asked.

"I got a call at the office. At about ten after seven. When Isabelle was with you. And I got this as I was leaving." She leaned over and handed him the envelope.

He opened it. She noticed the way his eyes widened as the fabric unfolded.

"You still think I'm hallucinating? You still think I'm paranoid? You still think this is a goddamn joke?"

He got up from the chair, came over to her, and put his arms around her. She didn't push him away, but she didn't relax into him either.

"I want a lock for the door to the other part of the apartment," she said, and began to cry again.

"We'll get a lock. And we'll call the police."

TEN

He SAID HE WAS DETECTIVE Scott and this was Detective Ramirez, and they held out their badges, which for all Isobel knew could have come straight from Cracker Jack boxes, and she thought it was just like a movie, but it wasn't a movie, because she couldn't get up and go home after the closing credits. She was home, more or less.

She opened the door wider, and the two men stepped into Pete's waiting room. Ramirez had a mustache like a mascara brush and an air, common to delicately built men, of someone on the lookout for a slight. Scott was bigger. His shoulders and biceps looked as if they were going to burst his shiny polyester jacket. His skin had the rich purple-tinged sheen of a ripe eggplant. She preferred Scott. He looked more like a cop.

"Is that the radio or your music?" Scott asked as soon as she closed the door. It was Pete's morning at the hospital, and she'd put on one of Hannah's old records and turned on the speakers all over the apartment. It was almost like having company.

She told Scott it was her music, or rather her grandmother's.

"The old London LP with Tebaldi singing Mimi, right?" Scott asked.

"I guess," Isobel said. They were Hannah's old records, and she'd grown up on them and still played them, but she never looked at them. She supposed she didn't even really listen to them. At least not the way Scott seemed to.

165

"Take care of them," Scott said. "They're gems."

They went into the living room. Isobel wondered if she was supposed to offer them coffee. She hadn't had much experience entertaining representatives of the New York Police Department. She saw the way Scott's head cocked when Tebaldi, who she'd never realized was Tebaldi, broke into an aria, and asked if they'd like coffee. Scott said they wouldn't. Ramirez didn't say anything, but when Welch jumped up on the arm of his chair, he stiffened.

Isobel pushed Welch off the chair. He headed for Scott.

Isobel stood. "I'll lock him up."

"It's okay," Scott said. "I like cats." He rubbed Welch's head. "What's his name?"

"Joseph Welch."

Scott looked from the cat to her, and his wide brow creased. "Like in the army-McCarthy hearings?"

Isobel nodded. He glanced around the room, then back at her. She waited for him to say something, but he just took out a small notebook and a pen and asked what the story was.

She ran through the whole history from the first phone calls to the stab wounds in her face in the umbrella. Then she handed him the file of letters and the slashed fabric. He went through the materials slowly. She watched his face as he read the letters. If he was shocked or offended or amused, his expression didn't show it. It remained impassive as he examined the shards of the umbrella. Then he put the letters back in the file, and folded the fabric, and handed it all back to her.

"Your husband thinks it's one of his patients?"

Isobel told him about erotomania and obsessive love.

Ramirez's hand moved to his genitals and sat cupped there like a codpiece.

Scott waited for a moment until the last notes of Tebaldi's aria faded. Then, as he glanced around the living room again, the

166

expression on his face changed from appreciation to evaluation. He stood. Ramirez stood, too.

"My advice to you, Mrs. Arlen, if you're really worried, is to get yourself a bodyguard."

"A bodyguard! I don't want a bodyguard. I want to find who's doing this and stop her."

He looked around the living room again. "Mrs. Arlen—"

"My name is Behringer."

"Mrs. Behringer, we have ten-year-olds shooting each other in the schools. We have drug trafficking and crack houses and car rings. Forget plain old theft. The only reason you report that is so you can collect the insurance. And as of this morning, the newspapers are on our backs because last night some guy called nine-one-one and had to wait twenty minutes for a squad car. So what are we supposed to do? Question all your husband's patients? Even if we had the time, I don't think he'd want us to. Trace the calls? You said they stopped. Take fingerprints off a torn umbrella? Stake out this place?"

Isobel knew he had a point. If she were reading about the incident in the metropolitan section of the paper over her morning coffee, she'd feel sympathy for herself but understanding for Scott. But she wasn't reading about it.

"In other words, wait till she does some real harm. Then maybe you'll be able to help."

Scott stood looking down at her. "Your husband's a doctor, right? Well, I got a medical problem in my family. My wife has this history of breast cancer. Her grandmother, her mother, and one aunt died from it. Another aunt and her sister have it. So she's supposed to get these mammograms once a year. A preventive measure, the doctor says. The only catch is, the insurance doesn't pay for a preventive measure. They only pay if she already has a lump."

He started toward the waiting room. Ramirez followed. So

167

did Isobel. Scott opened the door. Ramirez went out to the elevator and pressed the button. Scott followed him. Isobel stood holding the door.

"My husband isn't that kind of doctor. He's a psychiatrist."

"I wasn't blaming your husband. I was just making a point. The society we live in isn't exactly forward-looking, Mrs. Behringer."

The elevator door opened, and Ramirez stepped on. "Call us if you have anything more to go on," Scott said as he followed Ramirez. Then he turned back to Isobel. "Or if you ever want to sell those records."

She stood staring at the closed elevator door. She knew now what Pete had meant when they'd talked about his *Pentagon Papers* incident and he'd said she had too much faith in the system. She'd laughed at him then, because she of all people knew how evil and venal and thoroughly corrupt the system was. After all, she'd spent her life fighting it. But you didn't fight what you didn't believe in. And why shouldn't she believe? She had an American passport. She had a Social Security number. She had health and apartment insurance. And she wore a white middle-class face. Doormen were obsequious to her, and cabdrivers stopped when she hailed them, and bureaucrats were surly and inefficient but finally did for her whatever she was there to have done. Even when the police had picked her up at that demonstration years ago, they'd treated her like a misguided kid rather than a hardened criminal. One of them, a soft-voiced black cop who'd spotted the knee-jerk-liberal-let's-all-sit-around-and-strum-our-guitars-together bagel baby a mile away, had asked her out. But now for the first time in her life her cards and her insurance and her face didn't help. Now for the first time in her life her belief was shaken. Because now she knew the system wasn't just evil and venal and corrupt. It

168

was impotent. It couldn't do what it had been set up to do. It couldn't take care of her.

She went back into the apartment and locked and bolted the door behind her. Then she went down the hall to the kitchen, took a mug from the cabinet, poured herself a cup of coffee, and carried it to the table where she'd left the newspaper when the concierge had called from the lobby to say, with a thrill of curiosity in his voice, there were two detectives here to see her. The headlines were dry. Tax bills, government waste, the Supreme Court's attempt to roll back time. They infuriated from a distance, like a play seen through a scrim.

She paged through the paper. In one article Ross Perot was staging another comeback. In another Cher grieved for the rib she'd had removed for cosmetic reasons in her youth and demanded rights for Women-of-Age. On the op-ed page a mother whose son had been killed when a man had walked into a shopping mall, taken out a semiautomatic rifle, and opened fire demanded to know who had been responsible for releasing the man from the mental hospital, and why no one had paid attention to the threatening letters he'd sent to mall employees, and how everyone had ignored the warning signs and passed the buck and sat back and let her son be murdered.

That night Pete did something unprecedented. He took Isobel into his office, sat down at his desk, opened his appointment book, and named names. Not one of them sounded even faintly familiar to her. He tried describing some of the patients, but the women he wanted to make her see could have been any number of people she passed on the street, or stood next to in the elevator of her office building, or sat beside in the library. The only thing she did learn was that Pete noticed more about women's appearances and mannerisms than she'd ever dreamed.

169

* * *

The letter lay halfway down the pile of opened mail. Megan had probably been too embarrassed to put it on top. Isobel picked it up between her thumb and forefinger, the way she might pick up something soiled or contagious, and read it a second time.

This was no stab in the dark. And it wasn't a story she'd told dozens of people over the years. It was something Pete had told her. And apparently someone else.

She looked at the paper. For a moment the letters ran together, and the white sheet turned black with menace. Then she blinked, and the words took form again.

". . . the things he did with that woman in Provence that he won't do with you . . ."

It had happened when she'd known Pete for six months or so, when she'd still been obsessed with finding out about *before*. Not the incident itself, that had happened years ago, but Pete's telling of it. Well, not exactly telling. He'd made a slip, and she'd tried to pry the rest out of him. The rest had been some faintly kinky stuff he'd got up to one night when he'd been on vacation in Provence. Isobel had been in a quandary. From the sound of it, she didn't particularly want to get up to the same thing herself, but she couldn't help asking if he'd wanted to do that with another woman, why he didn't want to with her.

"I didn't even know her." For some reason, he'd thought it was a satisfactory explanation.

She couldn't believe Pete had told the story to anyone else. He'd barely told it to her. But then even Pete had been known to say things before the sweat had dried that he regretted the minute he'd stepped into the shower.

He was sitting in a chair in the bedroom watching *MacNeil/Lehrer* when she got home. Welch was curled in his lap. Pete's

170

eyes remained on the television screen, but he managed to pry his concentration away long enough to say hi.

She didn't answer him. She merely held out the letter.

He took it from her without looking at it and sat with it in one hand as he went on watching the screen.

"Read it, for Christ sake!"

Welch jumped off his lap and disappeared under the bed. Pete's eyes moved to her instead of the letter.

"Another one?"

"Not just another one. This one is special."

Now his eyes moved to the letter. His hand went to his forehead. It hid his face as he read.

"Who besides you and me and the woman who was there knows about that night in Vénasque?"

"No one."

She flicked the letter with her finger. "That's not the way it looks from this."

"You don't think I told anyone."

" 'You don't think I told anyone,' " she mimicked. " 'It isn't my handkerchief. You can't believe I'd do anything so despicable.' Well, someone's doing a hell of a good job making it look that way."

"And you believe them? Her."

The correction struck her as ominous. It showed too much control. Just like the balmy at-least-one-of-us-isn't-going-to-get-hysterical voice he went on in.

"Look, Isobel, if I did want to screw around—forget the fact that I probably wouldn't have got married in the first place—do you really think I'd take up with someone who sends crazy letters and makes voodoo dolls out of umbrellas?"

"Maybe you didn't know about the letters and voodoo dolls when you got mixed up with her. Maybe you broke it off or it was just a one-night stand or something, and now she's pissed."

171

"You've seen too many movies."

"It's a logical scenario."

He stood, crossed the room, and turned off the television. When he turned back to her, his face had an I'm-trying-to-be-patient cast to it.

"Then why would I lie about it? If it were past tense, especially past tense before I knew you, you'd be more curious than angry. Knowing you. So why would I bother to lie?"

She thought about that for a minute. "You said the letters were probably from a patient, either former or current, right?" Her voice was almost as reasonable as his, but he wasn't taken in. She could tell from the way his eyes narrowed that he knew what was coming.

"That's why. Because she is or was a patient and we both know how you feel about that. The cardinal sin. The primary taboo. Worse than incest. Fiduciary responsibility and all that. Hell, you probably couldn't even admit it to yourself, let alone to me."

He closed his eyes and shook his head back and forth. The gesture struck her as too melodramatic for him. He opened his eyes. "I did not sleep with a patient. Ever."

"Maybe not, but you must have got pretty intimate to tell her about Vénasque."

"You're the only one I told about Vénasque." The professional voice was getting thin.

She took the letter he was still holding and flicked her wrist so the paper snapped smartly. "Well, I sure as hell didn't tell her."

His eyes narrowed even more. The movement was so slight she wouldn't have noticed it if she hadn't been watching so closely.

"Why not? You tell Hannah about ménages à trois. I can

172

imagine what you tell Millie. God knows who you told about this."

"I didn't tell anyone. Especially not Hannah or Millie." She hesitated for a moment, then went on, though she knew it was childish. "I wanted them to have some shred of respect left for you."

An ugly rasping sound, like an electronic imitation of a laugh, escaped from his mouth. "Respect for me! They don't even know me. All I am to them is generic man. And they're terrified of him. The only difference is the way they deal with the terror. Hannah comes out swinging. Millie smiles and tries to manipulate. And you—" He bit off the last word.

"Don't stop now. Go on, say it."

"You play to them," he finished lamely.

"What do you want me to do, put them out on an ice floe to die?"

"Come on, Isobel, this isn't for them, it's for you. Everything you've done in your life has been geared to their reaction. It's not your fault. They set it up that way. But that doesn't mean you have to keep it going."

"Keep it going! I'd like to see you—" She stopped abruptly. Her breath rasped in the sudden silence. When she started to speak again, her voice was as low and controlled as his.

"You know what I love? Besides the fact that you say you don't practice on family. Every time we start out talking about you and this patient, who may or may not be crazy but sure as hell knows a lot about your sex life, we end up finding out the real culprit is me. Me and Hannah and Millie."

"That's not what I said."

"The hell it isn't." Now she was screaming again. "I tell you I feel responsible for them, and you tell me I'm sick. Well, not all of us are blessed with your godlike professional distance. The concerned word to me. The weekly call to your kids. If you had parents or grandparents, they'd probably get a Christmas card. Come to think of it, that's about all your sister does get."

He stood in front of the blank screen staring at her. She knew he wasn't going to answer. She could go on this way all night, flailing around with old grudges and half-remembered slights, apocryphal accusations spun from a single fact, not true exactly, but true enough to wound. But he'd stop. Pete always knew when to stop.

He walked past her now, out of the room, down the hall, across the waiting room, into his office, and closed the door behind him. She wanted to run after him, screaming that he didn't have to bother. He'd already closed the door between them. But she didn't run after him. She went across the hall to the study and shut the door behind her.

Half an hour later the door opened. "What do you want to do about this?" he asked.

"What do you want to do about it?"

"I'm not the one who's accusing you of screwing around with a patient."

"No, and you're not the one who's being hounded by a crazy woman who plants stained handkerchiefs and carves up pictures of you and sends letters which happen to be pretty damn incriminating."

"Incriminating! They're written by a crazy woman. You just said so yourself."

"Who knows some very personal stuff about you."

"These people can be very devious."

"They're not the only ones."

This time he slammed the door behind him.

A little while later she heard the phone in his office ring. At least she thought it was the phone in his office. But a few minutes later she was sure about the front door closing.

She sat listening to the lonely sounds of an empty apartment.

174

A radiator clanked. Something squeaked. A siren wailed by. It seemed to her there were more sirens lately, but that might be her imagination. A door opened and closed. At first she thought he'd come back. Then she realized the noise came from the Davisons across the hall. The apartment was suddenly silent again. There was nothing ominous about it unless you couldn't stand being alone, and she'd lived most of her adult life alone.

She waited a few more minutes, then wondered what she was waiting for. She was damned if she'd sit cooped up in one room all night. It was her apartment, too. At least it was supposed to be.

She opened the door to the study. It creaked on its hinges. So much for prewar graciousness. The damn place was crumbling.

She had an eerie feeling as she wandered through the apartment. She wasn't sure whether Pete had left or come back or what. As she went from one room to the next, she kept rearranging her face so she'd look as if she were expecting to find him, not as if she'd been caught red-handed looking for him.

She crossed the waiting room to the professional part of the apartment. The door to Pete's office was open. She wasn't going into it. She wasn't going to snoop. She leaned against the doorjamb, staring at the old oak filing cabinet and the inlaid wood desk that Mrs. Zelinski polished to a high gloss each week during Pete's morning at the hospital. There were brass fittings on the desk drawers, but she didn't think there were locks. She wasn't sure—she'd never thought about it before—but she didn't think there were.

She pulled herself up and away from the doorjamb. This was one of the reasons she'd never believed in marriage. It didn't bring out the best in people.

She turned and went into the kitchen. Halfway across the room from the table she spotted the paper. He'd anchored it

175

with the one-handed pepper mill he thought was such a great invention. She usually had trouble reading his handwriting, but she could make out this.

"Emergency. Had to go to the hospital."

She wanted to laugh. Only when she tried to pull her mouth up, it felt stiff and detached from her, as if someone had slipped her a massive injection of novocaine. What did he take her for, a cretin? He hadn't had an emergency since she'd known him. Once, during a hospital strike, he'd been on call. He'd walked around all weekend with a beeper strapped to his belt. She'd told him he looked like a drug dealer. It hadn't gone off. He'd predicted it wouldn't. After all, he wasn't delivering babies or on the qui vive for an organ transplant. But now suddenly, conveniently, he had an emergency.

She looked at the big Italian clock on the wall. She'd never liked that clock. It had too much of a Big-Brother's-Watching-You air. Five after nine. The letter about Vénasque had been bad enough, but this really was an insult to her intelligence.

She took a glass from a cabinet, put three ice cubes in it, half filled it with scotch, filled it with seltzer. She took a swallow, grimaced, took another swallow. That was better.

She called Welch. Nothing stirred. "Mr. Welch," she pleaded. There wasn't so much as a rustle in the apartment. She walked down the hall to the bedroom. "Welchie," she crooned in a sickeningly saccharine voice. But Welch was no fool. He knew the predatory cry of an overwrought woman.

She went back down the hall to the living room and stood at the window sipping her drink. The lights around the reservoir glowed like candles in the black water, a shimmering invitation to mayhem. Traffic raced down Fifth Avenue, oblivious of the furtive couplings in the Ramble, the rag-wrapped homeless sleeping watchful as animals on the benches, the muggers lurk-

176

ing along the paths. Right now was there an addict being rolled, a boy raped, a lost tourist knifed? And she stood watching, safe behind her double-paned windows, safe as houses. Safe as apartments? It didn't sound the same. She leaned against the window. The pane felt cold against her forehead. Her breath made a circle of fog on the glass. A man walking dogs came into view on the pavement below. She began counting. Three, four, five, six, seven, eight. The dogs tugged in different directions. The walker reined them in. The sweet reliability of man's best friend. She took her forehead away from the cold pane, went across the living room, into the dining room, out of the dining room, down the hall to the study. White walls and high ceilings and restored moldings whizzed past her. "Welch," she called. "Mr. Welch. Welchie." She rounded the corner into the bedroom. The damn baseball cap was still on his dresser. How the hell had the patient known anyway? Okay, so he sat there listening and nodding and when he finally said something he spoke in tongues making references to the major leagues and Monday-morning quarterbacking and Most Valued Players you'd still have to be a genius to know about the Dodgers or maybe just a snoop unless he'd told and let's face it if you're going to talk about kinky or maybe not so kinky she never had found out exactly what had gone on in Provence between him and that schoolteacher a schoolteacher for God's sake because he'd made an oblique reference to exotic Oriental practices and then wouldn't say any more which was just like him wasn't it the man of infinite understanding but not a hell of a lot of information though the reference to exotic Oriental practices had been enough because out of nowhere she'd remembered a novel she'd read years ago with a Japanese woman and a knotted handkerchief that she pulled out one knot at a time one two three four and how did she get to handkerchiefs again really only a crazy woman would plant handkerchiefs and cut up umbrellas and she was perfectly willing to buy the diagnosis erotomania or obsessive love or whatever he wanted to call it because not Pete never Pete but then how did you explain the words about Vénasque which weren't the rantings of a crazy woman but incriminating evidence no matter what he said because someone Pete only Pete must have told the crazy woman about nights in Vénasque and the Brooklyn Dodgers and stop! Two half-melted ice cubes lay in the bottom of the glass. She held the glass to her forehead. It was colder than the windowpane. The floorboards in the hallway creaked under her bare feet. The terra-cotta tiles felt as icy as the glass. Big Brother on the wall said nine thirty-three. The scotch slopped over the side of the tumbler. The sponge felt clammy in her hand. The pool of scotch disappeared into it. Magic, Millie used to tell her. Simple scientific principle, Hannah used to say. The floorboards creaked again. The hat came into view as soon as she turned the corner into the bedroom and she knew how the patient had known because it was his goddamn seduction speech or at least postcoital courting confession and she remembered lying in bed when she'd first known him sweat-slicked arms and legs tangled together listening to some stomach-turning story about a scout's coming to school when he was a kid and telling the coach he had a major-league arm only she hadn't thought it was stomach-turning at the time that was how besotted she'd been in this bed with sheets the color of a mangy mongrel though she hadn't noticed the sheets because it was all so edgily new though not necessarily better new wasn't necessarily better only newer which was what she'd thought that night after he'd stood out in the rain waiting for her and afterward she'd realized how the same things touch here touch there do this do that could feel so different and that night had been perfectly all right not astonishing not transcendent but really just fine except for the shadow in bed with them and stop! She was damned if she'd stand here staring at the bed with her glass empty again. Creaky floorboards and icy tiles and a puddle she'd missed cold and wet under the ball of her foot. That damn clock must be broken because it had barely moved since she'd made the last drink and she'd always hated that clock anyway what was it about his wife and Italian-made stuff like that hairdresser she'd taken up with for a month or so after Pete because she'd said she was tired of cerebral types but it sounded as if she just liked men who messed with her head in one way or another and boy she'd married a master they both had only she still was and she couldn't believe he wasn't what he'd seemed which was really what he'd let her be like the time she'd tried to pick a fight because she was accustomed to fights and didn't know there was any other way to do it and he'd just sat there and watched and listened while her voice had thrashed around as if it were trying to break out of the room and her language had smeared the walls with obscene graffiti and still he'd done nothing until finally in savage tear-stinging frustration she'd begun flailing and he'd got up and come over to her and made a circle of his arms not clutching she knew all about clutching but just a big loose bracelet of his long arms so the tips of his fingers had rested on her back just below where her hair swung against her collar in rage and no other part of him had touched any other part of her but she'd found herself standing not flailing or screaming or cursing but just breathing within the roomy orbit he'd made for her and maybe that was when it had happened not on the boat the way she'd thought but that night with his arms spread wide to encircle but not crush her and there went the scotch again over the glass on the table leaking across until she could barely read the words on the paper which was all

179

soggy and swollen from the liquid with dark blue ink oozing away and *Emergency* bleeding down the page so the *n* became a long undulating snake and the *c* an empty hole and the *y* a shaky line fading to nowhere.

ELEVEN

A SERIES OF CLICKS, LIKE A SUC-
cession of locks turning, woke her. She opened her eyes to the
cold white numbers glowing on the digital clock. Three ones. A
pain ran across her forehead from one temple to the other,
tight as a steel headband. She heard the heavier thunk of the
bolt sliding into place. The knowledge of the emptiness beside
her in bed hit her. The end of the evening seeped back.

She'd pushed herself to a point where she'd finally fallen
asleep or maybe just passed out. Even that ordinary act had
taken on a strange and confusing significance. Where was she
supposed to go to fall asleep or pass out?

She heard the sharp click of a light switch, though from here
she couldn't see any light. A shadow stirred at her feet. Welch
sat up.

She used to slam out and go back to her own apartment.
When she didn't have a place of her own, and sometimes even
when she did, she'd gone to Hannah and Millie. But she hadn't
wanted to slam out this time. She'd wanted to stay. She just
hadn't been sure where she was supposed to stay.

Down the hall another light switch clicked. Welch's head
turned toward the door.

She hadn't been able to decide whether she should go to
sleep in their bed, as if nothing had happened, or in the study
or guest room, because nothing had been resolved.

181

She heard the creak of parquet. It was that spot halfway down the hall where the floor hadn't been laid right in the first place or else something was rotting.

While she'd stood in the hall debating the sexual etiquette, her overheated mind had leaped back to one of the formative books of her adolescence. She still remembered the heroine, who'd finally made up her mind to lose her virginity, cowering in the bathroom trying to decide whether to come out of it wearing her dress or her slip or less. The heroine had decided on the slip, and Isobel had filed the information away for future reference, though she'd never drawn on it. But this was the other side of the coin. After you'd stripped everything away from each other, when there was nothing left between you but anger and distrust, where did you go if you didn't go away?

The sound of creaking shoe leather grew closer. Welch's ears made two alert triangles in the darkness.

Her mind was thick and cottony. She didn't remember making the decision, but somehow she'd ended up here in the bedroom.

She felt his presence before she saw him. She turned her head. The band of steel tightened around her temples. The shadow was a big man, bigger than Pete. Her body froze. Then she realized the bulk was his ski parka. It filled the doorway, shutting her back into the room. She didn't move, but she felt as if she were shrinking into a corner of the bed. He took a step forward, then stopped. The stillness surrounded her again.

The sound of tearing metal ripped through the darkness. Her nerves jumped. Welch darted under the bed. Then she realized he was unzipping his jacket. The fabric hissed as he took it off and dropped it on the back of a chair. He sat.

She went on watching him. His body was hunched over. He could be untying his shoes, or searching the darkness, or brooding.

182

She sensed that he didn't know whether she was awake. They went on watching each other in the shadows, connected by a thin wire of loneliness and suspicion. She felt the wire growing tighter, as if someone were cranking it in. Her body began to tremble from the strain. The more she tensed her muscles to stop the trembling, the worse it grew, until she felt the bed vibrating beneath her.

When she opened her mouth to speak, her teeth began to chatter. "I'm awake." The words rattled in the darkness.

His body jerked in surprise. She reached up and turned on the wall sconce on her side of the bed. They both flinched against the light.

"How was your emergency?"

Maybe he was so tired he didn't hear the sarcasm, or maybe he just pretended not to. "He's okay now," he said, and rubbed his eyebrows with his thumb and forefinger.

"What was it, a heart transplant or just stitching a couple of limbs back on?" As the anger hissed up, the trembling began to subside.

His hand fell from his face, and he sat staring at her. He went on staring at her for so long that she began to feel like the guilty one.

"It was the architect," he said after a while. "He finally did it. He cut one wrist and was just going to work on the other when his wife came home unexpectedly and found him." There was no smugness in his voice, and certainly no triumph. He stood. "And if you don't believe me, you can call the fucking hospital and ask."

"I believe you."

He didn't bother to answer her.

"I'm sorry," she said later when he'd got into bed, not beside her, not by a long shot, but at the other edge. "About the architect."

183

He didn't say anything to that either.

They hovered on opposite sides of the bed, rigid as two bodies laid out for burial, except bodies laid out for burial aren't waiting. She realized she was clenching her jaw and tried to relax it. The muscles in her right calf tensed into a cramp. She rotated her foot to ease the pain. She felt him stiffen at the movement. The silence in the room grew louder. The hiss of a radiator sounded like a scream. A siren screaming through the night hanging outside the window sounded like the end of the world. He turned on his left side with his back to her. The mattress shifted with his movement like ground opening in an earthquake. She turned on her right side with her back to him.

In the morning they moved around each other with labored politeness. Before he went down the hall to his office, he asked if she wanted coffee, but she could sense his eagerness to get away. She cast around for something to hold him, to make them solve this, but she didn't want to bring up Vénasque again, so she just said she'd get her own coffee. She sat in bed listening to the sound of him slipping away behind closing doors, one, two, three, and was relieved.

They returned to the motions of normalcy. He sat in the paneled library, dimmed and muffled by closed venetian blinds, listening for clues in the murmur of conversation that occasionally rose to a raging shriek or faded to an agonizing silence, but the clues he was after now were to his problem rather than the patient's. She attended meetings and wrote reports and turned up at the lunches and dinners and parties that were part of her job, but no matter where she went or what she did, she dragged along a sense of anxiety, heavy as an overstuffed briefcase. Sometimes she forgot what she was anxious about. Then she stopped for a moment and thought, and it always came back.

184

Megan no longer mentioned the letters, and now she put them at the bottom of the pile of mail, but once Isobel could have sworn she was smirking as she left the office. Another morning Isobel looked up from the latest letter and found Zoe standing in the doorway studying her.

"Did you want something?" Isobel asked.

"It can wait if you're busy," Zoe said, and Isobel was sure she saw a smug grin on Zoe's face, too.

For the next two days every time she passed Zoe in the hall or looked at her across a desk or even thought of her, she saw that same slick red crescent of mouth curling in cruel glee. It reminded her of an animal licking its chops. She knew the idea was impossible. For one thing, Zoe wasn't crazy. Ambitious, but not crazy. For another, Isobel and Pete agreed it had to be one of his patients. But she couldn't get the idea out of her head. Gradually a plan began to form in her mind.

She told herself she wasn't going to follow through. Then one night, when Zoe stopped in her office door at a little before six to say good night, and Isobel recognized the smirk again, she knew she was.

She forced herself to go on working for another twenty minutes. Then she got up from behind her desk and walked through the office, stopping to look into the various cubicles and rooms. She was the only one left. Even the cleaning woman had come and gone. She retraced her steps to Zoe's office, pulled out the desk chair, and sat. The top of the desk was neat. A few telephone slips were tucked into the blotter. The only decoration was a pewter twin frame with a photograph of a toddler in a tiny jeans jacket and a peaked baseball cap turned backward in one side and a picture of a grown man dressed the same way in the other. She rifled through the papers in the out box, then the in, though she knew she wasn't going to find

185

anything there. She was right. Not only was everything above-board, but it was all up-to-date.

As she reached for the handle of the top drawer, an image flashed through her mind. She was standing in her old bed-room on Central Park West, screaming about privacy and re-spect and simple human dignity, and Millie was facing her insisting she'd only wanted to straighten Isobel's underwear or her sweaters or her papers and pencils.

She opened the top drawer of Zoe's desk. Zoe wasn't exactly a closet slob, but she was a lot more messy where it didn't show. The discovery made Isobel feel, unreasonably, she knew, that she was on to something. She began going through the clutter. Among the discarded pens and loose rubber bands and dried-out stamp pads, there was a bank statement, which Isobel glanced at guiltily, and a fax from Club Med thanking Zoe for her deposit for one week for two adults and one child, and incriminating evidence, though not the sort Isobel was looking for.

She picked up the letter. "I am enclosing a résumé for your consideration . . ." She shook her head. Zoe should have told her.

She put the letter back, closed the wide center drawer, and opened the smaller one next to it. She worked her way down all three side drawers, through old birthday cards and a chipped coffee mug and a Pierre Deux picture frame with a wedding picture of Zoe and her husband and a flower-printed plastic makeup case. She closed all the drawers and sat staring at the pictures of the toddler and the man in the baseball caps. This wasn't the desk of a madwoman. It certainly wasn't the desk of a woman without a life of her own. Isobel stood and went back to her office. The words she used to scream at Millie made a trail of shame behind her.

*   *   *

Pete told himself he was wasting his time. The answer wasn't in old medical journals. It was somewhere in his current or past files. But he had to do something, even something futile, so that morning after he let himself out of the locked ward, he went down to the hospital library. It took him awhile, because they'd put the old *Index Medicus* he'd known so well on a computer he still had trouble getting around, but he finally tracked down the references and cross-references and carried a handful of journals to a table. He'd just turned to the first article when he felt a hand on his shoulder. As he turned to see who it was, he noticed the gleam of manicured nails and the blinding glow of a gold Rolex. He looked up to see Gabe Zeller grinning down, not at him, but beyond him to the journal.

Zeller leaned closer. " 'The Pathology of Love: Clinical Variants of Erotomania Associated with Folie à Deux,' " he read over Pete's shoulder. "Not a bad idea. Eating disorders, enabling, and codependency have been done to death, but that one's barely been touched. Not a bad idea at all," he repeated, and moved off toward the librarian, who was smiling at him as if she were hoping for an autograph.

Pete turned back to the article. He skimmed through it. There was nothing he didn't know, or at least nothing he hadn't known at one time and didn't now remember.

It was called, in addition to erotomania, de Clérembault syndrome, delusional loving, the *psychose passionnelle*, and old maid's insanity. The significance of that one had slipped by him in the old days. He wondered now which of the boys, sitting around with their cigars, had dreamed it up. Hey, guys, you want something catchy? Wait'll you hear this.

He skimmed another article. The patient was almost always female, though several cases of males had been documented.

That certainly limited it.

The rest of the information was familiar, too. Erotomaniacs

were resourceful and persevering and single-minded. They often spent years learning every detail about the objects of their obsession. Neither psychotherapy nor drugs yielded much success in treatment. Sometimes the only cure was transference of the obsession to another object.

The information wasn't new, but it was disheartening. Pete was just about to close the journal when the word caught his eye. Violent. The case history of a man who'd murdered the husband of an actress followed in clinical detail. Of course, the authors added, male erotomaniacs were rare.

He decided not to tell Isobel about his research.

It was as if a toxic substance had spilled across her life and contaminated every corner of her existence. There'd been a time when she'd come out of the apartment building each day and take a hungry swallow of the thin morning air. Now she hid in the shadows of the tall buildings, waiting for the doorman to hail her a cab and cringing at the dank cold that crept into her bones. Once she'd moved through the offices of Urban Heritage like a dancer stepping and stretching and strutting to the rhythm of ringing phones and humming machines and a hundred demands and questions. Now she crouched warily behind her desk like a woman under siege. The frown lines that had been faint as threads between her eyes were becoming dark and permanent as Magic Marker smudges. Her voice had become a suspicious whine. On the rare occasions when she and Pete managed to joke about something, their laughter sounded as shrill and ominous in the big apartment as an approaching siren.

They still turned to each other in bed. They made a point of it. That was the problem. Their determination was killing. No emotion could survive its onslaught. They were left with rote moves and hollow gestures and a barren no-man's-land that neither of them could find a way across.

The letters grew more hostile. Violence seethed just beneath the surface. Then the real intrusions began.

One Saturday a bottle of rat poison arrived in the grocery delivery Isobel had ordered by telephone. She called Gristede's to point out the mistake. The manager assured her in an aggrieved tone that the store did not carry rat poison.

A few days later the concierge called from the lobby to say there was a Federal Express envelope for her. Isobel wasn't expecting any urgent deliveries, but she told him to send it up.

Pete took the envelope from the porter. After he was gone, they stood in the front hall staring at each other over the red, white, and blue cardboard.

"We could soak it in water," Pete said.

"Nobody sends bombs through Federal Express."

She held out her hand for the envelope, but he said he'd do it.

"This is ridiculous." He began to pry the flap open.

"I'm not expecting disaster," she insisted. "Only unpleasantness. More rat poison or something like that."

Pete opened the envelope and looked inside. "A book." He held a small paperback out to her. A fat marmalade cat smiled up at them from the cover. "Doris Lessing" ran across the top in bold white type. "Particularly Cats" was written in smaller letters beneath. "Delightful and remarkable," promised the blurb from *Harper's*.

"So much for unpleasantness," she said, and took the book from him.

"Who's it from?"

She leafed through for a card, then opened it for an inscription. "Beats me."

189

He looked at the sender's space on the envelope. "Joseph N. Welch, Attorney-at-Law."

"It must be from Hannah. Trust her to find a book about cats by Doris Lessing."

"Why would she send it Federal Express?"

Isobel looked at the sweet-faced cat on the cover again. "The harasser wouldn't send something this benign."

"Are you sure there's no card or anything?"

She began to page through the book again. A paragraph highlighted in pink caught her attention.

> *In the end, the cats were rounded up and put into a room. My father went into the room with his First World War revolver, more reliable, he said, than a shotgun. The gun sounded again, again, again, again. The cats that were still uncaught had sensed their fate and were raging and screaming all over the bush.*

Isobel stopped reading. "It's from her," she said, and handed the book to Pete. He glanced at the paragraph, then closed the book and carried it down the hall to the incinerator.

Isobel went through the apartment looking for Welch. She found him asleep on the down comforter. She sat on the edge of the bed and began scratching his head. He flopped over and presented his stomach. She could feel the purr through her fingertips.

Pete stood in the door watching them for a moment. Then he walked to the bed and began scratching along with her. Welch rumbled like the IRT underfoot.

"A two-handed rub," Isobel said. "He thinks he's died and gone to heaven." Then she heard her own words and cursed.

Isobel swore she was going to pull herself together, but when she missed a hearing that was marked on her calendar in red

190

ink, and Becker called to inquire in his candied apple voice whether she was all right because he couldn't imagine anything except serious illness that would have kept her away, she knew she was losing it.

A few days later, as she was getting ready for work, she dropped the antique silver-backed mirror Millie had given her years ago. The glass shattered on the marble floor of the bathroom. She stood staring in disbelief at the hollow silver frame and the crazed cubist portrait of herself reflected in the shards of glass. Then she turned and walked through the splinters out of the bathroom and across the bedroom. A trail of high-arched crimson prints pursued her.

She forgot about the mirror during the day. Her cuts had been minor. But when Pete saw the bloodstains on the carpet that night, his face tightened.

"They'll come out," she said, though she wasn't sure they would.

He didn't answer her, but she knew from the look of disgust on his face that he wasn't worried about the stains in the rug. He was worried about the signs of her madness.

A few days later the first photographs arrived. Isobel found them in the pile of mail Megan had put on her desk. All three snapshots were of Pete. In one he was coming out of the Harvard Club. She knew it was the Harvard Club because she recognized the entrance. In another he was standing on a corner hailing a cab, though she couldn't tell which corner it was. In the third he was holding the door to a coffee shop for a woman Isobel didn't recognize. She got up and went out to Megan's desk. "Where did these come from?"

"They were in the mail."

"Without a note or anything?"

"Nope, just the pictures. I put the envelope with them, but there was no return address."

Isobel went back to her office and looked at the envelope. She knew even before she compared them that the heavy cream-colored bond would match the stationery the letters had been written on.

She went on looking at the photographs. There was nothing distressing about them, not even the one with the unknown woman. Pete often stopped for a sandwich with someone from the department after his mornings at the hospital. But there was something disconcerting about the idea of a person wandering around town secretly taking shots of someone you cared about.

They'd planned to go to an opening at the Guggenheim that night. Pete was waiting for her at the bottom of the wide swirling spiral. She saw him as soon as she came through the door, but he didn't notice her right away. He was standing with his weight on one foot and his hands in his pockets, watching the crowd milling around him. His mouth wasn't a thin ribbon, and his eyebrows weren't furrowed together in a single line, and he looked like a man waiting for someone rather than a victim hiding from someone.

He kept on looking that way after he caught sight of her, and she knew the kind thing to do, the smart thing to do would be to wait until they'd gone through the show and had dinner before she brought up the photographs. They might even manage to have a pleasant evening.

She crossed the lobby to him. He bent to kiss her hello. She said she was sorry she was late. He said he'd been early. He turned to go in. One hand reached for his arm to stop him. The other opened her handbag and went straight for the pictures.

She held them out to him. He took them without asking what they were. She watched his face as he looked at the photographs. His mouth stretched into a tight thin line. His eyebrows came together over his eyes. "Fuck," he muttered.

"Haven't you noticed someone taking pictures of you?"

"Do these look as if I'd noticed? If I had, don't you think I'd have confronted whoever it was, not to mention said something to you?"

She moved closer to him, but only to get a look at the pictures. "I just can't believe you didn't know. I mean, these were all taken at close range."

"For Christ sake, Isobel, haven't you ever heard of a telephoto lens?"

He was quiet for a moment, then asked in a more conciliatory voice if she still wanted to go through the show. She said they might as well since they were there.

They worked their way through the whole show, and it wasn't till they reached the last room that she turned and told the sleek-as-an-otter young man who was trying to impress his date with his knowledge of color theory to please shut up and let people enjoy the goddamn work.

The second batch of pictures arrived a few days later. There was nothing extraordinary about them, or there wouldn't have been if Pete were a celebrity whose most mundane acts were photo ops for a swarm of paparazzi. There were shots of him walking the streets of the city, and going into the neighborhood wine store, and coming out of the local Korean greengrocer's with a bunch of tulips. She remembered those tulips. They'd never opened. The ones from the greengrocer never did. But Pete hadn't known that at the time, and he was carrying the flowers in front of him and wearing a sweet, smug smile. It was one of those unexpected, intimate glimpses of him that made her heart swell, at least it used to, and she wondered again how the woman had managed to get it. "Haven't you ever heard of a telephoto lens?" Pete had snapped at her when she'd asked him the question in the museum.

That was when it hit her.

She went down the hall to Pete's office. He was sitting behind his desk staring at a file. It seemed to her he spent a lot of time that way lately.

"Lucy Price!"

He looked up from the file. "What?"

"The woman from the library. You said she was looking for a mother. But maybe what she really wants is to get mommy out of the way so she can have daddy."

"What are you talking about?"

"She lives with a professional photographer. She'd have access to a telephoto lens. And she'd know something about photography."

His eyebrows lifted in two quizzical peaks. "Access to a telephoto lens? We're not talking about high-explosive plastics, Isobel. This is a piece of equipment anyone with a credit card can walk into an electronics store or call a mail-order house and buy. Several thousand New Yorkers have. Besides, the woman who's doing this doesn't live with anyone. That's the point."

She thought about that for a moment. "Maybe she made up a boyfriend to tell me about and gave him a career she was interested in or at least knew a little about. She probably made up a lot of stuff. Even her name. Come to think of it, she'd have to make up a name if she were a patient. Do you treat anyone with a name even remotely close to Lucy Price?"

He shook his head.

"What about the initials? Any L. P.'s?"

"You're beginning to sound more farfetched than the letters."

"At least I'm trying to figure out who it is."

He didn't say anything to that.

"What about the patient Millie commandeered to help make the bed? She's a grad student, too. What does she look like?"

"Blond. Sharp features. Good body if you like them flat-chested."

"You've just described Lucy Price."

"My patient also lives with a flesh-and-blood boyfriend. Marty Sasoon's patient. That's how she came to me in the first place, remember?"

"Maybe they broke up, and she didn't bother to tell you."

He shook his head again, and his mouth began to settle into that thin line. She wanted to reach out and put her hand over his lips to stop him.

"Would you do me a favor? Would you just call Marty and find out if they broke up?"

She paced the room while he asked Claire Sasoon how the kids were, and talked to Marty about the possibility of playing squash that Saturday, and posed the question, and sat in silence listening to the answer.

"Well?" she asked as soon as he hung up.

"They're still living together." He looked at her from under those heavy brows. "And Marty wanted to know—he said he wasn't implying anything he just wondered—why I wanted to know. In view of that business a few months ago."

TWELVE

THEN SOMETHING STRANGE HAP-
pened. The mailings stopped. There were no more envelopes
full of snapshots and no more letters with inexplicable references to Isobel's family and Pete's past. Isobel warned herself it
was too good to be true. This was a hiatus rather than an ending.

But hope is a seducer. At the beginning of March, after three
weeks of silence and several days of warm weather that conned
the city into believing winter was over, she began to think
maybe they really were in the clear. Maybe the woman had
given up, or wised up, or found someone else to hound, which
Pete said was their best hope. Isobel didn't care why she'd
stopped; she just began to risk hoping she had. Pete began to,
too. She could tell, though neither of them dared mention it.
But he no longer went around looking as if he were clenching
his teeth. And she no longer jumped every time someone came
into the room. The sharp voices that made their words grate
against each other like two hacksaws began to blunt, then
soften. The air between them no longer vibrated with tension.

Then one evening, when she came home from the office, the
concierge told her there was a package waiting for her. She
stopped halfway to the elevator. She hadn't ordered anything
from a catalog or sent something from a store. Of course, it

could be for Pete. He was always getting books on this disorder or that dysfunction from psychiatric book clubs and journals. Still, the news made her uneasy.

The concierge asked if she wanted him to send it up. She imagined the patient, who was closeted with Pete in the soothing shadows of his office, jumping at the harsh sound of a buzzer and told the concierge she'd take it herself.

The doorman went to the package room to get it. While she waited, she asked the concierge how his son was doing at Fordham. He was still telling her when the doorman returned carrying a parcel the size and shape of a shoe box. Her shoulders sagged. Her briefcase suddenly weighed a ton. She wondered how she'd been naive enough to think it was over.

The doorman held the package out to her. She could barely make herself reach for it. Then she noticed the address sticker. Dr. and Mrs. Peter Arlen. The harasser had always sent things to her, never Pete. Even the pictures of him had arrived at her office, as if whoever was doing this were out to get her but didn't want to offend him. Everything fell into place. Millie was at it again, or at least her friends were. All last fall they'd been paying Millie back for the decades of wedding gifts she'd sent their children.

Isobel took the package from the doorman, tucked it under her arm, and headed for the elevator. The doorman followed her on, pressed nineteen, then stepped off.

As the elevator glided upward, she hefted the package again. Crystal, she'd guess from the weight.

At the service door she put her briefcase on the floor, got out her key, and let herself into the apartment. Welch strolled across the kitchen to meet her. He wasn't supposed to be there, but Freudian scruples were no match for feline perseverance.

She put the package on the kitchen table, took off her coat, and did a cursory run through the mail Pete had left there. She crossed the room and took a glass from the cabinet. Halfway back to the table, she remembered, returned to the cabinet, and took a second glass out for Pete. When she turned back, she noticed that Welch was sitting on the table sniffing the package.

She took a can of cat food from the cupboard and opened it. The mere scent was usually enough to lure him to the counter, but he went on nosing around the package. She dumped half the can into a bowl and put the bowl on the floor. Welch didn't even glance at it.

"You're supposed to send your compliments to the chef." She pushed him off the table and took a knife to the tape at one end of the parcel. He jumped back on the table and took a swipe at the piece of tape she'd loosened. "Knock it off," she said, and pushed him away again. He came around the other side. Maybe it wasn't crystal. Maybe it was food from one of those mail-order houses that specialize in Omaha steaks or Pacific salmon or unnaturally orange cheese rolled in soggy nuts.

She slit through the tape at the other end and narrowly missed Welch's paw. "Have you no sense of decency?" she asked, and pushed him off the table again. This time he circled once before he leaped back. It was enough time for her to slit the tape down the center of the package and pry open the sides. She'd been wrong about the gift. It was a shoe box after all. So it was probably Millie after all.

Welch sniffed at it frantically. She didn't blame him. She loved the smell of new leather. Only she didn't smell new leather. She smelled something faintly chemical. It occurred to her that the one thing Millie never bought her was shoes. And if she had, she wouldn't have sent them to Dr. and Mrs. Arlen. The uneasiness came creeping back.

She stood staring down at the package. Maybe she was being paranoid again. Or maybe she was being sensible.

Welch was still sniffing the box. She bent closer to it. The odor wasn't foul, merely acrid.

She picked up the wrapping. There was no return address, not even the name of a store. She didn't care if she was paranoid. She wasn't going to open it. She'd leave it in the back hall until Pete finished his last hour. Then they'd decide what to do about it.

Welch was rubbing his head against the corner of the box. She picked it up to get it away from him. He leaped for it and knocked it out of her hands.

The box fell to the floor. The stiff black corpse rolled out. The tail was a hardened curl. The legs were poker straight. The eyes were opened wide. Rigor mortis had produced a comic strip cat.

Isobel's mouth opened in a silent scream. Welch pounced. She howled.

She tried to push him away, but he came back from another direction. She yelled and pushed and swiped at him, and he scratched and bit and pawed deliriously at the warning he thought was prey. He was still wrestling with it in feral ecstasy, and she was still crying and shouting and trying to get the dead cat away when Pete came into the kitchen.

She slipped back into the dread as if it were an old coat or sweater she couldn't bring herself to give away. Each night as the cab pulled up in front of the building, anxiety laid cold fingers on her spine. Sometimes she stood with her hand on the doorknob of the apartment for minutes before she worked up the nerve to open the door and go inside. Walking down the long halls was like disappearing into the unknown. When she was alone in a room, her neck kept prickling until she turned around and saw that nothing was behind her. In a few months she'd come to hate and fear the apartment she'd once joked most New Yorkers would kill to live in.

One night when she was sitting in bed trying to read and trying not to hate Pete for the way he lay curled on his side, the lashes of his closed eyes casting innocent shadows on his cheeks, his breathing steady as a metronome, the bell rang. She looked at the clock. It was after midnight. She told herself there was nothing to worry about. The night doorman would stop an outsider from coming up unannounced. Crazy people didn't ring doorbells when they were about to do you in. But night doormen tended to be feckless. And who could predict what a crazy person would do?

The bell sounded again, longer this time and more insistent. Pete's lashes fluttered. He rolled over onto his back. His eyes narrowed to put the numbers on the digital clock in focus.

Normally Isobel would have been halfway to the door by now, but these were not normal times. She sat immobilized by the fear. He lumbered out of bed and stood for a moment, stunned by sudden consciousness, contemplating his own nakedness. The bell rang a third time. He tugged on a bathrobe and stumbled down the hall.

Isobel remained in bed, her back stiff against the headboard, her eyes straight ahead, listening to the sound of murmured voices. They rumbled softly, like the traffic nineteen floors below. It was not the sound of mayhem. Still, it went on for a bit.

She heard the door close and the sound of Pete's bare feet coming back up the hall.

"Who was it?"

"The Davisons' daughter. Her parents went to the country for the weekend, and she locked herself out."

"They must have a passkey downstairs."

Pete dropped his robe over a chair and sat on the side of the bed heavily. "That's why she rang our bell. She wanted us to call down to have them to bring the key up."

Isobel was incredulous. "She rang our bell rather than go down and get it herself?"

Pete turned on his side with his back to her. "Don't yell at me. I'm not the one who locked herself out."

"I wasn't yelling," Isobel said, but she knew her voice had been shrill with frustration.

Occasionally she tried to fight the fear. On one particularly bright morning when the sun seared the white walls of the apartment and bleached the menace out of every corner, she forced herself to slow down and go through the motions of getting ready for work as if she were a normal person living a normal life. She stood in the bedroom for a moment, taking her time, debating whether to play it safe with her winter coat or to risk her lighter gabardine trench. She decided she'd had enough of her winter coat and slipped into the other one. It took her another couple of minutes to find a scarf to go with it and a few more to find her gloves. Then she slung the strap of her shoulder bag across her chest, because though she was going only a few steps from door to cab, she'd heard stories of muggers who came careening by in lightning-fast running shoes or speeding cars, snatching bags before the victim knew what had happened to her. Finally she hefted her briefcase in her left hand and started down the hall toward the back door. She threw the bolt, pulled the door toward her, and took a step out of the apartment. Her foot came down on something soft and slippery. She felt it writhe beneath her weight. She looked down. A piece of hose slithered over the doorjamb into the apartment. She reeled back with a scream. The sound rose to a shriek and went on climbing until the terrible inhuman sound filled the apartment.

She was still shrieking when the suicidal architect came running down the hall from the waiting room. He was the one who pointed out that it was only a harmless garter snake and summoned one of the porters to get rid of it.

No one on the building staff, not even Felix, the eight-to-four concierge who'd known Pete in the days when he used to visit his uncle, could remember any rudeness or even a single unpleasantry from Dr. Arlen. Certainly no one ever expected him to make the scene he made in the lobby that morning, calling poor Felix, who should have been retired years ago, a retard and telling Angel that if he'd stop playing the Mambo King to every cleaning girl in the building and keep an eye on the goddamn door, which was what he was paid to do, this never would have happened.

By the time the shifts changed at four o'clock, the entire staff had heard the story. That morning most of them would have agreed that Dr. Arlen was an okay guy. Now they'd seen his other side, his and Mrs. Arlen's both, because when she came through the lobby a little later, she was even worse. Oh, sure, they were nice enough when everything was running smoothly, when you put the fish delivery they weren't home to receive in the staff refrigerator, and walked to the corner in the rain to get them a cab, and never lost a piece of dry cleaning, but just let one thing go wrong, and all of a sudden it was your fault that he took crazy people into the house, and she was scared of her own shadow, and, Angel told the other men with a knowing nod, the old honeymoon was over.

Pete told her he didn't have to go. Even this late in the game he could cancel his plans. And he wouldn't lose any money because the other guys would pick up his share of the condo.

The point was he didn't want to leave her alone, not if she felt uncomfortable staying alone.

Isobel sat on the side of the bed, watching him pull thermal underwear and silk turtlenecks and other pieces of clothing she hadn't known he owned from the drawers of his dresser and heard the murmur of desperation he was trying to suppress. It wasn't just that he wanted to go on this trip. He wanted to get away from her.

She said she'd lived alone most of her adult life and told him to have a good time. Then, after he left, she went into the living room and stood at the window, looking down at the sidewalk. A moment later Pete and Angel came out of the building. Pete was carrying his skis, and Angel had the duffel. A taxi pulled up. Angel flung the duffel in the trunk. The driver got out of the car. The three men began arranging the skis. They rolled windows up and down, and moved the skis one way and another, and gave each other directions. Isobel stood watching. She didn't know about the other two men, but Pete was having the time of his life. She could tell because she recognized the look of pure joy he turned on a total stranger and a doorman he'd recently called every name in the book, the look she hadn't seen in months.

She went on standing in the window after the taxi had pulled away. The trees in the park stood bare and brown under a discouraging winter sky. She couldn't figure out how it had happened. She was fairly sure that if they were asked, she and Pete would still say they loved each other, though God knows he'd never been exactly profligate with the words, and she was the first to say she wasn't sure what they meant. She was also sure that despite the past few months, they still trusted each other. And if those few weeks after the mailings stopped and before the dead cat and the live snake arrived were any indication, they even liked each other.

She shivered in the cold apartment and knew that the problem had nothing to do with loving or trusting or liking. It had to do not with how they felt about each other but with how they felt about themselves. Somewhere along the way, when things had begun to go badly, she and Pete had started to do something craven and vicious and corrosive to the adhesive that makes a man and woman hold fast. They'd started blaming each other for their own lives.

Pete had left on Friday morning. On Friday evening Isobel met her old friend Polly Markson for a movie. Afterward they went to a restaurant Polly had heard about from her performance art instructor. It featured leather-clad biker-waiters, fifties diner decor, and genetically engineered specialties like dwarf vegetables and elephant garlic. The restaurant, Isobel thought, just showed what life with a denigrating husband and without a career could drive you to. Nonetheless, each time Polly made a move to leave, Isobel ordered another cup of decaf espresso, or launched into a new story, or decided she'd love a glass of port. It was almost midnight by the time they hailed a cab heading uptown.

In the cab they had the usual debate about which of them would drop the other off. Isobel lived farther north, but Polly lived farther east. Isobel insisted they swing by Polly's apartment first. She was in no rush to get home.

It occurred to her as soon as Polly got out of the taxi. She didn't have to go home at all. She had a key to the apartment on Central Park West. She certainly knew how to come in without waking anyone. And tomorrow morning they'd be delighted when they got up and found her sleeping in her old room.

She wondered, if Pete was so worried about her staying alone, why he hadn't suggested it. Then she realized why. And she knew he was right. She was a grown woman. She lived in a terrific apartment. She refused to let a strange woman who was a victim of her own deranged love drive her out of it.

The cab turned west and headed rapidly toward Fifth. The streets were practically empty at this hour.

Pete might be right, but Pete was off skiing with a bunch of shrinks, while she was here in town being pursued by a woman who wasn't exactly a walking advertisement for their profession.

She looked up at the buildings as they sped past. Most of the windows were dark. It was a ghost city. She tried to imagine Pete somewhere in Utah. The only pictures she could summon were from an old movie with a lot of overly made-up actors glowing Technicolor bright against the blinding white snow and bursting into song every couple of minutes. He was that unreal.

The cab pulled up in front of the building. The driver flipped off the meter. She leaned forward to pay him. She gave him the address on Central Park West.

She opened her eyes to the chintz canopy of her old four-poster bed. The first time she'd taken Pete upstairs in this apartment, his eye had swept over the canopy and the shelves full of children's books and paperback editions of classics and come to rest on the Raggedy Ann that sat on the window seat. "Tell me," he'd said, "is there an admission charge for this museum?"

Isobel had bridled. "It's the guest room."

"Who're they expecting to visit, Alice in Wonderland?"

She got out of bed. One of her old flannel robes still hung in the closet. Across the hall in the bathroom, her mother had put out white towels with "Isobel" written on them in pink scroll.

Or maybe she hadn't put them out. Maybe she kept them there, just in case.

From downstairs she could hear the faint sounds of Hannah and Millie trying to be quiet. One of the voices began to climb. The other shushed it into silence.

By the time she came out of the shower their voices were louder. They'd heard the water and knew she was up. She crossed the hall back to her room. A glass of orange juice stood on a saucer on her old desk. She shook her head, but she drank the juice. Then she carried the empty glass downstairs.

She followed the sound of voices to the kitchen. Hannah was sitting at the table. Millie was standing at the counter with her back to the room. "I still think we should call the doctor," she was saying.

"What's he going to do? Tell me to take it easy? Fine, I'll give up my morning workout on the NordicTrack machine. Put me through a bunch of tests? To find out what? That I'm old."

Isobel stepped into the kitchen. Her feet recognized the familiar bumps and depressions of the brightly waxed blue linoleum.

"What's wrong?"

Hannah lifted her face to her granddaughter. Behind the thick trifocals, her eyes blurred, then refocused with watery pleasure. "Nothing's wrong. I felt a little light-headed this morning, and I made the mistake of mentioning it."

"Oh, now it's nothing," Millie said.

"I'm fine," Hannah insisted.

"Maybe you're premenstrual," Isobel suggested.

A faint light flickered behind Hannah's thick lenses. "You think everything is hormones? You never heard of existential angst?"

"Now you really are feeling better," Millie said to Hannah, and shot Isobel a grin of her own.

207

There were two conspiracies afoot in the room, and Isobel had the feeling she was the linchpin of both.

"What would you like for breakfast?" Millie asked. "Or should I say lunch? You really needed a good night's sleep. Cruz is off, but I went out early when I saw you were here and picked up a few things. Or I can make you some eggs."

"All I want is coffee and toast," Isobel said. "And I can get them myself."

Millie began taking containers and packages from the refrigerator. "Don't be silly. You have to eat."

"She's right," Hannah said. "It's almost noon. You ought to have something."

Millie's comment didn't surprise Isobel, but Hannah's did. Her grandmother had never belonged to the you-can't-start-the-day-on-an-empty-stomach, finish-your-milk, there-are-children-starving-in-Asia school of motherhood. But in the past few years something strange had happened. As Hannah's own appetite had shrunk, her hunger to see Isobel eat had begun to grow.

Millie took a container of blueberries from the refrigerator, and another of strawberries, and several different flavors of yogurt.

"Are you sure you have enough?" Isobel asked.

Millie stood examining the refrigerator to make sure she hadn't missed anything. "After I got the fish at Zabar's, it occurred to me you might want something lighter, so I stopped at Fairway. They had a special on the berries." She closed the refrigerator door, opened one of the cabinets, and began taking down china platters and silver trays and crystal bowls. Millie believed in the amenities. One day you stopped setting the table, the next you skipped a meal entirely, and before you knew it, your marriage was on the rocks, your children were going off to live in an ashram, and your home was the raw material of a garage sale.

She began unwrapping the packages she'd taken from the refrigerator. Her movements had an easy, economical grace. Though she rarely did things in the kitchen these days and had always had help, she knew her way around it. More than that, she was in control.

Isobel stood watching for a moment, then began taking plates from the cabinets and cutlery from the drawers. Her movements felt as familiar and effortless as her mother's looked. She hadn't set a table in this kitchen for years, but she still knew where everything was.

Millie's hands worked quickly over a platter, laying a base of lettuce, arranging smoked salmon, unwrapping a log of chèvre, while her voice skipped blithely from whether Isobel had slept well in her old bed, to the relative merits of eastern and western salmon, to the fact that she never would have thought she'd say this but she supposed it was all right, maybe even healthy for married couples to spend some time apart every now and then.

"She married him," Hannah said. "She didn't undergo surgery to have him joined to her at the hip."

Millie began slicing a tomato. "Say what you want, but I can see the change. This is the best thing that ever happened to her."

Isobel watched as Millie picked up a second tomato. "I gather by 'her' you mean me."

"And I'm not the only one who's noticed. Remember when you stopped by a couple of weeks ago and Alice Greene was here? She couldn't stop talking about how well you looked. She said she didn't want to say anything last time she saw you, but your face was getting a little pinched."

"Thanks a lot," Isobel said, and could feel the muscles around her mouth tightening.

209

"All of a sudden Alice Greene is an authority on beauty." Hannah turned to Isobel. "She's got more stitch marks behind her ears than a hem."

Millie began arranging the tomatoes around the platter. "I think she's right. You were getting . . . I don't know . . . a certain look. I didn't want to say anything, but unhappiness takes a toll."

"I wasn't unhappy."

"You didn't know you were unhappy," Millie corrected her, as she put down a slice of tomato, looked at it, picked it up, and moved it to another spot.

"Are we going to lacquer that or eat it?" Isobel asked.

"You see what I mean," Millie practically sang. "Pete goes away for a long weekend, and you're mad at the world." She picked up the tomato slice she'd just moved and put it back in its original place.

Isobel wondered if she was going to scream. "I thought you just said some time apart was good for a marriage."

But if Millie could talk while she worked, she didn't necessarily listen. "All I meant is that you look a lot better now than you did two years ago." She turned the strainer full of freshly washed blueberries into a bowl. "Younger, too." She stood staring at the bowl for a moment, then opened the cabinet, took down a larger dish that was divided into two compartments, and poured the blueberries into one side and the strawberries into the other. "And I don't think it's a crime against women to say I think that has something to do with Pete."

Maybe if Millie hadn't gone on fretting over those damn berries while she talked, or maybe if she hadn't kept chattering while she fussed, Isobel would have kept her mouth shut. But she stood there watching her mother move tomatoes back and forth and pour berries from one bowl to another, and all the rage at the telephone company, and the police department, and a strange woman who was hounding her, and Pete, who'd run away from her—most of all at Pete—settled on Millie's fragile shoulders. She opened her mouth and blurted out that if Millie would just take off her goddamn rose-colored glasses and face reality for once in her life, she'd see that Isobel looked like hell this morning because she'd been out too late last night drinking too much wine so she could face going home to that damn haunted apartment and that marriage in general and Isobel's marriage in particular weren't all they were cracked up to be.

Millie's hands froze over the bowl of glistening blue and red berries, then fell to her sides. She turned to face Isobel. "What do you mean?"

Isobel stood in the middle of the familiar kitchen cursing herself and wondering if she was ever going to learn. "Nothing. I'm just a little wired this morning. That crazy woman is beginning to get to me."

"I know about that woman," Millie said, "but what's this about you and Pete?"

"Nothing," Isobel repeated.

"That's not what you just said."

This time Isobel didn't answer.

"I knew it. I knew something was wrong when you didn't go away with him."

"I don't ski."

"You could have gone along to keep him company. You could have read by the fire, and taken long walks in the snow, and been with him in the evening."

Millie must have seen the same Technicolor movie.

"Look, I'm sorry I said anything. Pete and I are fine. Now can we just forget the whole thing?" But Isobel knew, as she picked up two of the platters and started for the dining room, that it was the one thing her mother was incapable of doing.

211

They filed into the dining room and sat at the table, Millie at one end, Hannah at the other, and Isobel between them. At first Millie merely asked questions. She was getting her bearings. But after a while Isobel began to notice a change. Millie's shoulders straightened against the back of the chair. Her voice grew more authoritative. She began to make suggestions. There were suggestions for professional help, which she didn't usually believe in, and personal self-sacrifice, which she swore by; for patching and fixing; for forgiving and forgetting; for turning over a new leaf and the other cheek. Millie had a plan for everything. She had a blueprint for Isobel's life.

Isobel sat listening while her mother's voice, firm and gentle as a masseuse's hands, pushed and prodded and kneaded and stroked, and suddenly struck a sore spot. She pulled herself up and away from the chair, as if she were pulling away from those skilled hands, and sat staring at Millie.

"What?" Millie asked. "What's wrong?"

Isobel went on staring. She couldn't believe it, but she knew it was true. "You're enjoying this!"

Hannah's breath shortened audibly. Millie's mouth opened like a wound. Then the words spilled out. "How can you say that?"

"I'm sorry," Isobel murmured, but the apology was no match for the words that had incurred them.

"You think I enjoy your unhappiness? You think I like sitting here watching you throw away another marriage?"

"Can we not start on that, please?"

"I don't understand you. I've done everything I know to help. I've practically stood on my head to cheer you up. And you tell me I'm enjoying this."

"She said she was sorry," Hannah murmured.

"I don't understand why everything in this family becomes my fault."

212

"Nobody was talking about fault." Isobel meant the words as reassurance, but somehow they came out as an argument.

"No, just about enjoying my own daughter's misery."

"That's not what I meant."

"Then what did you mean?"

"She didn't mean anything," Hannah said.

Millie's head swiveled to her mother. "And don't you defend her. She said I was enjoying this, and I want to know what she meant." Millie turned back to Isobel.

"I didn't mean you were enjoying my unhappiness."

"That's what you said."

Isobel hesitated. There had to be words that would explain this. "All I meant was that when I'm unhappy, you think I need you more. And you like that."

A few months ago Pete had said the same thing. At the time it had sounded eminently reasonable. Now the words hung between them, ugly and incriminating as soiled laundry on a line.

Millie stood and left the room without a word.

Isobel sat with her grandmother listening to her mother's footsteps cross the living room and fade up the stairs. She could feel the weight of Hannah's stare. She turned to face her grandmother. "I guess I should go after her."

"To do what?" Hannah asked. "Make it untrue?"

They finished their coffee and tea in silence. The only noise in the room was the thin sound of bone china clinking against its own.

Isobel cleared the table, and put away the food, and stacked the dishwasher. Hannah tried to help, but Isobel kept insisting she could manage.

They left the kitchen, went into the study, and sat at either ends of the sofa. The sound of Millie's footsteps creaked over their heads. They lifted their faces to the ceiling. The footsteps died. They looked at each other, then away.

213

The light began to drain from the steely sky. Isobel went around turning on lamps. They cast rings of amber in the shadowy rooms. The afternoon limped toward evening.

Hannah picked up the large-type edition of the paper, stared at it for a moment, then put it back on the end table. Isobel opened the magazine section of the next day's paper and began to leaf through it. The stock stuck to her perspiring fingers. She put the magazine down.

"I have to leave," Isobel said.

"You ought to," Hannah agreed.

Isobel went to the front hall, took her coat from the closet, and slipped into it. Then she stood for a moment, growing too warm in the overheated apartment. She turned around, crossed the living room, and went up the stairs.

She hesitated at the top. The door to Hannah's room was open. Her eyes moved to the dresser. An army of small pharmaceutical vials marched across it in neat lines. She could have sworn there were twice as many as last time she'd noticed them. She forced herself to look away and kept walking.

The door to her room was open, too. She hadn't bothered to make the bed that morning, but someone had turned the sheet down to a neat cuff, and tucked in the covers, and plumped the pillows. Someone had even put a pair of oxford pajamas Isobel vaguely remembered from the days when she used to wear pajamas at the foot of the bed. The overhead fixture was off, but the lamp on the night table cast a circle of light that reached to the Raggedy Ann on the window seat. It was a Norman Rockwell illustration, and it hit her with the same wallop of farfetched nostalgia. Cheap art frequently had that effect. Then her critical instincts took over.

She walked to the night table and switched off the lamp. Then she went down the hall to say good night to her mother.

Millie looked up from her magazine as Isobel reached the

door. Her eyes were wary; her mouth was stiff with unspoken grievances.

Isobel crossed the room, put a hand on Millie's shoulder, and bent to lay her cheek against her mother's.

"It's all right," Millie said, though her tone contradicted the words. "I know you didn't mean it."

Isobel straightened and looked down at her mother. Her hand was still on Millie's shoulder. "I'm leaving now." She felt her mother stiffen. She saw Millie's mouth open. She left the room before Millie could think of a reason for her to stay.

Millie waited until she heard the front door close, then went slowly down the stairs. Hannah was sitting in the same chair in the study. At first Millie thought she was asleep. Then Hannah spoke. "She's right, you know. Not just about you. About both of us."

Millie sat and smoothed her skirt over her lap. "I don't know what you mean."

"What Isobel said. You were enjoying it. Not her unhappiness, but the rest of it. We both were. We had her back."

"That's a terrible thing to say."

"Where did you get the idea the truth isn't terrible? Not from me."

When Millie didn't answer, Hannah lifted her face so she could get a better look at her daughter through the bottom of her trifocals. "At least you have an excuse. I should have known better. I should have learned from my mistakes. But you had an excuse."

"What are you talking about?"

"Harry."

"I won't listen to a word against Harry."

"No one's saying anything against anybody. All I meant—"

"You never liked him."

215

"I liked him all right. I just meant it might have been different if he'd been . . . different. Maybe you wouldn't have turned to her so much."

Millie stood and walked to the double windows. One shade was an inch lower than the other. "Harry was the best thing that ever happened to me." She gave the lower shade a smart tug, but instead of snapping up, it descended another inch. "A good husband." She tugged on the shade again. It sank lower. "A good father." She snapped it a third time. Now it was almost at the sill. "Everybody loved him."

"You know what I mean. If you'd had a real marriage all along."

Millie turned from the window to face her mother. "We had a child. A home. Companionship. What's more real than that?"

"All I meant was—"

"All you meant was something I mentioned, how long ago now, twenty, thirty years, that you refuse to forget. Well, let me tell you something. I'll take my marriage over yours any day. I never heard you and Pop laugh together. I never saw you hold hands. I never even heard you say a kind word to each other. You were always at him. Though God knows for what. It isn't as if he didn't take care of you. It isn't as if he didn't give you anything you wanted."

"Anything he wanted me to have."

"Oh, God, we're not going to start that again."

Hannah's mouth opened, then closed. When she finally spoke, her voice was low as a whisper. "You never know what goes on in another marriage."

"Exactly. So you can stop feeling sorry for me. And you can stop feeling superior to me, too. Because there are more important things in the world than sex. A lot more important. And I had all of those. After Isobel was born and that stopped, I still had respect and companionship and love. I'll take that over sex any day. And you would have, too, if you'd had the choice."

Millie turned back to the window and took another pull at the shade. This time it snapped out of her hand and flapped to the top with a sharp sound that tore through the room and made Hannah jump.

THIRTEEN

ISOBEL WAS HURRYING OUT OF THE apartment when she heard the phone ring. She wasn't going to answer it, because she was determined to get out of there, but curiosity drove her back down the hall to hear who it was. The woman on the machine identified herself as Sally O'Connell. It took Isobel a moment to put the name together with her favorite librarian from the Society Library. Sally would be calling about a book that had come in or one Isobel hadn't returned or something like that. Whatever it was, it wouldn't take much time. She picked up the phone.

"We have your notebook," Sally said. "The janitor found it in the Member's Room and brought it down to the front desk."

Three things occurred to Isobel at once. She might misplace theater tickets or even shoes, but she never lost papers from work. She hadn't been in the Member's Room in several weeks. And she didn't use notebooks. She preferred yellow legal pads.

"You mean my appointment book?" Isobel asked as she began digging in her handbag for it, though she knew that was impossible, too, because she'd had the book in her office yesterday.

"No, your notebook. You know, the one with the black and white marbleized cover, like the notebooks kids use in school. It has your name on it. At first I didn't realize it was yours. It says Mrs. Peter Arlen, and I always think of you as Isobel Behringer.

I mean, you never changed your card or anything. I wouldn't even have known the name if you hadn't added your husband to your membership last fall."

Something else occurred to Isobel. She'd occasionally called herself Isobel Arlen for convenience, but she'd never in her life identified herself as Mrs. Peter Arlen.

"Are you sure it's mine?"

"It says Mrs. Peter Arlen."

"Is there another Arlen who's a member?"

"I don't think so. Do you want me to check?"

"I think you'd better."

Isobel waited while Sally put her on hold. "You're the only Arlen," she said when she got back on the phone.

"Are you sure that's the name on the front of the notebook?"

"The writing's very legible."

Isobel didn't bother to tell the librarian that her own handwriting looked like a Jackson Pollock painting. For one thing, she could hear the impatience in Sally's voice. For another, she wanted to see this notebook.

The librarian held the notebook out to Isobel. "Do you want us to change the name on your card to Mrs. Peter Arlen?" There was a tinge of disapproval to the question.

Isobel told her to leave the card under Behringer and took the notebook. She had to struggle to keep from opening it right there at the desk, but she forced herself to tuck it under her arm. She didn't want anyone watching her when she looked at this book.

A handful of people were scattered around the Member's Room, but the only familiar faces were the muttering would-be novelist and the gigolo. Forget a job. Didn't the man have a home?

She took the seat at the end of the sofa. There was no one at the other end. She twisted around to make sure the chair that backed up against it was empty. A few years ago a nonmember had sneaked in, sat in that chair, and stolen twenty dollars out of the handbag Isobel had put on the floor beside the sofa while she worked. She'd had a feeling he was a nonmember at the time, and not merely because he'd kept squirming around in his seat, but she hadn't reported him, because he was black, or, as she'd put it now, Afro-American, and shabbily dressed, and the idea of thinking someone wasn't a member because he was black and shabbily dressed had filled her with shame.

She tucked her handbag into the corner of the sofa, put her briefcase at her feet, and sat back with the child's notebook on her lap. She remembered the thrill of expectancy she used to feel at the beginning of the school year as she wrote "Isobel Behringer" on the blank line beside the word *Name*. "Mrs. Peter Arlen" was written on the cover with the same bold, childish flourish. The *P* and the *A* swelled with pride. The *t* and the *l* stood proud. The *n* ended with a curlicue that reminded her of an illustrated manuscript. Seeing the familiar name written in that strange, overblown hand was like coming upon her own reflection pulled and stretched out of shape in a fun house mirror.

She opened the notebook. The writing ran from one edge of the page to the other, as if the writer were terrified of leaving even a fraction of paper uncovered. The scrawl started out overblown, like the name on the cover, then began to shrink as it moved across one line after another. By the time it reached the bottom of the first page, it was a demented chicken scratching.

Isobel's eyes returned to the top of the page.

*Arlen, Peter David, Cert P&N(P) 79. Direct Patient Care &
Medical Teaching. b 45 Rye NY. MD Harvard 71. Med. Intern*

(Brigham Hosp Boston Mass) 71–72 Res Psy (Einstein) 72-75 Instr Psy (Einstein) 77–79 Instr Psy 79–83 Asst Clin Prof 83–86 Assoc Clin Prof 86–(all at Colum P&S). Capt MC USA 75–77. APA.

She recognized the information. It came from the *Directory of Medical Specialists*. She knew, because when she'd first met Pete, she'd looked him up in it herself. She'd done it as a lark, right here in the library reference room. At the time she'd thought it was a perfectly innocent thing to do. Now the fact that someone else had done it, too, put the act in a new light. An image of Lucy Price sitting at the big oval table in the reference room, as Isobel had seen her a few weeks ago, flashed through her mind. She told herself that was ridiculous. Dozens of people used the reference room every day.

She went back to the notebook. The entries were dated. It was a journal, a diary of a life lived in the light and shadow of Pete's favor. He'd frowned when she'd walked into the office; he was angry with her. He'd smiled while she'd recounted a memory; he'd forgiven her. He'd seen her to the door at the end of an hour; he was trying to tell her he didn't want her to leave. His fingers had brushed hers when he'd passed her the box of tissues; he couldn't keep his hands off her. He was missing a button from a jacket; he was crying out for her to take care of him. Every word and gesture had a secret and magical significance. Isobel had sometimes been amazed at the shocks of love that jolted her at unexpected moments, but they were no match for the desperate thrills this stranger found in Pete's most minute and mundane acts. Only she wasn't a stranger. She was a patient. At least now they knew that for sure.

She went on reading. The details about Pete—his facial expressions, his words, his movements, his clothes—piled up. Gradually the horror began to dull, and a hypnotic stupor set

222

in. Then an entry stopped her. It was dated about a month or so after she and Pete had met.

> *11/3: A woman was coming out of the waiting room as I was going in. At first I thought it was the patient before me, but when I got inside the waiting room, the door to his office was still closed and a few minutes later the patient came out. Who is she? Does she mean anything to him? NO! A one-night stand. A hooker. A whore. A mistake in his loneliness.*

Isobel tried to think back a couple of years, but it was no good. This was New York. She passed too many people in halls, and on streets, and walking in and out of buildings. Besides, she tried not to look at Pete's patients. Those were the rules, even if she'd been breaking them by going through his waiting room that morning.

> *11/10: I saw her again. This time I followed her. I will keep following her until I know everything about her.*

Everything was underlined three times.

Isobel felt the paper sticking to her fingers. She wiped her hands on her skirt and went on reading. The familiar minutiae of her life spilled across the pages. Her name, her address, her phone number, where she worked and took her dry cleaning and had her hair cut, what time she left her apartment in the morning and her office at night, how often she went to the library or Pete's or Central Park West.

"She has an unnatural interest in me," Isobel had said the day Millie had brought the linens to the apartment, and Pete had countered that the patient simply had a natural interest in him. There was nothing natural about this.

Isobel went back to the notebook. It was a meticulously ob-

223

served chronicle of her days kept by a hostile stranger. Things she'd forgotten—places she'd gone, people she'd met, clothes she'd worn—came back to her through cruel and unforgiving eyes. Her jacket pulled across her shoulders, and her makeup was drab, and her shoes needed reheeling. She was a phony who gave another woman one of those French two-cheek kisses, a hick who walked around town staring up at buildings, a ball-cutting bitch who'd didn't care whom she beat out of a taxi. She was every flaw and weakness and epithet in the book. Isobel was beginning to wonder how much more she could stand when an entry dated a week before she and Pete had gone down to the judge's chambers stopped her.

9/15: A cat walked through the waiting room. It's the same cat I saw that bitch take to the vet. I'm sure of it.

Isobel thought of Welch wandering innocently through the apartment. He didn't even have claws. She remembered the Doris Lessing book and the dead cat and wiped her palms on her skirt again.

9/22: SHE *was there. Sitting in the kitchen wearing* HIS *shirt.*

Isobel remembered the incident. She also remembered that Pete had taken the patient's word against hers. She couldn't wait to show him the notebook.

9/24: I asked the doorman about the cat. He said it belongs to Dr. Arlen's new wife. How could he do this to me? She must have tricked him. She'll pay. I'll make her pay. And she won't even know what's happening until it's too late because I'll infiltrate and destroy from within. I've already laid the groundwork.

224

She'd sworn she wasn't going to jump to conclusions, but she remembered one of the first conversations she'd had with Lucy. Lucy had said she'd gone away for the weekend to see the autumn foliage. The entry was dated the end of September.

10/12: She carries a picture of him. He's standing behind the wheel of a boat. His hands are on the wheel. Beautiful hands. Imagine them on me. He's wearing dark glasses. Aviator. They make him look sexy and a little menacing. He's squinting up at something. Her? NO! Not her. SHE'S OUT OF THE PICTURE.

Isobel knew the snapshot. Anyone who'd watched her open her wallet to pay for a cup of coffee, or fork over a few dimes for a late fee at the library desk, or make a call from a pay phone could have seen it. But not everyone would have used the phrase out of the picture. Pete could say the city was full of flat-chested blond graduate students with an interest in photography, but only one of them had seen her do all those things in the past few months.

10/28: His daughter is Emily. I wonder if she'll resent me for taking her father away. He said he never thought any daughter of his would go to a dance with a boy who looked as if he had an IQ lower than the mean Fahrenheit temperature.

Isobel had sat in the coffee shop telling the story of Pete's reaction to his daughter's first date. They'd had a good laugh at it. Ah, men and their foibles, they'd agreed at the time. Ah, women and their need to shape and reshape their lives by putting them into words, she thought now as she cringed and hunched further over the book.

225

10/30: I have to stop the stories about men tying me up. I was trying to make him jealous, but I could tell from the way he looked that he was worried about me. He does care!!!

The entry didn't make sense. The graduate student and the one who picked up men and took them home to tie her up were two different patients. Then she recognized her own naïveté. There was no law, including the one of averages, that dealt Pete one patient to a disorder.

11/5: She just goes on and on, the dumb bitch. She started complaining about her stupid cleaning woman and all I had to do was push her a little. So now I know. He wears boxer shorts! I'll buy them for him in pure silk. He is so beautiful!!!

Isobel didn't know if that was worse or better than the story about Pete and his daughter, but she did know that she was never going to be able to convince him that it was not a betrayal but a normal women's conversation. At least it would have been if the woman were normal.

11/17: He spends every Sunday afternoon glued to the Giants' game. He hates her filthy mouth. I don't blame him. She talks like a whore. She has the mind of a whore. I know she tricked him into marrying her. But I'll fix that. I'll fix her. No matter what it takes. This is a solemn oath. Sealed in blood.

A dark red blotch almost blotted out the last word. Isobel ran her finger over the hardened substance and remembered the pathetic rituals of childhood. Pathetic, but not innocent.

11/24: He likes basketball and baseball, too. When he was young, a scout came to his school and said he had a major-league arm. He dreamed of pitching for the Dodgers. All that, and she paid for the coffee, too. Dumb cunt!

Now she understood. Lucy wasn't the patient Millie had enlisted to make the bed. Lucy was the patient who went in for rough sex. At least now Isobel knew how the patient had known he'd love the Dodgers' cap. But she was damned if she'd blame herself for the coffee. Kay hadn't had anything smaller than a twenty, and she couldn't pay for Kay's coffee without paying for Lucy's. Besides, it was only a couple of cups of coffee. Stop it! Stop defending yourself against a madwoman.

11/30: They fought about me! She said it was about the calls, but it was really about me. I didn't mean to make him stand out in the rain, but we must sacrifice for love. She said he was playing squash at the Harvard Club.

Isobel could still picture Lucy standing in the stairwell with her hands hooked in the back pockets of her jeans and her fine-boned face turned up as if she were sunning herself. "Hey," she'd called. "Hey, you guys. Have a nice weekend." Isobel's nails dug into her palms.

12/1: The Harvard Club is at 27 West 44th Street. I walked right in just as if I belonged. I do belong. We'll be married there. I even went upstairs to where the courts are. He played squash with Dr. Martin Sasoon.

Isobel didn't blame the Harvard Club. They'd only listed names. She'd given away secrets.

12/12: He wasn't unfaithful to me. He didn't know me then. That's why he went to Provence alone. If he'd known me, he would

227

have taken me. That woman meant nothing to him. She was a vehicle for his pleasure. Just like she is. But the time is getting near. I know because he kept me for an extra four minutes yesterday. I almost mentioned Provence then, because I knew his keeping me overtime was a secret message. He's just waiting for me to get rid of her. Then we'll be married at the Harvard Club and go to Provence together.

Isobel rested her head against the back of the sofa and closed her eyes. She'd stopped sweating. Her hands lay limp at her sides. She was exhausted. And ashamed.

She hadn't mentioned the incident in Vénasque to Hannah and Millie, but she had made a comment about it to someone else. She hadn't told the story. Not really. She'd merely made a reference, a joking reference, for Christ sake.

She warned herself not to fall into the old trap. The victim wasn't responsible for the crime. She hadn't been asking for it, as the old saying went. But she had been an accessory.

She'd been sitting right here on the sofa. It had been a Saturday afternoon, and she'd been working on the testimony for the landmark hearing on the Waverly house. She remembered, because there wasn't a lot she could say to justify saving it, except that it would mean twenty million dollars to save a lot of other buildings. But the truth wasn't exactly a cogent argument, and while she'd searched for one, she'd kept looking up, and gazing around the room, and staring out the window. Once she'd glanced over at Kay, who was sitting at the other end of the sofa. She had to laugh then, or at least smile, at the title of the magazine article Kay was reading. "The Best Sex I Ever Had."

"Okay," Isobel had said later when they were leaving the library together. "What was the best sex the author ever had?"

That was when Lucy had come up behind them. Isobel

hadn't seen her in the Member's Room. She must have been lurking in the women's room, just waiting to pounce. The little sneak.

"What are you talking about?" Lucy asked.

"The best sex ever. Kay was reading an article about it, and I want to know what it was."

"Nothing, really," Kay said, but they'd gone on teasing her until finally she'd given in and explained she'd been reading the article only because the writer's best sex ever was a lot like some pretty good sex her husband had owned up to having when he was in the service.

"But you still haven't told us what made it so great," Isobel insisted.

Accessory to the crime. She'd practically masterminded it.

"According to him," Kay said as they turned up Madison, "it was because he didn't know her at all."

"I don't get it," Lucy said.

"Men have this thing about anonymous sex," Isobel explained. Oh, she'd been helpful all right. "They think they can be more abandoned."

Kay laughed. "Not Pete, too? Tell."

And Isobel, the old laugh-a-minute raconteur, had been just dumb enough to. "He was on vacation in Provence."

"Oh, God!" Kay said. "A Frenchwoman. That makes it even worse."

"She was an American. A schoolteacher, of all things."

"At least he knew who she was. Brian didn't even know her name."

"For women, it's the zipless fuck," Isobel said. "For men, the nameless."

"But I still don't get why they think it's so great." Lucy had really milked it.

"What does Pete say?" Kay asked. "He's a shrink."

"Dr. Discretion? His lips are sealed when it comes to himself."

"Did he at least tell you what went on?" Kay asked. The question had finally stopped Isobel. She was sure it had. She didn't mind talking about male foibles in general, but she wasn't about to go into Pete's specifically. No matter what Pete thought. That was why she'd tried to change the subject. She really had tried. But Lucy and Kay had refused to change the subject. In fact, Kay had launched into a detailed description of exactly what her husband had got up to in that seedy motel with that nameless pickup. Isobel still found it hard to believe that the colorless man Kay had been arguing with the day Isobel and Millie had seen her had had that much imagination.

She opened her eyes and looked at the notebook again. The cramped demented words ran on, line after line. They led her down one page and onto the next, like an angler's line pulling her closer and closer. Pete said there were no accidents. She wondered if this was what Lucy wanted. She wondered if the loss of the notebook was intentional. She wondered if Lucy was reeling her in.

She turned another page and a card fell out. The red letters screamed "Sweepstakes." Bold black type beneath it promised a Mercedes sports car or two weeks in Hawaii or a Sony cam recorder. All she had to do was fill out the information below.

Isobel picked up the card and held it closer. She'd already filled out the information. Mrs. Peter Arlen was printed on the first line. There was an address beneath it. It wasn't Isobel's address. It wasn't even the address of Pete's first wife. It was an address on East Eighty-third Street. Someone was reeling her in all right.

She stood so abruptly she jostled the lamp on the table behind the sofa. The gigolo looked up from his magazine. The would-be novelist muttered angrily. Isobel didn't even stop to steady the lamp.

She came out of the library onto Seventy-ninth Street and started to run. As she reached Park Avenue, the light changed from green to orange, but she quickened her pace and raced toward the other side. A taxi careened around her. The driver leaned on his horn. A string of bilingual curses followed her down the block. It was hard to believe a total stranger could hate her that much.

The building was a soot-streaked concrete fortress with bars on the windows and a fire escape crisscrossing the front. You didn't have to be the head of Urban Heritage to recognize that it had no redeeming aesthetic value. For a minute she felt sorry for Lucy. Then she remembered the notebook and went into the vestibule.

A dozen names were punched on brown plastic strips next to the row of buzzers. "Mrs. Peter Arlen" was the fourth one down. Somehow that was worse than the notebook or the sweepstakes card.

Isobel pressed the button next to the name. She waited for a moment. She was just about to press it again when a rasping sound came out of the metal speaker next to the directory.

"Federal Express," Isobel barked into the speaker, though she doubted the words would be any more intelligible than the noise that had just come out.

The buzzer sounded. She pushed open the door.

The building had the sour eye-stinging aroma of a roadside rest room that's just been scoured. She didn't want to take the elevator, but she didn't see any stairs. She pushed the elevator button. It had a mushy out-of-order feel, but the digits in the plastic window beside the button flipped from five to four. It took forever for the elevator to reach the ground floor. The door scraped open. Isobel got on and pressed 2.

231

The elevator began to move. The cab shuddered and groaned as if it were breaking the sound barrier, though she could see through the window that it was barely moving. Finally it jolted to a stop. The sound of the door sliding open again grated on her like a nail going down a blackboard. She stepped out.

The hall was dark, but not so dark that she couldn't see that the tiny white and black tiles on the floor were cracked and stained. The numbers on the doors were barely legible. She was looking for 2 B. D was across from the elevator. She turned left and started down the hall. E was next. She turned and retraced her steps. One sign on the front of 2 B warned her to beware of the dog. Another said the premises were monitored by an electronic system. It was the home of a lunatic all right. Either that or an average New Yorker.

She pushed the bell. No buzzer sounded. No dog barked. There wasn't even the sound of footsteps. She pushed it again. Still no sound. She wondered if the bell was working or if Lucy was on the other side of the door peering through the peephole at her.

She rang the bell a third time. The door opened a crack.

"Ohmygod." The words escaped from Isobel in a single breath.

Kay Glass leered out at her.

Isobel stared at the face in front of her. This wasn't the slick, brittle Kay she knew, but the disheveled and distraught woman she'd glimpsed that day in the reference room. Her eyes were wide and wild, and her head was cocked to one side grotesquely as if she were listening to distant voices. But her own voice, when she spoke, was calm. "What do you want?" she asked, as if Isobel were an annoying door-to-door saleswoman.

Isobel put her shoulder against the door and pushed. Even

232

as she did it, she was amazed at herself. She had to be crazy to break into the home of a crazy person.

"I want to talk to—"

The words died as the door opened and she got a full view of the room behind Kay. Huge blowups of Pete stared down from the walls. She must have been following him around with a camera for months. Some of them were blowups of the snapshots she'd mailed. Others Isobel hadn't seen before. There were Petes for all seasons and all hours of the day and night, Petes alone and Petes in groups, head shots of Pete and full shots of Pete, Petes mutilated by the loss of an arm that had been around Isobel's shoulder or a hand that had held hers. Isobel's eyes darted crazily from picture to picture. Dozens of Petes smiled and frowned and stared back at her. She felt dizzy and reached out to steady herself against the door.

She closed her eyes, then opened them again and forced herself to look around the room more slowly. That was when she saw the rest of it. There were pictures of her, too. No, not pictures, collages. A slimily realistic photograph of a snake wound around her shoulders in place of Pete's arm. Large circles, like those used to mark a target in a firing range, were superimposed over a shot of her at the demonstration against Gorsky. An ax split the hood of the snowsuit with the JOE MUST GO sign pinned to the front, and red paint spurted from her small skull with sickening force. A wave of nausea washed over her. She tried to look away, but her eyes kept darting from one picture to another. Everything was oversized and out of shape and insane. It was a fun house version of her life. She dragged her gaze from the horror show back to Kay.

Now Kay's eyes were narrow slits. Her mouth was a lopsided smirk.

"So you finally figured it out," she said in the same maddeningly matter-of-fact voice.

Isobel started to back away. She knew. She had proof. And she didn't feel any safer.

"It took you long enough."

Isobel took another step backward.

"I'm glad. I'm glad you know."

Isobel kept inching toward the elevator.

Kay came out of her apartment into the hall. "He's going to leave you."

Isobel kept her eyes on Kay as she reached out to press the elevator button.

Kay was moving down the hall toward her. "He wants to marry me."

Isobel heard the squeaking and groaning of the elevator cables.

"Now he can tell you." Kay kept coming toward her. "Now that you know."

Isobel heard the elevator door scrape open behind her.

"You might as well give him up."

Isobel backed into the elevator.

Kay was closing the distance between them. "Because if you don't, I'll have to make you."

The elevator door began to shut.

"He loves me!"

Kay lunged toward the elevator and put her hand on the sliding door.

"He loves me and wishes you were dead!"

Isobel stood transfixed as Kay's fingers, clamped around the door, slid toward the wall. The space was getting smaller and smaller.

"Dead!" Kay screamed, and pulled her hand out just as the door closed.

FOURTEEN

"I SHOULD HAVE SPOTTED HER A mile off," Pete said. "You'd have to be blind not to."

Isobel agreed, but that was her dirty little secret. "Merely subject to blind spots," she insisted. "Yours happen to be women who are struggling to pull up their socks. Kay— Karen," she corrected herself, though she was having trouble getting used to the fact that Kay Glass was Karen Stone, "made you believe she was. The end of kinky sex. The hunt for a job. Even the new interests. How were you supposed to know she didn't really spend the weekend in the Bahamas taking a sailing course? Hell, you'd have to have Millie's training, not yours, to know she'd never gone any farther than the local tanning salon."

He shook his head. "I just can't believe I missed all the signs."

"Face it, slugger. She was bound to outsmart you. Sanity is no match for obsession."

Hannah and Millie agreed. Not that sanity was no match for obsession, only that he should have spotted her a mile off. Of course, they didn't come out and say as much. At least they didn't at first. Hannah even tried to blame herself.

"I'm sorry I ever introduced you." The halo of white hair trembled as Hannah shook her head.

"You didn't introduce us, Nana. She tracked you down to get to me. That's what she was doing at the Friday afternoon concerts in the first place."

Dark furrows, like time lines in an archaeological diagram, settled across Hannah's brow. Everyone, including her battery of doctors, insisted her mind was still sharp as a tack, but this obsession with other people's lives was too strange for her to contemplate, or too familiar.

"I feel sorry for her children," Millie said.

"She doesn't have children. Or a husband. She made all that up," Isobel explained.

"What about that man we saw her with that day we came out of the Harvard Club?"

"He could have been anyone, but Pete thinks it was probably her brother. He manages her trust fund. And insists there's nothing wrong with her."

Millie shook her head. "What's going to happen to her?"

"Pete convinced her to check herself into a hospital."

"They should lock her up and throw away the key." Hannah's libertarian principles were no match for her protective instincts.

A month later Isobel walked into the Member's Room of the library and found Karen Stone sitting at one end of the sofa. She'd known, as Pete had pointed out, that Karen would get out of the hospital eventually, but she hadn't expected it to be this soon. And she didn't believe in miracle cures.

Karen looked up and smiled brightly. Isobel turned around, walked out of the room, and went up to the other reading room on the eighth floor. She didn't like that one as much. It was smaller, the furniture felt more cramped, and instead of opening onto Seventy-ninth Street through long French doors, ordinary windows gave a narrow view of the building across the way. But the only person there was a man with a face so ordinary and good-natured he could have stepped out of a cold remedy commercial. When he barely glanced up from the book he was reading, she felt even more reassured.

She didn't tell Hannah and Millie about the incident, but they found out Karen was on the loose again. Millie ran into her in Zabar's.

"Would you believe it? She actually came over to me and tried to say hello."

"What did you do?" Isobel asked.

"I turned around and walked right out of the store. I was so upset I didn't even realize I was carrying a container of olives. I could have been arrested for shoplifting."

"I don't understand why Pete let her out," Hannah said.

"Because," Isobel answered, "Pete isn't the doctor in charge. He stopped treating her as soon as he got her to sign herself in. And because you can't keep a person in the hospital indefinitely."

"No one's talking about indefinitely. Just longer than a month."

"But how much longer? Tell me, Nana, how long after a patient's stabilized do you think she ought to be kept against her will?"

"Now you're quoting him."

Isobel was, because she and Pete had had the same argument, and the fact that Hannah had heard the echo only made Isobel more angry.

"I'm just asking a question. How long? Another month? Ninety days? A year? How long would you recommend? Or do you want to consult your civil liberties groupies down at the ACLU before you decide?"

Hannah didn't answer, but behind the thick lenses her eyes swam nervously, as if she were drowning.

"I'm sorry," Isobel said.

237

*　*　*

Hannah closed the book without putting a marker between the pages. That was one more she wasn't going to finish. She didn't understand the thinking behind large-type editions. They were printed for old people, like her. So what twenty-year-old marketing genius had got the idea that old people wanted to read about heaving bosoms, and fiery loins, and a bunch of born-again moralists apologizing for the recreational drugs they'd taken and the unsafe sex they'd had and the unconscionable sums of money they'd stolen in the last decade? Where did the people who made the decisions get the idea that when the eyes went, the mind went with them?

She put the book on the table beside her. All her life she'd looked forward to the time when she'd have the leisure and the freedom to read. For a while she'd even thought she'd finally go to college. It wasn't such a crazy idea. Lots of people went back to school late in life. Even in those days. After the children were grown and the boys were in the business, there'd be nothing to stop her. Nothing except Reuben, and she could have fought him.

She'd fought him about both boys, and lost. First there was the war, not the one between Reuben and her, but the one that concerned the world. When the boys came home from that, Reuben said what did they need college for. Not to run the business. He was proof of that. And Al, who'd crossed the Atlantic and fought in the ETO, and Sam, who hadn't fought but had crossed the Pacific as well as the Atlantic, agreed.

Hannah hadn't given up. She'd just turned her attention to Millie. Her daughter would get the education her own mother had denied her.

Hannah pulled her vision back from the past. She hadn't heard the front door open and close, but now she saw Millie coming toward her.

238

"Well, that's that," Millie said. "I put my fur coat in summer storage."

The comment sent Hannah back to the past again. Or maybe that was where she lived these days.

She'd never wanted a fur coat. In fact, the more Reuben had talked about buying her one, the less she'd wanted one. So when Millie had turned sixteen, Reuben had gone out and bought a fur coat for her. Hannah had been furious. Raccoon or beaver would have been bad enough, but whoever heard of a sixteen-year-old girl in mink? Reuben had just sat beaming as Millie had strutted back and forth across the furniture-cramped living room, turning the collar up over her ears, and swirling the coat around her, and throwing it open to stand with one hand on one hip in the exaggerated pose of a professional model.

Thirty years later Hannah had been vindicated when Isobel had refused the fur coat Millie had insisted she needed to go off to Bryn Mawr.

That was it! Hannah was surprised she'd never seen the connection before. At the time she'd thought Reuben had given in on college because it was for Millie. He'd always given Millie anything she wanted. Now she realized he hadn't given in to her. He'd outsmarted her. He'd told Hannah she could send Millie to college because he knew Millie didn't want to go to college. He knew Hannah had already lost.

She'd sent Millie off to Cornell with high hopes and a monstrous envy that she'd tried to hide because it was a shameful thing to envy your own daughter. Millie had had high hopes, too. Reuben had always told her the world was her oyster, and she knew all about the world from the magazines and the movies and the succession of maids who'd kept house for them while Hannah had helped Reuben with the business. She'd known all about football weekends and fraternity parties and proms. Classes, however, had come as a shock. Three months after Millie had arrived in Ithaca, she'd left school for good. But she hadn't returned home empty-handed. By then she'd met Harry. A year later they married.

"Did Cruz give you your digitalis?"

Again it took a moment for Hannah to drag herself into the present. She looked up and focused on Millie.

"She's been giving it to me every day for almost a year, and you still ask."

"Only because it's her afternoon off. I just wanted to make sure she didn't forget before she left."

"She didn't forget. And even if she did, I wouldn't."

"Fine. I'm sorry I mentioned it."

"I just don't like being treated as if I'm senile."

"No one said anything about senility. People forget things. I do all the time."

"People only forget what they don't want to remember. Ask your son-in-law."

Then why couldn't she forget this?

After she hadn't been allowed to try with the boys, after she'd tried and failed with Millie, it had been her turn. She hadn't asked Reuben. She'd told him. "I'm entitled," she said. "I worked all these years. I built the business with you. What did I take off when the children were born? Three weeks, a month each time; then I was right back there with you. So now it's my turn."

She sent away for the catalogs, and they came back, fat paperbound booklets brimming with promised wisdom and endless opportunity. She remembered the night she realized it wasn't her opportunity.

She and Reuben were sitting in the dining room of the old apartment on West End Avenue. The space was crowded with the heavy furniture that had been old-fashioned when Reuben had bought it. She saw him pick up the brochure. His hand grasped it so the big fingers obliterated the words on the cover. She started to say something, nothing mean or bitchy, just some comment, because it was such a strange thing for him to do, but he began to leaf through the pages, and she realized he just wanted to look at the pictures. As he sat there flipping through the photographs of young people sitting in lecture halls and bending over Bunsen burners and strolling campus lawns, the flesh grew tighter across his bony cheeks and his mouth shriveled until his face took on the peeled agony of a skull.

"I'm going to make some tea," Millie said. "Do you want a cup?"

Hannah shook her head. She couldn't speak because she wasn't here. She was back in the old apartment, hemmed in by the dark, oppressive furniture and family shadows and Reuben.

She remembered the rest of that night, too. She remembered, even after all these years, the anger Reuben had brought to bed. Not violence—he never crossed that line, because he had rules for himself as well as for everyone else, everyone except Millie—but a terrible simmering fury that had no place to go except up against her. The darkness sizzled with his rage, and when she reached out to soothe it, his wide shoulders began to heave. Then a terrible strangled sound, like a man gasping for air, broke from his throat, and the tears ran down his big rawboned face onto hers. And suddenly she was touching the suffering she'd been too resentful to admit all those years she'd worked beside him, first in the store, then in the office, his right hand, he used to say to other people, but never to her.

After that night Hannah hadn't had the heart to go to college.

She'd tried not to blame him. There were even times, the best times between them, when she'd managed to put the situation in a better light. Most marriages harbor some secret against the outside world. That had been theirs. But sometimes the bitterness returned.

She shook her head to drive it away now.

"If you don't want it, you don't have to drink it," Millie said. "I made it in case you change your mind."

It took Hannah a moment to realize Millie was talking about the cup of tea she was holding.

Millie picked up the book on the end table to make room for the saucer. "Do you want me to return this?"

Hannah shook her head again. She had to get rid of that memory. But Millie misinterpreted the gesture.

"Then you're not finished with it?"

Hannah forced herself back to the present. The book. Millie was asking about that awful book she'd brought her from the library.

"It's not worth finishing. You tell the librarian, when you take it back, if that's the best he can do in large type, he should save his money. Or the library's."

Millie put the book down, sat on the sofa, and picked up her own cup of tea. "I'm sure he's just waiting for your opinion."

"Why not? I'm a member. I pay my dues. You think you need a college degree to tell the difference between trash and what's good?"

"I think the library caters to a lot of people, and some people like this kind of thing, even if you don't." Millie picked up the book again and looked at the jacket. "I like this kind of thing. Of course, I'm not smart. Like my mother and my daughter."

"Maybe if you'd stayed, you would have got smart."

The words were out before Hannah knew she was thinking them. They hung in the air like telltale particles of dust suspended in a shaft of sunlight that penetrates a dim, seemingly well-kept room.

"I can't believe you're still harping on that! I'm a seventy-year-old woman, and my mother is still harping on the fact that I didn't finish college."

"Finish! You barely started. You threw away a golden opportunity."

"Golden for you."

"Golden for anyone who had the sense to take advantage of it."

Millie slammed the book down on the end table. The bone china cup rattled politely against its saucer.

"So why didn't you? And don't give me that story about your mother and the book burnings again. You could have gone after that. After we were all grown. You could have gone back to school then. You always said you were going to. Lots of people do. So why didn't you? I'll tell you why. Because it's easier to sit here and complain than to do something about it. Because it's easier to feel sorry for yourself and blame everyone else. You and Zelda-the-Blacklisted-Actress. Blacklisted, my foot. She didn't work because she was a terrible actress. And you didn't go back to school because you were too lazy or too scared or too something."

"I didn't go back to school," Hannah said quietly, "because Reuben needed me."

"For what? To run the business? That's another of your myths. That Pop couldn't have done it without you."

"He couldn't have." Hannah spaced the words carefully, as if she were putting down fragile objects.

"Why not? The boys didn't have any trouble running it without you after he turned it over to them. And Pop was at least as good a businessman as his sons. So tell me. What couldn't he have done without you?"

243

"I don't want to talk about it."

Millie could feel her face collapsing, the way it did when she was about to cry, but she couldn't stop herself. "You don't want to talk about it! You've been talking about it for as long as I can remember. All my life I've been hearing how Pop couldn't have done it without you. You even had him believing it. 'My right hand' he used to call you. So I want to know. I want you to tell me, finally, after all these years, what exactly couldn't this man who built a little store that sold boxes and string into a paper business that included a couple of forests in Canada do without you? What was so important that you had to leave your children home with maids while you went to business with him? What did he need you standing next to him every minute of every day for? Come on. Tell me. What exactly couldn't Pop do that you had to do for him?"

"What couldn't he do?" Hannah started, and told herself to stop before it was too late, and knew she wasn't going to stop, not now, not finally, when it didn't matter anymore. "He couldn't read the orders he filled, or the contracts he signed, or even the labels on the things he made. He couldn't—" She was about to continue the catalog of deficiencies, but she saw the look on her daughter's face and stopped. Millie's eyes were wide, the way she held them when she stood in front of the mirror debating a lid tuck, and her skin was as pale as the flesh tones of the portrait of the young Millie that hung above her on the wall.

"You're making this up," Millie said.

Hannah didn't answer.

"I don't believe you."

"He didn't want you to know."

"But the boys, Al and Sam, they worked with him, they would have known."

"We made sure they didn't."

244

Hannah hesitated. She knew she shouldn't say any more. She'd already said too much. And she knew it was merely the vanity of an old woman. But she couldn't help herself.

"That was one more thing he couldn't have done without me."

Hannah and Millie were still in the study when the house phone rang. Each of them sat up a little straighter at the sound. At best, it would be a visitor. They could find a way back to each other through a third person. At the least, it was a delivery of dry cleaning or a package, a mundane occurrence that would inch them back to the ordinary world where weaknesses were respected and secrets kept.

The swinging door to the kitchen caught and stayed open as Millie went through. Hannah watched her as she took the receiver off the wall.

"That's impossible," Millie said after a moment.

"What is it?" Hannah called.

"Are you sure?" Millie said into the receiver.

"What's wrong?" Hannah asked.

Millie stood with the receiver in one hand and her other on her forehead shielding her eyes as she listened.

Hannah recognized the gesture. She pushed herself up out of her chair, made her way into the kitchen, and stood leaning on one of the kitchen chairs for support. "What is it?"

Millie shook her head.

"What's going on?" Hannah insisted.

"Tell her we're not here," Millie said into the phone.

"Tell who we're not here?"

Millie hung up the house phone. "That girl. Kay Glass. What did Isobel say her real name was? Karen Stone."

"What does she want with us? Hasn't she made enough trouble?"

245

The house phone rang again.

"Don't pick it up," Hannah said.

Millie glanced at the phone, then back at Hannah. "How can I not pick it up? Louie knows we're here." She took the receiver off the wall again.

The pain was beginning in Hannah's legs. She tried to take a deep breath, but she felt winded.

"Tell her we can't see her now," Millie said into the phone. "We're busy."

"Tell her we can't see her anytime." Hannah held out her hand. "Let me."

Millie ignored her and went on listening to Louie. "Tell her if it's that important, she can write me a letter."

"She has nothing to say to us," Hannah said.

Millie put her hand over the mouthpiece. "Now someone else is on the line. The whole building's going to know." She took her hand away from the mouthpiece. "Yes, Louie, I'm still on. No, Mrs. Pearson, there's no trouble." There was another silence. "Thank you, Mrs. Pearson, but we don't need help. Everything is under control. Send her up, Louie."

Millie put the receiver back on the wall, but it took her a moment to meet Hannah's eyes. "What did you expect me to do? That Mrs. Pearson in eleven A got on. All I had to do was let her hear me telling Louie not to let someone up, and it would be all over the building that we're hiding from someone. They'd think it was the IRS or a bill collector or something."

"What do you care what people think?"

Millie started out of the kitchen without answering. Hannah followed. She made her way through the dining room by leaning on one chair after another. She told herself not to hurry, but she wanted to get to the front hall to make sure Millie didn't let that crazy woman in.

Millie was opening the door as Hannah reached it.

Karen stood in the hall with her hands jammed in her trench coat pockets. Her hair was limp and greasy. Her skin had a cheesy pallor. Her head drooped on her neck like a dead flower on a stem. She raised her eyes to them without lifting her face.

"I know you don't want me here." Her voice was almost a whisper. Hannah had to take a step closer to hear it. Millie just stood there with her hand on the doorknob.

"I know you must hate me." She paused again, as if she were waiting for them to answer. They didn't deny the statement, but neither of them could manage to come out and agree with it either.

"I just wanted to come and say I know all that, and I'm sorry." She waited again. When they still didn't say anything, she finally lifted her head. "The whole time I was in the hospital, I kept thinking that I had to apologize to both of you. I told my doctor there that, and he said it would be all right." She waited again. Neither of them spoke. "That's all." A thin, sickly smile pulled her mouth out of shape. "I just wanted to tell you how sorry I was."

"So now you have," Hannah said.

"If I could just explain." Karen didn't exactly take a step. She merely leaned forward so her hand was on the door frame and her upper body was cantilevered into the apartment. "I mean, I know it must seem crazy to you, but that's the point. I was crazy. I just went crazy for a while. I'm okay now, but I wasn't then. I mean, I just lost control." The rush of the words propelled her forward so she was standing just inside the door.

"That's why I was in the hospital. God, that was a nightmare." Her shoulders drooped until she was leaning against the wall next to the door. "I mean, I know I did some things that weren't right, but nobody ought to be locked up that way. With people watching you all the time. You know what a judas

247

hole is? They watch you through a judas hole. And they take everything away from you. Even my belt." Her face swung to Millie. "Can you imagine what that was like? I mean, you know the way I dress. Good stuff. I even have a Chanel suit. Chanel, for Christ sake. Shoes, too." Her voice was beginning to race. "And there I was walking around like some bag lady because they took away my belt. You know what kind of belt it was?" She moved her face closer to Millie's. "Guess what kind. Think of something really chic, really expensive. Go ahead, guess."

"I can't," Millie said quietly.

"Try. You have to try."

"I don't know."

"An alligator with a Kieselstein-Cord buckle! But I got it back. I told them if I didn't, I'd sue. Do you want to see it?" She began to rummage in her bag. "I know I have it here somewhere."

"It's all right," Millie said. "We believe you."

Karen's hand swung up and landed on Millie's arm. "But the belt is important. It shows what they did to me. Just because of him. Because they were jealous. Everyone there was jealous of me."

The sound of telephone extensions ringing throughout the apartment stopped her. They rang a second time, then a third.

Millie hesitated. Karen's hand was still on her arm, and she was still holding the door open. She glanced at Hannah.

"You get it," Hannah said. "I'll stay here."

Millie shook off Karen's arm, closed the door, and started toward the study.

Karen turned to Hannah. "You ought to get off your feet. I know about your condition. I'm very knowledgeable about these things. A doctor's wife has to be." She took a step toward Hannah. "Let me help—"

"I'm fine," Hannah snapped, but her breath felt short as she said it. "And you're not a doctor's wife," she went on, though the effort of the words made her chest ache. There didn't seem to be enough air in the room. This crazy woman was using it all up.

Millie came back across the living room and into the hall. "You have to leave. I just talked to—" She stopped. "You have to leave."

"I only want to apologize. I'm not going to hurt anyone. I just want to make you understand. You have to understand."

"We understand," Millie said. "And now you have to leave."

"But you don't," Karen whined. "No one does. It's not—"

"You have to go."

"—fair. He loves me. Me!" she shouted. "I have to make you understand that." Her hands, which hung at her sides, balled into fists and hit the wall behind her. "He's always loved me." They hit the wall again. "Ever since the first day I walked into his office." A third time. "I knew it right away." Her fists were beating against the wall, punctuating her words. "I know things like that. I'm extremely perceptive. Ask anyone. Ask him. He knew I knew. We both did. He loves me." Her mouth twitched around the words. "He loves me!" She whipped her face back and forth from one of them to the other. "Me me me me me." The words pounded like a hammer. Then suddenly her body caved in under the assault and slid to the floor like a rag doll. Her head flopped forward. Her legs splayed out in front of her as if they had no joints. Her shoulders shook and heaved.

A sharp-edged glance ran between Hannah and Millie.

"I'm going to call Dr. Arlen," Millie said softly.

Karen's head jerked up and bounced against the wall with a crack. Hannah and Millie recoiled at the sound.

"No!" The word was a wail of pain. "I'm not supposed to be

here. Don't tell him I'm here. You can't tell him. Please don't tell him."

"You need help," Millie insisted.

"Go call him," Hannah said.

"No!" Karen threw her head against the wall again. It hit with another sharp crack. She threw it back a second time, then a third and a fourth. The sound of each contact crashed through the room like thunder.

"Stop!" Millie shouted the word. Hannah gasped it.

Karen's face contorted into a maniacal smile as her head went back and forth against the wall. The lamp on the table beside her trembled from the vibration. A crimson spot began to form on the white paint.

"Stop it!" Millie pleaded.

Hannah opened her mouth, but she had no breath to push the words out.

Millie bent and tried to take Karen's head between her hands to hold it still, but Karen continued to hurl it back and forth. Now it looked as if Millie were bashing Karen's head against the wall.

Hannah felt the fingers begin to tighten around her left breast.

"Don't," Millie pleaded as she hunched in front of Karen, her hands going back and forth with Karen's head.

"He loves meeee!" Karen wailed.

The cracking sound came faster. The lamp shuddered. The blood spot spread on the pristine white paint.

Hannah's breath was trapped in her chest. She opened her mouth to let in more air. Her body jerked and heaved with the effort. The fingers in her chest twisted her heart and wrung it out like a piece of wet laundry.

Karen hurled her head back against the wall, then forward.

It butted Millie's shoulder and sent her sprawling backward onto the floor.

Hannah felt the pain in her chest explode as her body flew apart into a galaxy of swirling particles. And still, from a great distance, the sound, crack, crack, crack, echoed in her head.

FIFTEEN

I SOBEL DIDN'T BOTHER TO HANG up the phone. She jabbed the button to get another line and dialed 911. It rang once. Her fingers drummed the desk. The realization hit her as it began to ring a second time. The voice on the other end of the line would ask what the emergency was. She tried to phrase an answer.

A woman has conned her way into my mother's and grandmother's apartment.

Is she armed? Is she threatening their lives? Is she holding them hostage?

She wants to apologize to them.

She hung up the phone, grabbed her handbag from the bottom drawer of her desk, took her coat off the hanger on the back of her office door, and started down the hall to the elevators.

The first thing she noticed as she reached the street was the mass of glowing off-duty signs heading up Madison Avenue like a swarm of fireflies. It was the changing of shifts, and every taxi driver in the city was heading for his garage.

A cab stopped near her for a red light. Through the closed window, she gestured and pleaded, though she knew it was hopeless. If the apartment were on the way to a bridge, he might consider picking up a little extra cash, but even the most recently arrived non-English-speaking cabby knew Central Park West wasn't on the way to Queens or Brooklyn or wherever the hell the garages were. She opened her handbag, but before she could pull some bills from it, the light changed and the driver sped off.

A gypsy cab pulled up in front of her. She'd never been in a gypsy cab in her life. Hannah, in some vague way, had always connected them with strikebreaking scabs. Millie believed that every gypsy cabdriver was a closet rapist and murderer. The driver grinned an invitation at Isobel. His eyes shrank to narrow slits. The gold of his left incisor glinted maliciously. It wasn't a face to inspire confidence. She opened the door, climbed in, and gave him the Central Park West address.

He drove as if his life depended on getting there without stopping for a single light, and for once Isobel didn't protest. He ran two lights in a row and half a block from the apartment slammed his brakes to a bone-bruising stop at the third. Isobel's arm stiffened to keep from crashing into the wire-grated plastic window separating the backseat from the front. As she ricocheted back against the seat, she saw the white van with the black lettering and red cross on the side double-parked in front of the building and the crowd simmering around it with obscene curiosity, and knew she was too late.

She grabbed a bill from her wallet, thrust it through the slot in the wire-grated window, and jumped out of the cab. As she began to run, her heel twisted in a pothole and she went down on one ankle, but she regained her balance and kept going until she reached the wall of backs and shoulders that ran from the entrance of the building to the ambulance.

She tried to pry through. A woman snarled at her. A delivery boy with a baseball hat turned backward cursed at her. Under normal circumstances, she'd know she was asking for trouble, but the trouble was already here, so she kept pushing and shoving until she broke through the wall to the small circle of space beneath the canopy. She was just in time to see two quick-stepping men coming out of the building with a stretcher between them. The hump on the litter was so small it could have been a heap of clothes stuck beneath the coarse blanket. Two feet pointed skyward. At the other end a small ash-colored face lolled, its eyes closed, its lips black-tinged and slack.

Isobel had never seen a dead body. She'd been told about her father's and her grandfather's deaths after the fact, and she didn't count the painted and rouged manikins she'd come across at wakes and viewings. But without having seen death, she knew this was what it looked like.

Then even as she realized that, she noticed something else. The thin rough blanket didn't cover Hannah's face. Somewhere inside Isobel hope flapped its mangled wings. Even the sight of Karen lurking in the lobby wasn't enough to kill it.

Millie came out of the building a step behind the stretcher. Her eyes were flinty. The fine bones beneath her skin looked surprisingly solid. Then she caught sight of Isobel, and her face collapsed into soft folds as she began to cry. Isobel put her arm around her mother's shoulders, and together they walked beside the stretcher as it bobbed toward the ambulance.

Isobel's eyes ached from the fluorescent glare. Her stomach heaved at the stench of antiseptic and medication and fear. She stood beside her mother as they watched the stretcher disappear down the hall and the double doors to the cardiac care unit swing closed behind it.

A woman who might or might not have been a nurse—she had the familiar air of anger born of defeat, but she was wearing slacks and a cotton blouse—told them there was a dayroom down the hall where they could wait. Isobel opened her mouth to say something, but the woman cut her off. "We'll let you know as soon as we have any information."

In a room about the size of Isobel's office, ten or twelve people sat on a sofa and two chairs, and perched on tables and windowsills, and leaned against the wall. One woman was scolding a little boy while she wiped his nose. Another was nursing a baby. An old man sat with his arm around an angry-looking younger one while he crooned soft Spanish sounds into his ear. Two women hissed at each other. The room was like a mound of yeast fermenting with love and rage and family tension.

The old man glanced up and saw Millie and Isobel standing in the doorway. He lifted his arm. It caught the attention of the rest of the family as if he were a conductor signaling the first note. Without a word two small boys who were sitting together in one of the chairs stood. The man gestured Millie toward it.

Isobel settled her mother and went down the hall to the pay phones. Pete's answering machine picked up on the third ring. She wanted to scream into it, as if the volume of her voice could break through the mechanical wall of silence that screened him and the patient he was closeted with. She fought to keep her voice normal as she told the machine what had happened.

By the time she got back to the dayroom, the family had left. Millie was sitting alone like a child with her hands folded on top of the handbag on her lap and her knees together. Her eyes were on the floor, and as Isobel stood for a moment watching her, the room lurched like the supporting beam of a scale, and the maternal burden shifted. She became her mother's mother.

She stepped into the room. Millie looked up with inky eyes. "Did you call Pete?"

"He's with a patient. I got his machine."

"He doesn't pick up for an emergency?"

"He doesn't know it's an emergency. He keeps the sound off so it doesn't disturb the patient's hour."

"Patients." Millie sighed and shook her head.

"He'll listen to it as soon as the hour is over." Isobel looked at her watch. "In about fifteen minutes."

Millie turned from Isobel to stare at the opposite wall. "I wish he'd get here. I know they'll take better care of her when they know she's related to someone on staff."

Isobel clamped her mouth shut. She'd always agreed with Hannah, who professed solidarity with her fellowman, but at this moment she understood Millie, who made no bones about wanting to be singled out and lifted above and distinguished from.

"At least he could get in there and find out what's going on," Millie insisted.

Isobel said she'd see if there was any word and went back down the hall to the nurses' station. As she walked, the familiar thoughts ran through her head like a mantra. Hannah was ninety-four. She'd had a full life. People have to die sometime. But it didn't work. Age had nothing to do with it, and Hannah's life had been full of dead ends and unfulfilled dreams, and Isobel wasn't ready.

Another woman stood behind the desk now. This one was wearing a white uniform, but the expression of weary hostility was the same. She was telling Isobel there was still no word when a man Isobel recognized as Hannah's doctor came through the swinging doors Hannah had disappeared behind. Isobel left the nurse in mid-sentence and crossed the hall to him.

She introduced herself. As he stood looking down at her, the silence between them swelled. At least it seemed that way to Isobel. She tried to read his face for signs, but all she could see was a stubble of five o'clock shadow that looked, this close, like the black circles in an Andy Warhol painting. There was also a thin thread of dried blood above his Adam's apple.

257

"I just spoke to your husband," he said. "We've managed to stabilize her."

Later Isobel would be struck by the sequence of those sentences. Now all she heard was the second one.

"Then she's all right?" The words rushed out of her in a breeze of relief.

"For the moment." Isobel stood listening while the doctor listed the various machines and procedures and medications that were shoring up her grandmother. As he talked, the exhaustion slid from his face, and his voice began to throb with wonder, like a boy opening the envelope with the secret code ring or walkie-talkie wristwatch he'd sent for with fifty cents and a bunch of box tops.

"If your husband has any questions, have him give me a call," he said as he began moving away from her. There was a beat, just enough time for the gleanings of some tax-deductible sensitivity-training boondoggle in Barbados or Palm Springs to float back. "Or if you or your mother have any questions, of course."

She started back to the dayroom. Her feet skimmed over the mottled gray linoleum, patterned to camouflage dirt and blood and the spillage of human life. As she rounded the corner into the dayroom eager to give Millie the news, she came face-to-face with Karen Stone.

No matter how hard she tried later, Isobel never could get the next few minutes clear in her mind. She was screaming at Karen to get out, and Karen was insisting she just wanted to know if Hannah was okay, and Millie was crying. Later Karen would insist Isobel had lunged at her, and maybe she had. All Isobel knew was that she had to get Karen out of the room, off the floor, and away from her family. She was pushing and pulling Karen, and Karen was trying to fight free, and Millie was pleading with them to stop, and suddenly there were more people in the room. An orderly, and then the nurse, and then the other woman who wasn't wearing a uniform, and another orderly. The nurses were shouting, and Isobel saw one orderly trying to hold Karen and felt with a sickening terror the other pinning her arms to her side. People were screaming and scuffling, and a crowd was gathering at the door, and the orderly's arms felt like a straitjacket around her. She was struggling against him and shrieking at the nurses to get that woman out, and Karen was insisting she had a right to be there, and one of the orderlies was shouting at them both to calm down. Then suddenly, behind the crowd blocking the door, Pete's face loomed into view. Isobel was still thrashing against the straitjacket of the orderly's arms as Pete shouldered his way into the room.

It was all over in a few minutes. One of the orderlies ushered Karen from the floor, and the out-of-uniform nurse assured them she wouldn't be let up again. On his way out of the room, the orderly who'd pinned Isobel's arms to her sides told her he was sorry. She said it was okay, she understood that he was just doing his job, but it wasn't okay, because she could still feel his big arms wrapped around her and the panic rising as she kicked and twisted and fought against him. She could still feel what it was like to be entirely helpless.

Hannah was graduated to a private room before the week was out. Millie spent the entire day there, moving back and forth between the two plastic-upholstered chairs, waiting for Hannah to need something, even if it wasn't her.

Isobel stopped in every night on her way home from work. She hated going from the loamy green aroma that floated off the park on those spring evenings into the nose-stinging reek of the hospital. She hated the elevators full of blank-faced visitors and gossiping staff and bathrobed patients who hung their heads as if they'd checked their dignity with their street clothes. She hated walking into the room every night to find, in place of her grandmother, a shrunken puppet dangling from a maze of wires and tubes that monitored and measured and fed.

Still, each night as she entered the room, Hannah managed to smile, and each day the doctor said she was getting stronger, and Isobel knew things were far better than she had any right to expect.

Then one evening, as the taxi pulled up in front of the hospital, Isobel saw Karen on the sidewalk. She crossed the pavement to the curb and stood there as if she were a normal person waiting for a cab. For one illogically hopeful moment, Isobel thought maybe she did want a cab. Then she realized she was crazy even to hope.

Karen went on watching Isobel as she paid the driver and got out of the taxi. Though she knew it wasn't possible, she hesitated for a moment to see if Karen would take the door from her. Karen didn't move. Isobel closed the door and started across the sidewalk to the hospital entrance. Karen fell in step behind her. She wasn't merely following her; she was dogging her steps like a shadow.

"He's mine," Karen hissed in her ear.

Isobel fought to keep from turning around.

"He's going to divorce you and marry me."

Isobel stepped into a section of the revolving door. As soon as she did, she knew it was a mistake. Before she could move, Karen slipped in behind her. They were locked together in the small wedge of glass-enclosed space. Isobel could barely breathe. She felt Karen's body pushed up against her back. She shrank under the hot force of Karen's breath on her hair. She pushed the door forward and took a step. Karen's shoes came down on her heels. Karen's hands grabbed her shoulders. Karen's body shoved and jostled and bumped them forward.

The distance was an arc of only a few feet, but it seemed to be taking forever. Through the glass, Isobel saw the world turning in slow motion around her, the street, the shrubs beside the door, the wall of the building, a corner of the lobby. And all the time Karen kept hissing in her ear. "He's mine. He's mine. He's mine." Then fresh air hit Isobel in the face, and she broke free.

She crossed the lobby to the security guard lounging against the desk and told him what had just happened. He didn't even bother to pull himself upright. "Who'd you say it was?" he asked.

Isobel turned to point out Karen. She was gone.

When Isobel got home later that night, she told Pete about the incident. He said he'd speak to the head of security at the hospital.

The next night Karen was waiting again. She dogged Isobel's steps from the cab to the entrance, whispering behind her all the way. At least Isobel had the sense to go through the swinging door.

"I don't know what to do," Pete said when Isobel got home that night. "We can keep her out of the hospital, but we can't keep her off the street."

"Can't you hospitalize her again?"

"Not against her will. She isn't threatening anyone's life. Making it a living hell," he went on before she could protest, "but not threatening bodily harm. Besides, she isn't my patient anymore."

"Whose patient is she?"

"That's one of the problems. She won't stick with anyone. She stopped seeing the guy who was treating her when she was in the hospital. Then she made an appointment with Marty Sasoon—he was one of the names I gave her—but she never kept it. As far as I know, she isn't seeing anyone."

The following night Isobel entered the hospital through a

different pavilion. "I don't know why I didn't think of it before," she told Pete when she got home.

The next evening Karen was waiting at the other entrance.

Looking back at it later, Pete realized he should have known something was up as soon as Marty Sasoon suggested a drink, but at the time he didn't suspect anything because if they rarely had a drink after a game of squash, they occasionally had a drink after a game.

They went down to the Cambridge Room, which was the only place in the club you could get a drink late on a Saturday afternoon, and settled into leather chairs in front of one of the two empty fireplaces that yawned like maws at either end of the room. The great men of history, or at least Harvard, gazed down at them from the wainscoted walls. Their looks were stern—have you been living up to the standards of a scholar and a gentleman?—but Pete preferred them to Teddy Roosevelt's hapless elephant, which cast a dusty gray pall over the great hall, or the portrait of a brash young JFK trying to look mature and trustworthy in a corner of the dining room.

They ordered drinks, and the waiter came back with them and a plate of potato chips and pretzels and cheddar spread on Ritz crackers that only a mahogany-paneled club or a neon-and-plastic bar would still dare serve. Pete leaned back in his chair, and took a swallow of the drink, and felt the smoky smoothness of the scotch make his tired muscles hum, and never dreamed of what was on the way. He could remember the club when women weren't allowed in most of the rooms most of the time, and though even then he'd opposed the policy in theory, he'd always known it had its advantages in practice. When a couple came in, and Sasoon's eyes did a thorough strip search of the woman, Pete appreciated the advantages even more. Marty Sasoon was one of those men whose senses quickened visibly, like a hunting dog who'd picked up a scent, whenever a woman entered the room. To be fair, Pete supposed all men reacted in one way or another. Marty was just less subtle about it.

When he turned back to Pete, his face was suddenly serious. Pete was surprised. He'd been expecting a joke or at least an evaluation.

Their chairs were at a forty-five-degree angle with a small table between them, and now Marty listed to one side so his body was closer to Pete's, though he turned his head to face the room, as if they were two spies in a grade B movie pretending they didn't know each other. When Marty spoke, his voice was so low Pete had to lean still closer to hear him.

"I just want you to know I haven't mentioned this to anyone else, and I don't intend to. What I'm going to say doesn't go beyond this room."

Amazingly enough, at least it seemed amazing to Pete later, he still didn't expect trouble. He assumed the confidence had to do with Marty rather than himself, though if he'd been listening carefully, he would have picked up on the creamy undercurrent in Marty's voice. It was the voice of a Roman watching Christians being thrown to the lions or a rational human being sitting in a dark theater watching a horror movie.

"It's about that patient you sent me," Marty went on. "Karen Stone."

"I thought she never kept the appointment."

"She made another. I've seen her a couple of times now." Marty sighed. "Jeez, this is a mess."

Pete put his drink on the table. He'd warned Marty when he'd asked if he could refer Karen to him, and Marty had said sure, because whatever else you could say about Sasoon, he was a good therapist and an ethical guy, who didn't believe in treating only the easy patients who were going to get better and

263

write you a letter a year later thanking you for the experience. But now Karen Stone was hounding him and his wife, and he was going to blame Pete.

"I was afraid of this," Pete said.

Marty's head swiveled to Pete. "Shit!" he whispered. "I was sure that was the last thing you'd say. I was sure you had nothing to worry about. Even after that business last winter, I was sure. You know the time I mean. When my patient came in and told me he thought you were—"

"I know the incident you mean." Now Pete was whispering, too.

"To tell you the truth, I'd never have given this a moment's thought if it hadn't been for that. I mean, this Karen Stone isn't a woman with a steady grasp of reality. But Jesus, Pete, first that guy, then her, and now when I start to ask you about it, the first words out of your mouth are 'I was afraid of this.' It sounds like even if nothing happened—and believe me, I'm not suggesting it did—you gave her some encouragement."

"I meant," Pete said evenly, though he could feel the sweat coming out on his upper lip, "I was afraid she was hounding you and Claire."

Sasoon's hand went up like a stop sign. "That's not the problem. In fact, I haven't seen any sign of that."

"Then what?" Pete asked, though he already knew.

Sasoon listed closer and dropped his voice to a murmur. "Karen Stone says you were screwing her."

Goddamn women! Manipulative bitches! The words came out of nowhere and whirled through Pete's consciousness like a tornado. Then they faded, and silence slid over the room, hard and slick as a sheet of ice. He clutched the arms of his chair, but he couldn't stop himself from careening wildly over its treacherous surface. In an instant he saw the futility of his defense, the wreck of his career, the inescapable eternal shame that would pursue him no matter how far or often he moved. He saw people's pity turning into suspicion and hardening into condemnation. He saw his children's mistrustful eyes and his colleagues' averted faces, and recognized for the first time that what he'd mistaken for an ethical, even honorable streak in his character was nothing more than craven vanity.

"I wasn't," he said softly.

Sasoon was still staring at him. "I'll take your word for it, Pete. Like I said, I wouldn't even have brought it up if it weren't for that incident last winter. If you ask me, the whole profession has gone off the deep end about this kind of thing. Like rules for how long after you stop treating a patient you can start screwing her. I mean, who's crazier, the APA or the patients? But I thought I ought to mention it. Just so you'd know. Not that I'd say anything to anyone else. You don't have to worry about that." He glanced around the room again. "As far as I'm concerned, this whole business stops here."

The old Pete, the one who'd walked into the room half an hour earlier, would have said there wasn't any business, and if Sasoon thought there was, he ought to report it to the proper board. At least that was what the old Pete had believed he'd do.

"Nothing happened," this Pete said. "You have my word."

"Jesus, I'm glad to hear you say that." As Marty's voice soared to the high ceiling, the couple at the other end of the room turned to stare, and Pete knew from the brash heartiness of the words and the slick smile pasted on Sasoon's mouth that whatever he said, he'd always believe, or at least suspect, that Pete had done something unconscionable or at least unethical with one of his patients, and maybe more than one.

Then Sasoon's voice died, and he leaned over and put his hand on Pete's arm. "But if you don't mind a little advice," he went on in his hushed, conspiratorial tone, "watch what you tell patients. About your personal life, I mean. This girl seemed to know some pretty intimate stuff. Most of it probably isn't even true. You should have heard her on the subject of you and some X-rated business in Provence. Talk about sexual fantasies. But the point is she shouldn't have known you were in Provence in the first place. I know not everyone agrees with me. Hell, in California they hold group therapy sessions in their goddamn hot tubs. And the other day I heard about a guy who videotaped his new baby's delivery to *share* it with his patients. New Age bullshit. Feel-good therapy. If you ask me, the less they know about us, the better. In other words, old buddy, keep your lip as well as your fly zipped."

"That's outrageous," Isobel said when Pete told her about the conversation. "If he's such a hotshot shrink, he ought to be able to spot a crazy like her. And he should know you better."

Pete didn't point out that he hadn't spotted a crazy like Karen, and that Isobel did know him better and that hadn't stopped her from suspecting him. He didn't even tell her how terrified he'd been, and maybe still was because he had a feeling this wasn't going to go away that easily.

He merely shook his head and shrugged. "In this society we're all guilty until proven innocent."

SIXTEEN

T HEY DECIDED TO TRY THE POLICE
again, now that they knew who was harassing them, but neither
of them expected much. There were no SWAT teams to combat
psychological mayhem.

Nonetheless, Isobel made the call. Detective Scott answered
his phone with a grunt. She identified herself. He asked if she'd
decided to sell those records. She explained that wasn't why she
was calling and heard the boredom seep back into his voice.
She told him about Karen's identity and the latest incidents.

"Did anyone see her leave the snake? Were her fingerprints
on the dead cat? Did she break into your mother's apartment?"
He sighed, and she thought she detected a faint breath of sympathy. "Look, Mrs. Behringer, I'm not saying I don't believe
you, but that doesn't mean I can just go over there and arrest
her."

"But there must be some way to stop her."

He sighed again and told her she had to bring charges.

"You mean, file a complaint at the precinct?"

"I mean go to the DA's office." She heard a muffled sound,
like a yawn. "But I wouldn't get my hopes too high. Harassment isn't even a crime. It's a violation."

"I knew it wouldn't do any good," Hannah said when she
called to find out what the police were going to do. "We live in a

267

corrupt society. Crooks in Washington stealing the people blind, CEOs firing workers right and left while they pay themselves millions of dollars a year, police taking bribes and beating up—"

"Enough!" Millie's voice came over the other extension. "Could we forget society's corruption and just figure out what to do about Isobel?"

"You don't have to do anything about me," Isobel said. "I can take care of it."

"Only you haven't," Millie pointed out. "What you need is a good lawyer." The emphasis was on the word *good*. Millie had always believed that if you went to the senior partner of the firm or the head of the department, the men—women didn't figure in this scheme—with the right diplomas on their office walls, and the requisite respect, and the unconscionable incomes, you were bound to win your case or come through the operation with flying colors. Isobel knew better, but her mother had given her an idea.

Pete had said she had too much respect for the system. Scott said the system didn't cover this because harassment wasn't even a crime. So what she needed wasn't a good lawyer, but a smart, shady one who made a career of manipulating the system and getting around the law. What she needed wasn't a criminal lawyer, but a lawyer with a criminal mind. She thought of Ed Becker. She couldn't go to Becker, of course, but there had to be more where he came from. She remembered the attorney who'd sent her the two-hundred-dollar black lace teddy. He'd got the company that was running the mail-order scam off with a small fine. In view of that, and the fact that she'd had the teddy credited to his account, he couldn't still be angry.

She checked her Rolodex as soon as she got to her office that morning. Augie Shaw's name was still on it.

He remembered who she was, though he didn't seem

pleased to hear from her. He told her he was living with someone. She didn't remind him that when he'd sent her the teddy, he'd been married to someone.

"A model," he said. "Twenty-eight years old," he added.

She wished him luck and got around to the reason for her call.

"Sure, I'll give you a name." Confidence began to ooze back into his voice. "But tell me something. I mean, I don't want to pry, but how come you're calling me? You must know other attorneys. All those Oliver-Wendell-Holmes-Learned-Hand clones you used to hang out with."

She hesitated. It was always a mistake to bank on other people's self-knowledge. Mass murderers really believed they loved animals, and organized crime figures prided themselves on their generosity to aging mothers and small children. She was willing to bet that when Augie Shaw looked in the mirror, he saw an honest man fighting for survival against misguided naïfs and irrational laws and an entrenched establishment. She doubted that the word *crooked* was in his vocabulary. "Because I want someone tough," she said.

Shaw laughed. "I've got just the guy for you. Only she's a woman. You'll like that." He laughed again, and Isobel remembered that when she'd told him she couldn't accept the teddy, he'd asked if she was a lesbian. As Isobel took down the lawyer's name, she couldn't help thinking that though she'd never wanted to be a man, there were times when she wouldn't mind a dash of male vanity.

A vicious-looking primitive mask dominated the reception area. Isobel's first thought was that it was a peculiar artifact for a law office. Her second was that this was exactly the kind of law office she was looking for.

The receptionist's bloodred talons were in keeping with the

decor. When she picked up the phone to announce Isobel, she curled her fingers under, like Welch pulling in his remembered claws, and used her knuckles to punch the keyboard buttons.

A moment later Sheila Lewin blew into the reception area like a fast-moving weather front. She was small and delicately built, but she'd perfected her handshake on a men's wrestling team.

She herded Isobel back to her private office. The primitive masks there were smaller but no less nasty. Isobel was strangely encouraged.

Sheila Lewin asked what she could do for her. Isobel went through her story. Then she handed over her folders. Scott had been good, but Sheila Lewin was better. She might have been studying a timetable for all the emotion her face gave away. She closed the folder and looked up at Isobel.

"Let me tell you my philosophy of life, Ms. Behringer. I don't believe in getting angry. I believe in getting even."

Isobel had to hand it to Sheila Lewin. She delivered the line as if she'd just coined it.

"I'm not after vengeance."

"Of course not. Just your fair share. On the other hand, I have to warn you, even with all this evidence"—she tapped the folders that lay on her desk—"it's not going to be easy. Especially since you've been married less than a year and you kept your job. Culpability has no effect on the distribution of assets. In other words, just because he screwed around doesn't mean you can't get screwed financially."

Isobel shook her head. "I didn't make myself clear. She made all that up about an affair."

Sheila Lewin leaned back in her big swivel chair. Her eyes were skeptical slits. Her mouth was a disbelieving cut in her small face. She gave off cynicism like a scent.

"She's crazy," Isobel went on. "Only a crazy woman would do the things she did."

Sheila Lewin shrugged. "Look at *Fatal Attraction*. Glenn Close was a homicidal maniac, but that didn't stop Michael Douglas from jumping into bed with her."

Isobel felt hope sliding away. She hadn't expected Augie Shaw to refer her to a legal scholar, but she had hoped for an attorney who knew the difference between box-office bonanza and legal precedent.

"What I'm trying to say," Isobel went on evenly, "is I'm not here about a divorce."

Sheila Lewin's eyes widened into a disapproving stare. "Then why are you here?"

"To find some legal means of keeping this madwoman out of my life."

Sheila Lewin thought about that for a moment. "This is a different issue entirely."

"That's what I've been trying to tell you."

The lawyer looked at the ceiling, as if she were consulting divine guidance, then back at Isobel. "I suppose we could go to court and try to get a restraining order."

Isobel leaned forward in her chair. Now they were on to something.

"The only problem is the courts don't take cases like this seriously. At least not until they get violent. I'm not even sure I'd want to take it on."

"Augie Shaw said you liked a good fight." Isobel hated the wheedling tone in her voice, but surely if serial killers were entitled to representation, she should be able to find a lawyer to take her case.

"A restraining order is just a means. I'm interested in ends. Even if you get to court, you probably won't win. And if you do,

271

you won't get enough in the way of damages to make it worth my while."

Sheila Lewin stood. Isobel did, too.

"Take my advice," the lawyer went on as she began easing Isobel toward the door. "Stop letting this woman get to you. Take control. It's a question of empowerment." She stopped at the door and turned to face Isobel. "You've been giving this woman the power to hurt you. Once you decide to take responsibility for your life, once you realize you hold the power in your own hands, she won't be able to do anything to you."

A week later Isobel got a bill from Sheila Lewin for $250. It wasn't steep by legal standards, but it seemed high for a quick movie review and a few lines of psychobabble.

Sheila Lewin had cautioned her, Detective Scott had warned her, the woman in the police precinct and the counselor on the New York Telephone harassment prevention hot line and Pete had all told her, but it took a baseball bat to the head to convince her that she couldn't do anything about Karen Stone until Karen Stone did something violent to her. On the last Wednesday in May, the Wednesday before Pete and Isobel were supposed to get away for a long and restorative Memorial Day weekend, Karen obliged.

As demonstrations went, this one wasn't impressive. At least it wasn't as serious as the protest several months earlier that had made the local evening news on all three networks and got Isobel's picture in the *Post*. It was merely a handful of Gorsky's henchmen, posing as unemployed construction workers, strutting the open-legged macho roll in their name brand, pump-inflated, hot-off-the-back-of-a-truck athletic shoes in front of City Hall, where the public hearing on Gorsky's redevelopment plan was taking place. Even the two cops on duty had drifted off from the picket line, as if they were embarrassed to be assigned to such a Mickey Mouse demonstration.

Isobel barely noticed the protest as she came out of the building onto the steps. First, the view of the Brooklyn Bridge, suspended from the pale spring sky like an intricate spider web, caught her attention and held it, though she'd seen it dozens of times before. Then she noticed a woman from the Landmarks Preservation Commission and hurried down the wide flight of steps to catch up with her. The woman stopped at the bottom, Isobel reached her a few seconds later, and the two of them stood talking about the hearing and pointedly ignoring Becker, who was lurking a few feet away. But Isobel was acutely aware of Becker's presence, and she noticed when the toothy crescent that was his smile suddenly turned upside down and the color drained from his face. Becker yelled and lurched toward her, and Isobel's arms came up instinctively to ward him off, which was why the baseball bat Karen Stone had swung missed Isobel's head and cracked against her forearm with a crisp home run sound. Then Karen was lunging at her, and Becker was struggling to hold Karen back, and the next thing Isobel knew two cops had moved in and wrestled Karen Stone to the ground.

The officer who booked Karen Stone told her she was allowed one call. She used it to call Pete. He was with a patient, so the machine answered. Karen left a long, if somewhat confused, message. The gist of it was that she hoped this wouldn't affect their relationship.

The miraculous news was that Isobel's ulna wasn't broken. The good news was that now they could go to the district attorney's office.

*   *   *

273

Madeline Whittier had a body that made the most enlight-ened man think of sexual harassment, and a granite face with a narrow prominent jaw that dared him to try. In the four years she'd been an assistant district attorney, she'd made an impres-sive reputation trying sex-related cases. She was known as a dedicated lawyer, a tough prosecutor, and a firm believer that if you scratched a man, you were likely to find a potential per-petrator.

She stood behind her government-issue desk and directed Isobel and Pete to two government-issue metal and plastic-up-holstery chairs. When she sat again, she swiveled her own chair to face Isobel and place Pete outside her line of vision. When she asked if they wanted coffee, she still managed not to look at Pete. Isobel said no, thank you. Pete didn't bother to answer.

"So here's the problem, Ms. Behringer. We have a woman who's harassing you. A very sick woman who's harassing you. Right?"

She stopped as if she were waiting for an answer. Isobel nodded.

"Good. Now our problem is to find a way to protect you and not just to stop her but to help her as well." Again she waited for corroboration. This time Isobel took longer, but she finally nodded a second time.

"Good," Madeline Whittier said again. "We're in agreement. I think you'll also agree that Rikers Island isn't the answer. We're not going to help this woman by putting her in a poten-tially violent situation. She doesn't deserve that." Again Made-line Whittier hesitated.

What about me? Isobel wanted to say. I don't deserve to be in a potentially violent situation either. I don't deserve to be stalked and beaten. But Madeline Whittier sat staring at Isobel with flinty eyes that made her think of the women who'd settled the West and won the vote and fought for legal birth control, the women Isobel had always wanted to be, so she didn't say anything at all.

This time silence was all Madeline Whittier needed. She leaned across her desk toward Isobel and went on in a confidential tone. "Karen Stone is an intelligent woman. Her IQ would surprise you. She's well educated. And there was a time when she had her act together. She used to work as an editor in a medical publishing house. She was also smart enough to win you over as a friend." Madeline Whittier paused to let that sink in. "In other words, the only difference between someone like Karen Stone and someone like us is a tough break in the parental sweepstakes or a chemical imbalance. There but for the grace of God and all that. What I'm trying to say is putting this woman in prison would be like putting your sister or your roommate or your best friend in prison." She leaned back in her chair but kept her eyes fixed on Isobel's face. "Can you live with that? The question isn't rhetorical. Can you go to your office in the morning, come home to your apartment at night, do all the ordinary things we take for granted knowing that because of you, another woman—okay, I'll say it, a sister—was spending several years behind bars?" Her eyes narrowed. "Perhaps you've never been in a prison, even a women's prison, but I have, and it's not exactly Canyon Ranch. It's mean and dangerous and spirit-crushing. Do you think you can live with that? Do you want to live with that?" Madeline Whittier rested her prominent chin on her fist and went on staring at Isobel.

Isobel sat staring back and wondering how she'd got to be the villain. "Maybe not," she said finally, "but I can't live with her in my life either."

Madeline Whittier leaned forward again with sudden enthusiasm. "No one expects you to. Here's what I'm suggesting. We forget criminal prosecution. You get an order of protection—

275

that will keep Karen Stone away from you—and we insist she get meaningful psychiatric help."

"She's had help," Isobel said. "She was in the hospital. She was in treatment." She glanced at Pete. He didn't return her look.

"I said meaningful psychiatric help," Madeline Whittier repeated.

This time Isobel couldn't look at Pete, but she didn't have to. She sensed something coiling inside him.

Madeline Whittier turned her chair a few degrees farther away from Pete. "I think it's worth a try, Ms. Behringer. What about you?"

Isobel didn't answer. Madeline Whittier went on waiting. For a busy assistant district attorney, she suddenly had all the time in the world.

Isobel said she was willing to give it a try.

SEVENTEEN

Women roved Fifth Avenue and Madison and Lex showing too much sweat-glistening flesh for their own good. Hard hats in midriff-exposing jerseys, and white-collar workers in short-sleeved polyester shirts, and middle management men in suffocating summer-weight pinstripes followed them with eyes as hard as the light glancing off the sunbaked sidewalks. Water dripped from overhead air conditioners, and fumes rose from steaming sewers, and melting upholstery stuck to hot thighs in the backseats of taxis as drivers leaned on their horns and cursed in Russian and Pakistani and Dominican patois. The underclass piled into broken-down third- and fourth-hand cars that were sure to overheat before the end of the day and headed to Jones Beach or Riis Park or Rockaway. The merely poor bragged about having the museums and movies and outdoor concerts to themselves. Strangers with cameras slung around damp necks stopped Isobel on street corners and asked directions in French and Japanese and exotic American dialects. She answered with exaggerated pronunciation in a too-loud voice and clutched her handbag as she spoke. It was summer in the city, and she loved it.

She loved the tables that spilled out of restaurants onto sidewalks and the diners who lounged at them with the self-conscious languor peculiar to New Yorkers trying not to rush. She loved the neighborhood children with sunburned noses and chlorine-bleached hair who streaked off buses into the arms of waiting Filipino and Hispanic and Irish and black women. She loved standing in the living room at dusk when the buildings of Central Park West seemed to rise straight from the violet reservoir to the rouged sky in lurid parody of all those Tintoretto and Canaletto and Turner views of Venice. She loved being able to hear the Philharmonic and the Metropolitan Opera concerts in the park while she sat in bed beside Pete, and she loved being able to get up and close out the heat and the noise when the temperatures rose and the concert was rock. She loved not having Karen Stone in her life.

Thanks to Karen, they never had got around to renting a house or planning a real vacation, and since neither of them played the role of houseguest particularly well, they spent most of the summer in town, but one weekend in late July, when the Tuckers had to fly to Chicago for a wedding, they asked Isobel and Pete to keep an eye on their house and pool and tennis court in East Hampton.

Isobel left her office early on Friday, and Pete rescheduled his last three appointments, but they still managed to hit the height of the rush-hour traffic. At least it was hard to imagine that it could get worse as the afternoon progressed. While they sat in a line of cars waiting to inch onto the FDR Drive, a religious fanatic hustling roses grew ugly after Pete refused to buy one of his flowers. When they finally got on the Triborough Bridge, a woman talking on a cellular phone almost ran them off it. But after a while the traffic started to thin, and Isobel noticed that the muscles in Pete's jaw began to relax. Outside the car the air was still foul with heat and exhaust and neon signs for fast food and cut-rate electronics and twelve-theater movie houses, but inside, the temperature was comfortable, and a local jazz station came in clearly. Pete began to play stride

278

piano on the steering wheel. Every now and then Isobel looked at the faces behind the windows of the other cars. It seemed to her that most of the mouths were set in grim lines, and the cheeks were hollow with loneliness, and the eyes stared blindly at the road or hostilely back at her. She turned back to Pete.

By the time they crossed the Shinnecock Canal, the last rays of the sun were turning the surface of the water into a shimmering Impressionist palette of pink and mauve and purple. Pete turned off the air-conditioning, and they rolled down the windows, and the heady smell of honest-to-goodness grass made them swoon. She looked at his profile silhouetted against the twilight sky and felt that same solid-state hum she remembered from the night on the boat. Then she stretched and sighed and rubbed the back of his neck just beneath the hairline where the skin was smooth and vulnerable. Usually when she did that while he was driving, he shook his head and told her to knock it off because it was soporific, but now he just played a few more bars on the steering wheel.

They reached the house just as the shadows on the lawn were fading into the darkness. Pete carried their duffel into the bedroom while Isobel read the instructions the Tuckers had left. Then they went around opening windows and trying various switches. When Pete flicked one beside the glass doors, a deck came suddenly alive and a pool glowed eerie neon blue in the darkness beyond. He slid open the door and went out onto the deck. Isobel followed him.

Crickets and katydids sawed the night, and the ripe smell of low tide drifted across the yard. They looked at the pool, then each other and, without exchanging a word, began pulling off their clothes. As they hit the water, an explosion of shrieks and splashes drowned out the insects. Then the only sound was the gurgle of the pool drains as the water surged back and forth and the quiet roar of human sighs.

279

Later when they began to talk again, Isobel admitted there were worse things in the world than being a cliché.

They'd sworn they wouldn't go anywhere except the fish store and the wine shop and the farmers' market. On Saturday afternoon Pete nosed the dusty Toyota in among the Jaguars and Miatas and vintage Mercedeses parked in front of the farmers' market, and Isobel took an environmentally and aesthetically correct straw shopping basket from the stack on the grass, and they plunged into the crowd. Fruits and vegetables and breads and cheeses and salads billed as gourmet were stacked and spread and arranged. Everything, including the shoppers, was on display. The women, depending on their body types or at least their self-images, wore sarongs that covered them from waist to ankle, or T-shirts that covered them from neck to thigh, or string bikinis that barely covered them at all. Several of the older men, presumably veterans of the sexual wars, sported postage stamp bathing suits. Their sons, who'd inherited a world where everyone let everything hang out, layered baggy swim trunks over baggy boxer shorts. Sunglasses glinted, and oiled skin gleamed, and straw hats and baseball caps jostled each other for position.

"They ought to charge admission for this," Isobel said.

"They do," Pete answered, and put a five-dollar bag of vegetable chips back on the rack.

They were standing in the checkout line watching the show when the sound broke from Isobel as if she'd been wounded. "No!"

Pete's attention snapped back from a woman in a bikini top and spandex bike shorts. "What's wrong?"

"She's here."

He didn't ask who. His head turned one way, then the other. "Where?"

"Right there." She gestured toward a bench on the lawn in front of the takeout food counter where a woman sat eating a focaccio sandwich.

Pete's eyes followed. He stood staring for a moment. Then he turned back to Isobel.

"Take off your sunglasses, slugger."

She looked again. She didn't have to take off her glasses. Even through the tint she could see that the woman had curly ash-streaked hair, and a thin, nervous body, and only the faintest resemblance to Karen Stone.

Gradually the specter began to fade. First the dread, as stifling as the polluted yellow sky that stretched over the city, lifted. Then one hot purple twilight in mid-August, as Isobel came off the running track, she realized the hatred had dissolved, too. Maybe it was her own feeling of sweaty achievement, or the young couple tangled together on the grass in sublime oblivion, or the voices of other runners thrusting and parrying in the shadowy public privacy of the Engineers' Gate, but she could hear romantic promise ripening in the city night as clearly as rural ears discern corn growing, and as she walked home through the soft darkness, she felt hopeful and happy and deeply sorry for Karen Stone.

This time Isobel had no reservations about sending Pete away for the weekend, though her motives weren't entirely altruistic. She knew he loved to sail, but she suspected he was less enthusiastic about living cheek by jowl with five other men in forty-two feet of damp teak and fiberglass. In Hemingway stories and Hollywood buddy movies and light beer commercials, guys liked nothing better than going off together to beat up on nature and animals and each other, but in Isobel's experience, men like Pete, domesticated men who lived with women rather than beside them, didn't really want to leave their best

281

audiences and full-time help for longer than an afternoon. She'd encouraged Pete to crew on the overnight race, because she thought he'd have a good time while he was away, and because she was certain he'd be eager to come back.

For her part, she was looking forward to spending the weekend alone. She'd catch up with friends, and read all those books piled on her night table, and watch old movies on the VCR. She didn't even tell Hannah and Millie that Pete was going away. It might not have been the courageous or even adult way to handle it, but it was an effective way to handle it.

On Friday night she had dinner with two friends from her abortion rights days, on Saturday lunch with Polly Markson, and by Saturday night she was glad to be alone. She was sitting in bed eating sesame noodles and watching Bette Davis befriend Paul Henreid's daughter in Claude Rains's mental hospital when the phone rang. She cursed, pressed the volume button on the VCR remote control, and picked up the receiver.

"Please don't hang up. Please."

She recognized the voice immediately.

"This isn't a crazy call or anything like that. I promise. It's Karen. Karen Stone."

"I know who it is."

"Please don't hang up."

Isobel pressed the power button. Bette Davis faded. "What do you want?"

"I have to apologize."

"The last time you apologized my grandmother ended up in the hospital."

There was a silence. Isobel was about to hang up when Karen spoke again.

"I know. And I feel awful. Believe me, if there were anything I could do to undo the mess I made, anything at all, I'd do it."

"You can leave us alone."

There was another silence.

"I have," Karen said finally. "All summer, right?"

"Am I supposed to be grateful for that?"

"No, of course not. I was just trying to show you that I'm not sick anymore. I'm in treatment again. With a woman this time. I didn't want to go to her at first. The court said I had to." She laughed. It was a nervous sound, but it wasn't a crazy sound. "I forgot. You know all that. And I'm on Stelazine. It really helps."

"You were on Stelazine before." Isobel recognized her mistake as soon as the words were out. She wasn't supposed to know what medications Pete's patients were on, or if they were on medication at all. She wasn't supposed to know anything about Pete's patients. On the other hand, she wasn't going to let Karen think she was putting something over on her, again.

"I was supposed to be, but I never took it. I lied and said I was taking it, but I didn't. I wish now I had. It really makes a difference."

"I'm glad."

"There's another reason I called."

Isobel waited.

"God, I'm so embarrassed."

Isobel was surprised. Embarrassment implied a sense of reality, appropriate behavior, maybe even a conscience.

"When I think of what happened," Karen went on, "when I think of the things I did, I cringe. I mean, have you ever felt that way? Have you ever done something—nothing as awful as what I did, but something really dumb or cruel or just really embarrassing—and every time you remember it you cringe?"

Are you kidding? Isobel wanted to say. Sometimes it seemed her whole life was made up of unconscionable acts and unkind comments and overly effusive words. Just the other day she'd let out a groan in the shower, and Pete had called from the bedroom to ask what was wrong. "Nothing," she'd yelled, because she was too ashamed to explain that what was wrong, so wrong that it made her groan in shame at the memory, had happened a good fifteen years earlier. And now she kept her mouth shut with Karen, too.

"I know I can never undo all the terrible things I did. Dr. Kohler says the important thing is to understand why I did them and to go on from there. That's why I'm calling. Not to keep apologizing, but to thank you."

"There's nothing to thank me for." The words came out all wrong. Isobel hadn't meant to sound like the lady of the manor.

"Are you kidding! You think I don't know that you could have brought criminal charges against me? I could have ended up on Rikers Island. I may not be the mental health poster child of the year, I may be on Stelazine, but I'm not so out of it that I don't know how much I owe you. So that's why I called. Just to say it. Thank you."

The silence seemed to Isobel to go on for an inordinately long time. "You're welcome," she said finally.

"Will you tell Dr. Arlen I said thank you to him, too?"

Isobel said she would.

"I hope you don't mind my calling on a Saturday night like this, but I've been trying to get up the nerve to do it for a long time, and then all of a sudden tonight I just said, 'Do it.'" There was a small, self-deprecating laugh on the other end of the line that Isobel remembered from Kay Glass. "God, I sound like an ad for athletic shoes."

"It's okay," Isobel said. "I know what you mean."

"Actually, it was really nice of you to listen. Especially on a Saturday night in August, when the rest of the world, people with normal lives—who am I kidding? people with lives—are all in the Hamptons or the Berkshires or the south of France. To tell you the truth, I don't know what I'd have done if you'd hung up on me. Probably taken the entire bottle of Stelazine." Now her laugh had a shrill edge. "I'm just kidding. Anyway, you can't OD on Stelazine."

"There must be other people you can call. Friends." Isobel was ashamed of her own hypocrisy. Women like Karen didn't have friends to call and hang on to by a telephone wire until they'd beaten back the desperation. "Your brother."

"He thinks I should move to California. He says I could start over. He means I'd be out of the way. A remittance woman."

"I'm sure he doesn't mean that," Isobel said, though she knew from what Pete had told her that he did. "Look, Karen, I'm glad you're feeling better, but I really have to go."

"Oh, God, I'm sorry. I didn't mean to keep you on the phone like this. Pe—Dr. Arlen must be furious. I'm so sorry. Really. It's just that it's so good to have a normal conversation with someone again." Karen laughed. "Who am I kidding? When have I ever been normal? It feels so good to have a conversation."

"You ought to get out."

"I've been out all day. The boy at the admissions booth in the Metropolitan Museum said, 'How many?' The man behind the counter in the coffee shop said, 'What'll you have?' And the woman in the booth at the movies just slid the ticket through the opening and didn't say anything at all." Karen's voice veered dangerously close to a sob. "If you hadn't talked to me, I don't know what I would have done. I'm scared, Isobel. Really scared. I can feel myself slipping. That's why I'm trying to keep you on the phone. I know I should let you get off. I know I shouldn't keep babbling like this. But I can't help it. You're my lifeline."

There was a time when Isobel would have wondered how she'd gone so quickly from being a nemesis to a lifeline. Now she knew there wasn't that much distance between the two. "I think you should call your doctor, Karen."

"She won't be there."

"You can leave a message on her machine. If she doesn't get it tonight, she will in the morning."

"The morning," Karen repeated as if it were next year.

"I can't help you," Isobel insisted, "but she can."

"I suppose you're right."

"You know I'm right."

"I suppose so. I'll call her."

"Good."

"But you're wrong about one thing," Karen insisted. "You can help me. You already have. Thank you."

"It's all right."

"No, it's not, but thank you anyway. Thank you, thank you, thank you," Karen said, and hung up without saying good-bye, as if she didn't want Isobel to hear the tears. But of course, Isobel already had.

Paul was handing Bette a lighted cigarette when the phone rang again. A woman's voice identified itself as Dr. Kohler and asked for Karen Stone. As the camera panned to a starry sky, Isobel switched off the movie and explained that there must be a mistake. Karen Stone didn't live here, though she'd spoken to Karen a little while ago. In fact, Isobel went on, she was the one who'd urged Karen to call Dr. Kohler. The woman on the other end of the line asked whom she was speaking to, and Isobel explained that, too.

Dr. Kohler took a moment to consider things. "She must have been foggy," she said finally. "Sometimes trifluoperazine has that effect."

"I thought she was on Stelazine."

"I'm sorry. Trifluoperazine is the generic name. One of the

side effects can be a mental fogginess. I can't imagine why else she'd leave the wrong number."

Isobel could imagine. It wasn't that far in the past.

"Unless, of course, it's the vestiges of wanting to be you," Dr. Kohler, the mind reader, said. "I don't have to tell you we have a long way to go. We've made progress," she added quickly, "but we still have a long way to go."

"So I gathered from her call tonight."

"How did she sound?"

Isobel thought about that. At one point Karen had joked about taking an overdose. But otherwise she'd been fairly rational and occasionally funny and mostly pathetic. Even the desperation had been different. The old Kay-Karen wouldn't have known she was slipping.

"A lot better than I expected," Isobel said.

"Yes, she's responding well to the medication."

"But not in good shape tonight. She said she was scared. You could hear it in her voice. And . . . I'm not a professional, and she said she was just joking, but she made some comment about taking the rest of her pills. All at once. Tonight."

"Oh, my God!"

The words gave Dr. Kohler away. She belonged to the new school of therapists who didn't believe a sprinkling of human concern was a plunge into the murky unprofessional waters of countertransference. Isobel knew Pete would disapprove, but for Karen's sake, she was glad.

"I hesitate even to ask this, Mrs. Arlen. I mean, I know this isn't exactly a conventional hour for a consultation. But we might or might not have a suicidal woman on our hands. Could I speak to your husband for a moment?"

Isobel said she was sure Pete would be happy to talk to her if he were there, though she knew he wouldn't be in the least

287

happy about it, but explained that he was away for the week-end.

"I see." The words were clipped, and Isobel had the feeling that what the woman saw was Pete lurking in the background while Isobel lied for him.

"I can have him call you when he gets back tomorrow night."

"Unfortunately tomorrow night may be a little late. Do you know where she was when she called?"

"I assumed she was home. I mean, I didn't ask, but that was the way she sounded. She said she'd been out all day. She'd gone to the museum and the movies, but she sounded as if she were home then."

Dr. Kohler said she'd try Karen there, and apologized for bothering Isobel at this hour, and then, after she'd said good-bye, added one more thing. "Thank you."

"For what?"

"For listening to her. Professional help can do only so much. She needs a life. And that means connections with other people. You could have turned your back. A lot of women in your position would have. As Karen's therapist, and as someone who cares about her, I just wanted to thank you for not doing that."

Isobel sat thinking about the conversation for a moment after she hung up the phone. She knew what Pete would think of Dr. Kohler. Unprofessional at best, dangerous at worst. And she knew what he'd tell her. You can't cure pathology with kind-ness. But she was still glad she hadn't hung up on Karen.

It was after ten when the doorbell rang. Not even the build-ing staff would come to the door at that hour. They'd ring from the lobby. Then she remembered seeing the doorman loading the Davisons' car that morning. Their daughter must have locked herself out again. The girl was a nuisance, but Isobel could tell just by looking at her that she was having a rotten adolescence, so she hadn't said anything to the Davisons the last few times it had happened, and she knew she wasn't going to make a fuss now. She put her book on the night table, got out of bed, and went down the hall to the door.

She bent to put her eye to the peephole. The small round lens distorted the view, and the woman was standing with her back to the door, but Isobel would recognize those narrow, tense shoulders anywhere. She threw the bolt and opened the door.

The figure turned around. Karen's face creased into a tentative smile. Only the figure looked more like Kay than Karen. It wasn't just the well-cut linen trousers and shirt or the freshly streaked and styled hair. It was the general air of careful grooming. She no longer gave off the soiled rancid aura of madness.

"I'm sorry. Again. But after I talked to Dr. Kohler—you were right about that, thanks—I went out for a walk, and before I knew it, I found myself here. I mean, if we were friends, we could have gone to a movie or dinner or something, and it would have been perfectly natural for us to come back to your apartment or mine for coffee or iced tea or something. I mean, friends do that, right?"

Isobel had been wrong. This wasn't Kay. It was a pathetic child.

"Friends do that sort of thing. But friends don't turn up unannounced in the middle of the night." Isobel hated the prissy grammar school teacher tone of her own voice.

"They do if they're suicidal."

"Did you tell Dr. Kohler that?"

"I was just kidding."

"It's not something to joke about."

Karen dropped her head. "I know. I'm sorry."

289

Isobel stood staring at the top of her head. "How did you get upstairs without having the doorman announce you?"

Karen looked up and shrugged. "There was a whole group of people in front of me. I guess he just assumed I was with them." She stopped, shook her head, then went on. "All right, I admit it. I attached myself to those people because I was afraid you'd tell the doorman not to let me up."

Isobel leaned against the doorjamb and crossed her arms over her chest. She wasn't exactly blocking the way, but she wasn't about to invite Karen in, either.

"Listen, Karen, I'm sorry you're having a bad night. But I can't help you. I don't hate you. I understand that you were sick. And I'm glad you're doing so well. Really I am. But you can't start dropping by. We're not—" Isobel took a deep breath. It was the honest thing to say. It was the only possible thing to say under the circumstances. But as she stood face-to-face with a woman who had no family, no friends, no job, and no life, a woman you used to like, it wasn't an easy thing to say. "We can't be friends. It just isn't possible. After what happened."

Under the starched linen blouse, Karen's shoulders sagged. "I know. I even told Dr. Kohler. She said you'd forgiven me, but I knew."

"It has nothing to do with forgiving."

"Then you don't believe people can change?" It was a question rather than an argument.

Isobel thought of the tug-of-war she'd been waging with Hannah and Millie for the past year. "Just tell them no," Pete insisted in a maddening paraphrase of some crazed Republican lack-of-visionary. It wasn't that easy, but she was trying, and she knew from the things they didn't do more than the things they did that they were, too.

"I hope they can."

Karen stared at her for a moment; then she shook her head

and grinned. "God, we sound like something out of a twelve-step program. My name's Karen, and I'm crazy. I haven't done anything crazy today, but I may do something crazy tomorrow." She squared her shoulders and put her hands in the pockets of her trousers. "Thanks for listening to me. I won't bother you again. I promise." She took a step toward the elevator, then turned back to Isobel. "No, that's not true. I have one more favor to ask."

Isobel waited.

"Could I use your bathroom? My teeth are floating, and I'd rather not disgrace myself in your lobby. I've made enough trouble in the building," she added with a pathetic smile.

Isobel hesitated. She thought of her conversation with Dr. Kohler. The shrink had thanked her for not turning her back. As Karen's therapist, she'd said, as someone who cares about her. Pete wouldn't approve. He'd say Dr. Kohler had a problem with countertransference, or overinvolvement, or at the very least unprofessionalism. But Pete hadn't had much success treating Karen, and Dr. Kohler seemed to be having some. She felt guilty for thinking that, but it was true.

"I'll just be a minute," Karen pleaded.

Forget Pete and Dr. Kohler. This had nothing to do with schools of treatment. This had to do with simple human decency. It was unconscionable to refuse to let another woman use your bathroom.

She opened the door wider. Karen stepped into the apartment. As she glanced around the waiting room, Isobel noticed that she actually winced.

"It's down there," Isobel said.

"I know." It was a sigh of embarrassed wistfulness.

Karen went down the hall and closed the bathroom door behind her. Isobel sat in one of the Barcelona chairs, then stood. She didn't want to be sitting when Karen came out. It

291

was too much of an invitation for Karen to sit in the other chair. She paced from one end of the waiting room to the other, then back. It took only four or five steps each way. She tried just standing there, but that felt awkward, too. She walked down the hall and into the kitchen and began straightening things. She pushed the canisters against the wall, and centered the spoon caddy on the stove, and aligned the knives on the magnetic bar on the wall. Welch strolled in and sat beside his bowl. She reminded him he'd already had dinner. He went on staring at her with unblinking eyes. She took a morsel from the box of cat treats and held it out to him. He ate it from the palm of her hand.

She was surprised when she looked up and saw Karen in the doorway. She hadn't heard the toilet flush or water run or the door open and close.

"I'm sorry about the cat, too," Karen said.

"Let's not start that again."

Karen leaned against the doorjamb and looked around the room. "I used to fantasize about what was behind this door. Once I even peeked. You were sitting at the table reading the paper. In Dr. Arlen's shirt." She shook her head. "Oh, God, I'm so sorry."

"Please," Isobel said. "It's over." She took a step toward the door, but Karen didn't move. Her eyes swept the room again and came to rest on the Sub-Zero refrigerator. Isobel was still ambivalent about that refrigerator. When she'd first moved into the apartment, she'd thought it was just fine. Then Millie had informed her it was better than that. All her friends' children were putting Sub-Zeros in their kitchens. After that Isobel hadn't been exactly ashamed of it, but she couldn't manage to regard it as an innocuous appliance either.

"I always wanted one of those," Karen said.

"It was here when I moved in."

Karen's eyes moved from the refrigerator to Isobel. "That must have been rough. Moving into another woman's apartment, I mean."

"It was terrific. I hate renovation and redecoration and all that."

"But still, living with her things. Your predecessor. Aren't you jealous? Or at least uncomfortable?"

It wasn't the first time another woman had asked the question. She gave the same answer she always did. "Maybe I would be if she'd left Pete or if he still cared or something."

Karen shook her head. "I wish I were as strong as you."

"I'm not strong. I'm logical. How can I be jealous of a woman he can't stand?"

"I'd be." Karen smiled. "But then I'm crazy. Or at least a textbook case of transference run amok."

Isobel took another step toward the door. Karen didn't seem to notice. She was still leaning against the doorjamb, and her eyes were focused on the middle distance, as if she were thinking about something else. "I can't imagine what it's like being married to him. I mean, I used to fantasize all the time when I was crazy. But now, well, I can't imagine what it's like."

"It's marriage," Isobel said, and took another step toward the door, but Karen still didn't get the hint. Her eyes came back to Isobel.

"It must be wonderful."

Isobel didn't know what to say to that. If she agreed, she was giving away secrets. If she said it had its ups and downs, it was betrayal. "It's getting late."

Karen's eyes moved to the big silent clock on the wall, then back to Isobel. "It's only ten-thirty. What's the rush? It isn't as if he's waiting for you in the bedroom." Karen flashed an embarrassed smile. "Dr. Kohler told me he was away for the weekend."

293

Isobel was furious. Pete was right after all. First you got emotionally involved with patients, and the next thing you knew you were giving away things that were none of their business.

"It's still late."

"I just wanted to thank you."

Isobel tried to make her voice light. "You've already done that. A couple of dozen times."

"But I have to make sure you know how grateful I am. Professional help can do only so much. I need a life. And that means connections with other people. You could have turned your back. A lot of women in your position would have. I just want to thank you for not doing that."

Isobel recognized the words. Then she realized there was nothing unusual about that. Patients frequently mouthed their therapists' phrases.

"You're welcome. Now you really do have to go."

"You're going to send me away. Just like that? Aren't you worried about what I might do? After all, you told Dr. Kohler I was suicidal."

Dr. Kohler was sounding more incompetent by the minute.

"I only told her what you said to me."

" 'I'm not a professional,' " Karen began in a singsong voice, " 'and she said she was just joking, but she made some comment about taking the rest of her pills. All at once. Tonight.' Isn't that what you said?" she finished in a flat, angry tone. "Well, who gave you permission to talk to my doctor? Who the fuck do you think you are anyhow? You think just because you're married to him that gives you the right to call my doctor and discuss me with her?"

"Dr. Kohler called me," Isobel said as gently as she could.

The anger drained from Karen's face as quickly as it had appeared, and her mouth curled in a wide smile. "That's right, she did, didn't she? Because I left her your number. Isn't that what she told you? That I must have left your number by mistake because of the medication. What were her exact words? She must have been foggy. 'Sometimes trifluoperazine has that effect.' And you said you thought I was on Stelazine. Jesus, that cracked me up. I was laughing so hard I was sure you could hear me on the extension."

Incompetent was too polite a word for Dr. Kohler. "You were on the extension when Dr. Kohler called?"

"Come on, Isobel. How dumb can you be? There is no Dr. Kohler. I told this would-be actress who lives on my floor that I wanted to play a practical joke on a friend. And you went for it. Sometimes I wonder how he puts up with you. I mean, even the actress was surprised. Of course, she ascribed it to her talent. You'd have thought she got a rave review from Frank Rich instead of just put one over on you."

"Fine. You and your friend had a good laugh. Now you'll have to leave."

Karen took a step into the room. "What's the rush?"

"The rush is that you don't belong here. I never should have let you in in the first place. There's an order of protection. If I have to, I'll call the police."

"Don't be silly." Karen took another step into the room.

Isobel fought the urge to take a step back. "I mean it. You have to leave. Now."

Karen took another step toward her. This time Isobel couldn't help herself. She stepped back.

"You don't have to be afraid of me," Karen said. Then she laughed. She stood in the middle of the room and glanced around the kitchen. "This really is a great room. I think you're right. I don't think I'm going to do a thing to it."

"Karen, why don't you go home and call your real doctor?"

Karen's eyes snapped back to her. "Why don't you shut up?"

Karen took another step toward her. Isobel retreated again.

295

She felt the counter against her back. Karen's arm swung up. Isobel ducked to the side. Karen's hand hit the long magnetic strip on the wall. A serrated bread knife and two paring knives clattered to the floor. Welch streaked out of the room. Karen's hand swung above her head. The broad blade of a Japanese chef's knife glinted in the light.

Karen's hand fell. Isobel screamed and jumped to the side.

Karen's lips pulled back in a tight grin. "I was just kidding." Her elbow was bent now, and the shiny blade was only inches from Isobel's stomach. Karen twisted her wrist. The light from the overhead fixture danced on the blade. "What's the matter? Can't you take a joke?"

Isobel said the words in her head to make sure her voice sounded calm, but when they came out, she could hear the terror. "Put it down, Karen."

"You should have listened to me. I told you to leave him. I warned you. You should have listened."

Karen's wrist went back and forth. Light glittered off the steel. Isobel couldn't take her eyes from it.

"And then I found out he went away for the weekend and I knew. He was sending me a sign."

Short breaths rasped through Karen's open mouth. Her wrist twitched more rapidly. The light dancing off the blade made Isobel's eyes ache. She could reach for the knife, but even if she were the stronger of the two, and she wasn't sure she was, all Karen had to do was move her hand forward. The hard bright steel would slide into Isobel's flesh.

She dragged her eyes from the knife to Karen's face. "You're right. It was a sign."

"What?"

"This weekend." Her voice was thin as tissue paper. She prayed it wouldn't tear. "It was a sign to you. Because he didn't just leave me for the weekend. He left me for good."

296

Karen's eyes narrowed as she took in the information. Isobel waited. The blade of the knife shone like a candle.

"I don't believe you."

"How can you not believe me? You just said you knew it was a sign."

"You'd say anything now."

Isobel felt the air go out of her lungs. It was hopeless. She inhaled again. "He told me everything."

Karen's hand twitched. Light exploded off the knife. "What do you mean everything?"

Isobel tore her eyes away from the shining blade. "How he felt about you." She had to force the words out. "How he was in love with you but couldn't admit it because you were his patient."

The knife was flashing back and forth so fast now it took Isobel's breath away. "He told you that?"

"Put the knife down, Karen, and I'll tell you everything he said."

Karen's wrist kept moving. "At the hospital they said I was imagining it."

"You weren't imagining it. He loves you."

Light glinted off the blade.

"If you don't believe me, I'll show you. It's all in your file. Months and months of entries."

"You saw them?"

"I found them. That's why we fought. I found them yesterday. Pages and pages about how much he loves you."

"Really?"

"Do you want to see them?"

Karen's wrist twitched. A streak of light leaped off the blade. "Where are they?"

"In the file cabinet. In his office."

297

Isobel waited. Karen didn't move. The blade shone flat and cold and steady.

"Come on, I'll show you."

Karen didn't even blink. Isobel heard her own breath scraping in and out. She prayed Karen didn't notice it. "Come on," she said again, and took a tentative step toward the door.

Karen stood immobile. Isobel took a second step, then a third. She kept going toward the door. When she got to the hall, she didn't dare turn around, but she could hear Karen behind her, and she could sense the knife.

She moved around Pete's desk to the tall oak filing cabinet. Karen followed her. There were three drawers. Pete used the bottom one for personal papers. She reached for the second drawer and pulled it open. It rolled out with a solid whir. The sound must have startled Karen because she lifted her arm. Now the knife glittered near Isobel's throat.

"Why don't you put that down?" Isobel said.

"Show me the file."

Isobel bent and began going through the folders. She'd overshot her mark. She was in the *T*'s. She moved her hand toward the front and began walking her fingers through the files. "Rider," she murmured, as if to herself. "Ruben. Stevenson. Here it is. Stone." She straightened and looked at Karen. "See for yourself."

Karen bent to the file. She rested her right hand, which was holding the knife, on the drawer, and reached for the folder with her left.

Isobel threw her body against the drawer. It slammed in. Only Karen's hand kept it from closing. Karen screamed. Isobel pushed the drawer again. Karen screamed again. Isobel kept pushing. She pushed with her hands and her hip and her foot. And Karen screamed and screamed and screamed. But Isobel couldn't stop. She pounded and shoved and kicked.

298

Only when she saw blood spurting over the files and heard Karen's screams turn into a long howl could she open the drawer. The sight of Karen's mangled hand made her sick to her stomach.

She took the knife and brandished it at Karen. If she'd stopped to think, she would have wondered if she could have actually used it, but she wasn't stopping to think. The bloody mass of Karen's hand was proof of that.

She backed Karen into the patient's chair on the other side of Pete's desk. With the knife still in her right hand, she used her left to pick up the phone and dial 911. Then she sat in Pete's chair. The knife was shaking. She realized her whole body was trembling. She began to cry. She sat that way until the police came, crying and trembling and every once in a while telling Karen how sorry she was about her hand.

EPILOGUE

Thishis time Pete didn't tell her she was indiscreet or reckless or any of the things he'd been saying she was for the past year. And she didn't blame him for bringing Karen into their lives in the first place. They didn't need mutual recriminations. They had a knife-wielding psychopath to draw their fire.

And this time the district attorney's office didn't talk about the danger of putting Karen in a potentially violent situation. They brought charges. Karen was sentenced to a year in prison.

Isobel told herself she was safe, at least for a year, and waited for the nightmares to stop. The worst part of them wasn't Karen's face, leering into her own helpless one night after night, or even the knife that went on glinting endlessly in the blinding light of her unconscious. The worst part was her own bloodthirst. She kept slamming and kicking and punching the drawer closed until the rage hurled her awake. Then she'd lie in the quiet room, hearing the thumping of the strange heart inside her chest and the pounding of the wild blood in her ears. But there were other times when the force of her fury couldn't break through to consciousness. Then in her dream she'd howl. She'd howl at the top of her lungs until her pathetic mewlings woke Pete, and he'd shake her back to life. After that she'd make him turn on his side, and she'd turn, too, and wind herself around him and hold on, though she knew he couldn't stop her from falling.

But what really horrified her about those nightmares, what made them linger the next morning like the acrid aftertaste of a hangover, was the sense that Hannah and Millie had been in them, too. She was never sure what they were doing there, because the fragments always faded in wakefulness, but once when she was helping Millie make the bed around Hannah, who wasn't feeling well enough to get up that day, she saw her mother's softly lined hands smoothing the blanket and her grandmother's gnarled fingers lying on the wide cuff of sheet, and, with a horrible shock, recognized the mangled bloody hands of her nightmares.

Gradually the dreams became less frequent, and she began to feel safe, or as safe as a woman who'd been stalked by a crazy person, and who lived in Manhattan in the last decade of the twentieth century, and who had people she loved hostages to fortune, dared to feel. And of course, her fears were justified.

A year and a half later, around the time Karen Stone was scheduled to get out of prison, Hannah went into cardiac arrest. She died alone in the study of the duplex on Central Park West. Cruz was in the kitchen. Millie had gone to the library to return some large-type books Hannah hadn't been able to finish. Isobel was at her office.

Several months earlier Hannah had given Millie an envelope to open after she died. "I'm not being melodramatic," Hannah had said. "No family skeletons or beyond-the-grave confessions. It's just instructions about what I want done."

They were precise. She did not want a funeral. She especially did not want a religious ceremony. She'd be damned if she'd have some rabbi who'd never known her, and wouldn't have thought much of her if he had, saying fatuous things over her, especially since she'd have no opportunity for rebuttal. She wanted to be cremated. And she didn't want anyone making a fetish of the ashes.

"She had to be stubborn. Even to the end," Millie said.

Isobel looked away. Her mother's usually cared-for face had the shriveled dusty look of a deflated balloon. Isobel wondered if it would be easier to grieve for someone you'd loved without ambivalence. Then, as she reached across the table to take her grandmother's letter, her hand brushed her mother's, and she realized there was no such thing as unambivalent love.

Isobel read through the letter and was about to hand it back to her mother when she noticed the envelope. Her own name was written below Millie's, then crossed out. She sat staring at the two names. Hannah must have addressed the letter to her originally, then changed her mind. She'd decided to put the burden on Millie. She'd decided to let Isobel off the hook. The weight of obligation fell away, and Isobel floated free in her loss.

Millie adhered to Hannah's wishes. Isobel was surprised. She'd been sure her mother wouldn't be able to resist some ceremony.

What Millie did next surprised Isobel even more. She sold the big apartment on Central Park West and bought a smaller one in Florida. Most of her friends had moved there years ago, she explained. She'd hung on in New York only for Hannah, and for Isobel. But now Hannah was gone and Isobel no longer needed her. Millie hesitated. She might have been waiting for Isobel to contradict her. She might simply be thinking about what she was saying. Isobel remained silent.

Several months later, as they walked through the empty rooms of the duplex, Isobel listened to their shoes tapping out a lament on the bare parquet floors and felt another surge of loss. She told her mother she'd miss her. Weeks after Millie had

303

moved, Isobel was amazed to find it was true. She didn't miss the incessant phone calls and the care packages and the surprise visits, but she was as ambivalent about freedom from love as she was about love.

She was sure the nightmares would stop now that Hannah was dead and Millie was gone, but they continued to stalk her. They didn't recur often, or even regularly. Sometimes they vanished for weeks or months at a time. Sometimes they stayed away for so long she began to think they were gone for good. But they always returned.

One night when she opened her mouth to scream in the dream and no sound came out, when she strained and struggled and thrashed against her strangled silence, the violence of her movements tumbled Welch from the bed and awakened Pete. He put his arm around her in a classic lifesaving grip and hauled her back to consciousness. She could feel her stricken heart hammering against his palm.

"It's okay," he whispered, though they both knew it wasn't.

They lay with his chest against her back like a shield while she fought to drive her fear back into its cage. Gradually her heartbeat became regular. He relaxed his lifeguard's grip. Welch came out from under the bed.

They turned so that her chest was against his back and she could hang on to him. Welch did a reconnaissance march up and down their legs, then arranged himself over their feet. She felt the motor of his contentment through her toes. She heard Pete's breathing settle into the steady cadence of sleep. She tightened her arms around him. He shifted within her hold, then muttered in his sleep and rolled away from her.

The dream, like the reality, would always be there, a grim possibility waiting to happen, a stark reminder of the fragility of her happiness. Still, she felt the space between Pete and her, less a void than a vacancy, and carefully, stealthily, so she wouldn't wake him or dislodge Welch, moved closer. She wound herself around him again. Then she leaned her cheek against his shoulder, and closed her eyes, and waited for sleep.